Tales from the Indian Jungle

Tales from the Indian Jungles

KENNETH ANDERSON

Rupa & Co

Published 2001 by
Rupa & Co.
7/16, Ansari Road, Daryaganj
New Delhi 110 002

Offices at:
15 Bankim Chatterjee Street, Calcutta 700 073
135 South Malaka, Allahabad 211 001
PG Solanki Path, Lamington Road, Mumbai 400 007
36, Kutty Street, Nungambakkam, Chennai 600 034
Surya Shree, B-6, New 66, Shankara Park,
Basavangudi, Bangalore 560 004
3-5-612, Himayat Nagar, Hyderabad 500 029

ISBN 81-7167-466-6

Typeset Copyright © Rupa & Co. 2001
Typeset in Classical Garamond by
Nikita Overseas Pvt Ltd
19-A, Ansari Road,
New Delhi 110 002

Printed in India by
Gopsons Paper Ltd
A-14 Sector 60
Noida 201 301

Contents

Contents

Introduction

THE MAN SITS WITH HIS BACK TO A TREE AND THE LIGHT FROM THE campfire waxes and wanes, throwing him into sharp relief along with the tree-trunk against which he rests, to fade the next instant into obscurity and gloom. Leaning against the tree beside him is a .405 Winchester rifle of ancient vintage.

Someone throws a fresh log on the flames and myriad sparks soar upwards, lighting the heavy boughs of the great tree that overshadows the camp. For an instant the man's countenance, too, is lit brightly and we see that he has a beard and moustache, and that firmly held in the corner of the mouth is an old briar that has long gone out. A battered 'Gurkha' hat, its brim curled up at the left side, slopes rakishly to the right upon his head.

The man is speaking. He appears to be telling a tale and it is clear that he is so intent upon it, so absorbed, that he has forgotten his pipe and all else around him.

The flames die down, then flare up again, their momentary gleam revealing the absent look in the man's eyes, as he lives again the incidents he describes. The past has become so real that he is oblivious of his audience, squatting around him on the ground beside the fire, listening to his words.

The sparks fly upwards to merge, fade and disappear in a thick spiral of smoke that curls yet higher until it is lost in the gloom of the heavy foliage of trees that encircle the camp and accentuate the jungle night.

Except for the crackle of the flames and the drone of the man's voice, the forest is lost in silence, and a heavy, oppressive, uncanny quiet that we feel cannot last much longer. And we are right. The roar of a tiger breaks suddenly through the blackness, to be answered by the scream of an excited elephant. 'Aungh-ha! Ooongh! Aungh-ooongh!' comes that awful sound as the tiger stalks boldly down the jungle aisles, while the distant trumpeting of the elephant 'Tri-aa-a-ank! Tri-aa-a-ank!' announces that the challenge has been met.

But the man seems not to hear these sounds, so engrossed has he become in the story he is telling. He appears to be of the jungle himself, and we get the impression that he belongs there. This is home for him and here is the place he would want to die; the jungle is his brithplace, his haven and his resting place when the end comes.

Let us give heed, then, to what he tells. Stories of the denizens of the forest; tales of incidents, macabre and ghostly sketches of himself. The man seems happy as we listen and he warms to his theme.

For he loves to speak about the jungle and its people, and who should know that better than I.

For I am that man!

One

Ghooming at Dawn

THE POOJAREE AWAKENS US WITH HIS PERSISTENT SOFT CALLS OF *'Dorai, Dorai; yeancheko, knarl munni agadho!;'* meaning, 'Master, master; wake up, it's four o'clock!'

He whispers the words into our ears, first mine and then yours; for to touch either of us with his hands would be considered disrespectful. Have not the poojarees, for as long as man can remember, been regarded as outcasts, whose very proximity to any ordinary person—let alone their touch—is abhorrent in the extreme?

We sit up abruptly, for in the jungle a tardy awakening may spell the difference between life and death, to view the glowing embers of the fire whose light barely extends to the trunks of the giant trees of the forest that hem us in on three sides. On the fourth we see a whole stretch of water, lit by the stars, which is the Cauvery river, and we hear the dull rumble

1

as the flood swirls past us, appearing out of the darkness of the jungle night and vanishing just as swiftly.

We are camped in the open upon the river bank, a few yards from the fringe of the forest and only a short distance from the water's edge. The poojaree has remained awake all night, to stoke the fire that protected us while we slept from an unwelcome visit by some wandering elephant that might have come for a drink, or perhaps an unusually daring crocodile. The sands of the river bank on which we have been sleeping have been a deterrent to our smaller but equally unpleasant foes such as snakes and scorpions, who do not like crawling on such a surface.

We throw off our light coverings, for it is comparatively warm. The heat from the embers has helped to protect us from the dew. I place a small kettle of water on the fire to brew some tea, that ever-refreshing drink that is always welcomed by persons who sojourn in wild places, and while the water boils accompany you the few paces to the water's edge for a quick wash of teeth, face and hands.

By the time we return, the kettle is boiling, and soon we sit with a steaming mug in hand, while cold buttered *chapatties* and some ripe bananas—called plantains in India—a complete breakfast, unfit for kings perhaps, but of which there is no equal for good health.

This brief meal is soon over, and now we attend to the rifles that we are going to carry on this early-morning 'ghoom' of the foothills that start less than a quarter-mile away and rise steadily and culminate in a peak called Ponachimalai, over 5,000 feet high and about six miles distant as the crow flies.

My silent, but trusted friend and companion over many years and through many adventures, a somewhat battered .405 Winchester of which everybody makes fun, needs little or no attention. Like me, it is an old-timer that seems to look after itself. In any case, it appears very inferior to that 10-shot U.S. 3006 Springfield rifle of yours, which you rightly treat with such care.

It is still dark when we leave camp. Our poojaree companion is eager to accompany us, but as we are embarking upon a prowl during which I would like to try to show you a few interesting things, I decide to leave him behind on the pretext of looking after the few possessions we have brought. A hunter, pure and simple, Byra, our poojaree friend, would greatly disapprove of my pointing out to you some grand old sambar stag instead of shooting it; while if I draw your attention to the mother-love of a spotted doe, offering herself as a target in an attempt to shield her fawn, he would be positively annoyed with me for not pulling the trigger and bagging both mother and fawn.

The air becomes chill within a hundred yards, and seems to grow even colder as we start to climb the sloping ground to the summit of the first foothill.

It is still dark and we progress slowly. Stumbling over stones and brushing through the undergrowth will certainly betray our movements and turn the first phase of our little walk into a failure. For it is the season when the *jumlum*-tree casts its purple fruit so prolifically over the ground, and this astringent delicacy is an article of diet absolutely irresistible to sloth bears, who will cover miles in a night to visit such a tree. Only yesterday I noticed a grove of these *jumlums* close to the riverside and barely two furlongs from camps, with the tracks and droppings of many sloth bears that have been visiting them each night to feed upon the fallen purple fruit.

The hillock we are now ascending is adjacent to the grove and will form the direct line of retreat for the sloth bears that will be still gorging there. As is their custom, they will begin

3

to make for rising ground as soon as the false dawn breaks. That time is close upon us now, and a momentary lightening of the sky heralds this curious phenomenon.

But within a few minutes a pall of darkness once again envelopes the land, till a wider spreading glow in the eastern sky, perhaps twenty minutes later, announces the true dawn and the beginning of another day.

This false dawn deceives not only the hunter new to the forests, but the inmates of the jungle as well. Junglecocks begin to crow, peafowl awaken to voice their brassy calls, carnivores on the prowl turn back to the lairs, and the hyenas and jackals that have been sneaking after them in the hope of a meal from what is left of their kills, turn back to their burrows in the ground and under the rock, where they shelter during the day.

The grumpy and greedy sloth bears that have been concentrating their energies on gormandizing the fallen *jumlums* will also be deceived by the false dawn. Reluctantly they will abandon the few fruits they have been unable to force down their throats and will make for the haven of the hillsides where they will be left in peace, there to spend the hot hours of noontide sound asleep in some cave or grassy hollow in the ground, or perhaps beneath the shade of a gnarled old tree.

But we ourselves are not misled and hasten to take up our positions before the short-lived glow lapses into pre-dawn darkness. We should be in hiding if we are to hear the sloth bears' approach and perhaps glimpse one of them in the light of the true dawn when it breaks. It would never do to be surprised in the murk of that short-lived twenty-minute interval.

The sloth bear shares with its relatives of all lands the evil reputation of being irascible, excitable, resentful and aggressive should one stumble upon him unexpectedly. Scores of jungle dwellers in India carry horrible scars because they happened to encounter a sloth bear coming round a corner or floundered upon one sound asleep. Many have lost eyes and noses under their raking talons.

This rock, which we have come upon, will suit our purpose admirably. It is about four feet high by perhaps six long. Both of us can crouch behind it and await the coming of a bear. It is, of course, just a chance that may or may not come off, for after all the bears have the whole jungle to roam in and there must be many other *paths* and byways by which they could climb the hillock without passing in this particular direction.

We chance our luck and wait in silence for a few minutes, hearing only our own breathing. Then the faint thud of a stone, somewhere at the base of the hillock, raises our hopes. Only an animal, generally clumsy in its habits or in search of the grubs that hide under such stones, would have betrayed its presence by making such a noise. Decidedly not a deer, for it would be afraid; and certainly no tiger or panther would advertise its passing. The other possibility might be an elephant. This we will know in a few moments.

Now we can hear the sound of laboured breathing, as if some old man is climbing the hillock with great difficulty. This removes any doubt that a sloth bear is indeed approaching sniffing at holes under the rocks and at the roots of bushes in search of grubs and other succulent morsels.

The eastern sky is beginning to brighten with the approach of the real dawn, but it is still dark behind the rock where we crouch, when the bear reaches us. You are to my right, and the bear is to the right of you, maybe ten feet away. I press your arm tightly and you understand my unspoken signal to remain motionless. It might not see us, for it is notoriously short-sighted. It is also very deaf. It might attack should we betray our presence, and we do not want to shoot it, for normally a bear does us no harm.

The snorting and the grumbling, the huffing and snuffing pass. All we can glimpse is a black blur against the bushes; then the bear has disappeared as it ascends the hill and the sounds of its progress grow fainter.

The dawn breaks apace and the sky to the east across the river displays a pattern of ever-changing colour, starting from dark grey and deep purple and trailing off into violet, green, blue, orange and vermillion, till at length the sun's rim rises above the jagged heights of distant mountain peaks. Its diffused rays are not yet bright enough to keep us from staring with unshielded eyes at that glorious fiery ball.

In salute, birds large and small, far and near, burst into song. The twittering of a hundred *bulbuls*, the call of the black-and-red crow-pheasant, the cry of a brain-fever bird rising to crescendo, fall upon our ears from the hillside, while from the heavy cover by the river we hear the challenge of junglecocks, 'Wheew! Kuck-kya-kya-k'huckm,' and the metallic notes of a far off peacock 'Miaoo! Miaoo!'. We can imagine it with the glorious plumes of its tail spread like a large fan, strutting and dancing before a bevy of admiring hens.

Crack-a-a-ack! We hear the sound but once, rather faint but quite unmistakable. Something heavy is coming up the hill, perhaps another sloth bear, but I think not. Bears are continuously noisy, while this animal, except for that initial accidental sound, is otherwise, silent.

We crouch quietly behind the rock with just the tops of our heads and eyes showing. To remain absolutely still is the first secret of successful concealment in the jungle. Even if an animal sees you, it will not be able to make you out provided you remain absolutely motionless. The second factor, of course, is the direction in which the wind is blowing. The sense of smell rather than of sight is far more developed in most wild creatures, particularly members of the deer family. Provided the wind is not blowing directly from you to the quarry, and provided you remain absolutely still, you have a good chance of ambushing practically any animal successfully.

We put this to the test a moment later when the bushes before us part with a faint rustle to reveal the head and shoulders of an enormous sambar stag. His giant antlers are spread in perfect symmetry, and he is near enough for us to see their gnarled thickness, equal to your forearm, at the base.

The stag is closer to us than the sloth bear was a moment earlier, and directly in front, yet he does not see us. He hesitates cautiously before advancing into the clear space on the other side of the rock behind which we are hiding. Then he steps forth and we see his massive body in all its grandeur.

He is an old animal, as revealed by his dark brown colour, the shagginess of the mane around his neck, and the long coarse hair on his flanks, which is not quite thick enough to cover completely the skin on his sides. These factors and the massiveness of his antlers indicate the stag's advanced age.

Now I will show you how inquisitive a sambar can be. Plucking a thick stem of grass at my side, I allow the plumed end to protrude above the rock, while holding the stem between finger and thumb. Then I begin to twirl it around and the effect on the stag is instantaneous. Soundless and slight as is this movement, it registers on those ever-watchful eyes. He stops abruptly, his two large ears flicking forwards and backwards, and then forwards again. Impatiently he raises his right leg bent at the knee-point, and stamps it hard upon the ground. His hoof makes a metallic click against a stone.

The stag repeats this action while staring harder than ever at the stem of grass which I continue to revolve. All his suspicions are aroused now as his instinct warns him that something strange is going on. He has seen stems of grass many a time swaying in the breeze. But never has he seen one twirling round and round!

We can read the stag's thoughts behind those staring eyes. Instinct alerts him and urges him to flee. But curiosity impels him to find out more about the stem of grass that twirls around in such a peculiar fashion. The sambar takes a step forward, hesitates for a full minute, and then comes forward again. Every muscle in his frame is taut, attuned to flee at a moment's notice; but he just cannot overcome his inquisitive urge.

This natural inquisitiveness among the deer and antelope families is the reason why thousands of them are slaughtered each year by experienced poachers, who do just what I am doing at the moment, or adopt some other trick to entice them to their doom. The stag is so close now that he could be transfixed by a spear-throw; and he is coming even closer! Clearly this foolish animal must be taught a salutary lesson and I decide to give him the fright of his life.

Springing up from behind the rock, I yell ' Wroff! Wrooff! Wrooff!' at the top of my voice. To say that the stag is taken aback by this sudden apparition of a human with a tiger's voice describes the situation mildly. He rears up on hind legs, slips on a stone, falls to his knees, struggles erect and lets out a strident cry of danger.

'Oo-onk!' he screams.

Then he lays his antlers back along his sides so as not to get them caught in the branches of trees, and crashes down the hillside. So precipitate is his flight that we can follow his movements by the rattle of displaced stones till he reaches the shelter of the heavy forest beside the river. There the stag evidently halts to see if he is being pursued, and resumes his warning to all the jungle that danger and death lurk upon the hillside.

'Oo-onk! Dha-ank!' he bellows, again and again.

The general excitement is taken up by the watchman of the band of langur monkeys that have been feeding contentedly in the *jumlum*-grove. We can just glimpse him from where we hide, standing erect on two legs on a tree-top as he strives hard to catch sight of the danger that the sambar has announced. Try as he may, he cannot see us. Obviously he is puzzled and wants to identify the nature of the foe. Then the big male langur decides he must do his duty to his band and the other wild creatures at large by joining in the alarm and passing on the warning.

'Harr!' he screams gutturally; and then a moment later, 'Harr! Harr-harr!' in quick succession. The forest is disturbed in right earnest now, and from the far side of the river a jungle-sheep, about to quench his thirst, takes fright, scampers away and voices his dog-like bark as he goes, 'Kharr! Kharr! Kharr!'

A herd of spotted deer, grazing somewhere on the other side of the hillock on whose slopes we are hiding, hears the commotion and passes on the warning. 'Aiow! Aiow! Aiow!' call the hinds to each other in quick succession. In the distance an elephant trumpets shrilly.

The excitement dies down at length and we decide to resume our early-morning prowl, for there is nothing to be gained by continuing to hide. The sambar has made too great a commotion for anything further to come our way.

Do you see that shrub with the tapering leaves resembling the tea-plant that thrives only in higher altitudes? Many such bushes grow all around. It is known as the 'vellari' plant. The leaves, in a compress or poultice form are very useful in relieving rheumatic pains and swellings of any sort. The five-pointed leaves of this large tree, green above and silver-white below, produce excellent effects when applied to raw wounds or a contusion; the silver-white side is placed in contact with the troubled area. That little plant that grows on the hard ground, barely a foot high, with the silver-grey, almost spiked leaves, is said to be a remedy for poisonous snakebites, and that other tiny plant with white, daisy-like flower and the serrated leaves, is renowned for stopping bleeding where the juice from the leaves is squeezed into a wound. It also lowers high blood pressure in a patient as rapidly as can any medicine prescribed by a doctor.

Truly the jungle is filled with all manner of herbs and plants whose leaves, stems, seeds, flowers and even roots are remedies for most of the maladies from which the human race suffers. They grow in the forests and also in civilized areas, even along the railway track.

You must often have noticed the myriads of pink and white flowers peeing out from among the green leaves of the common Indian periwinkle shrub that thrives practically everywhere, particularly on railway embankments. Forty leaves of this plant, brewed like tea and drunk in a large cupful of water or milk every day, stimulates the pancreas by helping the secretion of insulin, thus controlling diabetes. But there are other roots and leaves that are even more effective in treating this malady, one of them a little creeper common in every jungle. It is known as the 'sugar killer' because, after chewing only one leaf, sugar loses its sweetness and tastes like sand in the mouth, this effect lasting for about three hours.

But we are digressing and in the meanwhile have arrived at the top of the hillock and begun our descent on the other side. We must move cautiously now, for in places the going is steep, and should one of us dislodge a stone or make some noise, the family of spotted deer that has now stopped calling and that we hope to see soon, will surely take alarm. Luckily the breeze is blowing up the hill, so they will not scent us.

We reach the base of the hillock and tread our way around bushes of thorn and lantana on tiptoe till we arrive at a grassy glade. There, feeding placidly, is a herd of at least forty of the deer we had hoped to find. Fortunately, none of the hinds on sentinel duty have observed our approach and we stop just in time behind a crop of young redwood trees.

The sight before us is magnificent. The stags are in the centre of the group, antlers spread and tapering, as they toss their proud heads and sniff the air before stooping to graze again. Around them on all sides are the does and fawns, the former ever alert, with ears cocked forwards and twitching to catch the faintest sound. Now and then a head and neck dips quickly to earth to grab a mouthful of grass or leaves, but is raised again quickly, ever observant, always vigilant.

The fawns have no such responsibilities and death will strike many of them down cruelly and suddenly, before the survivors learn that the great secret of continued existence in the jungle is to be 'ever watchful at every moment; for death lurks everywhere.'

They gambol and play among themselves, one chasing the other round and round. A few of the very young members nuzzle up against their mothers, slyly dipping their tiny heads under udders hanging temptingly close, to sneak a drink of milk. The mothers in turn stop their feeding now and again to lick their little offspring affectionately, but never for a moment do they halt their close scrutiny of the surrounding jungle for a possible foe. Their eyes seem to stare in every direction, with ears strained forwards to catch the slightest sound, and nostrils dilated to detect the faintest scent of danger.

On a tree directly above the grazing deer is a small family of langurs. Two of these jump to earth and playfully chase a spotted fawn. Then one leaps back to a low branch where, hanging by its legs, it grabs the fawn by the tail and half lifts if off the ground. The fawn enjoys the game but its mother does not seem to approve.

A scene apparently of utter peace, beauty and tranquillity. But out of the corners of our eyes we notice the faintest of movements beneath a large bush, well away to our left. We look harder at the bush, but the movement has now ceased.

A hind with her young fawn, grazing close to that bush, has seen it too. She raises her head abruptly to stare hard, both ears cocked forwards and muzzle aquiver. The she raises her right foot to stamp the ground and voice the first syllable of her warning cry, 'Aiow!'

But it is already too late. An elongated form, golden and spotted in the rays of the early morning sun, springs from under that bush and in two bounds reaches the little fawn. In the next second it is dead, while the panther glowers and growls over the small quivering body.

Then we witness a scene that is as touching as it is magnificent. The fawn's mother, forgetful of her own safety, rushes forward to defend it. The panther leaves the little carcass and springs upon the hind, seizing her throat and bearing her to the ground. Her hoofs drum out their death-agony on the green grass, already stained a deep red by the blood that flows from her torn throat.

I watch you as you raise your 10-shot Springfield to cover the still growling panther, in order to exact what you feel is just retribution for the murder that has just been done. But I stretch out a hand to hold the muzzle and deflect your aim.

'Don't shoot, John! It's the law of the jungle. The panther has killed for food, not wantonly.'

The panther hears my voice, then sees us. In the next instant it has vanished. But it will come back.

Two

The Bellundur Ogre

BELLUNDUR IS A HAMLET SITUATED ON THE SHOULDER OF A HILL AND
about three miles from the village of Tagarthy, in the district
of Shimoga, in Mysore state.

For centuries this part of Mysore has been the home of
tigers, which had become so numerous as to have almost
eliminated, simply by devouring them, their lesser cousins, the
more subtle but far less powerful panthers that also, not long
ago, roamed in large numbers through the area. These lesser
cats, as a matter of fact, had created havoc in their time. Far
bolder and more clever, and more difficult to circumvent, they
could hide themselves better, being smaller than tigers; they
haunted the precincts of villages which they raided systematically
each night after sundown, carrying away fowls, dogs, goats,
sheep and calves with equal disdain and impartiality.

Humans they seldom harmed unless they were wounded,
but on those rare occasions when they were guilty of this

13

'crime, to exact retribution against them was difficult because of the cover afforded by the dense jungles of the area, well watered as they were by heavy monsoon rains.

When my story opens, however, tigers were the ruling factor, while in Bellundur lived a necromancer who was reputed for his ability to provide charms and talismans of all sorts for all purposes. These last were said to be particularly efficacious in procuring a loved one, or contrarily, in ridding yourself of one whom you did not love quite so well. They were also rumoured to be very effective in securing a job that had been applied for or the success of petition.

Among his other abilities, this magician was far famed as possessing the power, by charms and incantations, to 'tie up' the jungle, so that any hunter operating in that area would meet with total failure. The game would either not appear before his rifle; or if they did, the rifle would not go off; or if it did go off, the bullet would not strike the quarry even at a few yards' range. I had met this character some years ago, and have written about him in one of my earlier stories.* Like most members of his calling, he enjoyed a little flattery. Otherwise, I had found him quite friendly and had found nothing wrong in his weakness. After all, we all like to be flattered.

But the 'Ogre of Bellundur,' about which I am going to tell you, began its career in more or less the usual way, as a very ordinary and inoffensive tiger. Nothing was heard of it in its younger days. Evidently it had confined its attentions to killing and eating spotted deer, sambar and pig, which swarmed everywhere in those times. Then the government began encouraging programmes of cattle-rearing, and as rich pasturage abounded, herds of cattle were introduced which

---

* See *Nine Man-eaters and One Rogue.*

multiplied into many thousands within a short period, to the detriment of the wild deer and pig that previously had grazed undisturbed.

'The Ogre,' as it came to be known later, now made its presence felt by varying its taste for wild game with a liking for prime beef, and this inclination grew rapidly to the exclusion of any other kind of meat. It killed and it ate, and it ate and it killed, till it had accounted for many herds of cattle and the villagers at last began to feel that something should be done.

The Indian villager is a man of unbounded patience, an attribute easier to understand if one observes his complete apathy, his capacity for resignation and for accepting whatever misfortune it may be the will of God to bestow upon him. So, when I tell you that at last the villagers had had enough of this tiger and were determined to put a stop to its depredations you will realize that the Ogre had really gone too far. They decided to set a trap, catch it and then kill it.

A deep rectangular hole was dug in the centre of a game trail; the mouth was carefully concealed by thin interlaced bamboos covered with leaves and twigs, and the bait, in the form of the least valuable calf in the village, was tied to a stake at the farther end of the rectangular pit. A direct approach to the bait from any other direction except across the rectangular pit was made impracticable for the tiger by a vast mass of thorns packed tightly around it on both sides and beyond, leaving only the one approach open.

Everything went according to plan and on the third night the tiger fell into the pit.

The following morning all the inhabitants of Bellundur village turned out, including the necromancer, to gloat over their erstwhile enemy and throw firebrands at it, before putting it to death by the simple but rather slow process of spearing it from above. Evidently nobody had a gun, and the question

15

SKETCH MAP: OGRE AND GOWNDNORAI TIGERS
(Chapters 2 and 3)

N

Amligola village

To Chordi

Valley of Death

Bellundu village

Tree where the Gowndnorai and panther were shot

Park-like Jungle

Forest bungalow

Two huts where Ogre was shot

Tagarthy village

of cruelty, of course, did not occur to anybody. For was not this animal the tiger which had killed and devoured so many of their cattle?

Not only did the inhabitants of Bellundur have no guns, but they did not appear to be very rich in spears either. I discovered afterwards that just two people had spears, or articles that might pass as such. One was a short affair, less than four feet long and entirely blunt at the end. The description fitted more a crowbar than a spear. The second was a true spear and belonged to the local temple. It was reputed to have been used in a war two and a half centuries ago, but was now as blunt as the aforementioned crowbar, having been employed many times for digging yams out of the earth. In any case, the shafts of both weapons were too short to reach the tiger from the surface of the pit, but this mattered little, as each of their owners was confident that, with a single throw of his particular weapon, he could transfix and kill the imprisoned beast.

Much argument is said to have arisen as to who should cast his weapon first. Finally, but I do not know on what grounds, the owner of the crowbar won the dispute. Taking careful aim, he hurled his weapon; no sooner had it left his hand than its blunt point was deflected and the side of the weapon rather than its blunt point, struck the flank of the tiger with a dull thud.

As might have been expected, the tiger did not take lightly to this form of treatment. It roared its defiance and glared up at its tormentors. There was widespread tittering amongst the assembled crowd as the second spear-man, after glancing contemptuously at the crestfallen owner of the crowbar, prepared to make his cast. The 250-year-old spear flew downwards to its target, the blunt point embedding itself fairly in the tiger's hindquarters.

Now Bellundur was totally unarmed! And the Ogre lost its temper. With a burst of unexpected energy, it sprang upwards to the rim of the pit, groping with the talons of its forefeet. They reached it, held and embedded themselves in the soft soil. The hind feet, kicking the air madly, found purchase against the sides of the pit and levered the beast upwards. And the next moment the tiger was free, leaping out of the mouth of the pit like a demon from hell, and far more dangerous.

Just one of the crowd stood in its *path* to freedom; all the rest had fled. The tiger leaped over the man before it, kicking backwards with all four feet extended, and the claws of one of those dreadful feet met the back of the man's skull before he, in turn, could gather his wits to run. It was only a glancing blow, comparatively light considering the force that the tiger had put into it, for if the paw had struck the head fully the skull would have been smashed like an eggshell. As it was, the tips of the claws caught in the skin at the back of the man's neck, and the weight of the tiger, as it leaped over the man's head, did the rest.

Then the tiger had gone. The man fell where he had been standing but he was quite alive. The whole of his scalp, removed neatly from the bone, now hung over his face, the long hair streaming down before him instead of behind. It took three days for this man to die, for to the very last moment he lived in the hope that his scalp could be put back. He was the Ogre's first victim although admittedly unintentionally so.

Naturally, with the healing of his wound, the tiger grew cunning. Other baits were tied out for it with various forms of traps, but they were studiously ignored. All its killings of cattle thereafter were done in broad daylight, generally in the afternoons while the herds were placidly resting after having grazed all morning and their attendants were huddled asleep in the shade of the bushes. Those who were awake or had been awakened by the short cry of the stricken victim, at first attempted to drive the Ogre off by shouting and throwing stones. But the Ogre soon put a stop to such tactics by leaping upon one of the graziers and mauling him severely. Strangely enough this man made a complete recovery, though the lesson that had been given was salutary enough. Thereafter, at sight or sound of the tiger all herdsmen fled, leaving their charges to its mercy.

The situation at Bellundur went from bad to worse. Cattle owners could no longer trust their animals to the forest for grazing, but endeavoured to feed them at home, and this of course cost a lot of money. Correspondingly, the tiger's hunger grew as the supply of Bellundur beef was cut down, so it extended the range of its operations to include Tagarthy and some of the smaller neighbouring hamlets. Its fame for daring as a cattle-lifter began to spread far and wide.

That was how a gentleman, whom we shall call Mr Johnson, came to hear about the tiger.

Johnson was an officer in railway service who had lately been transferred to the area from some other part of India where tigers did not exit. This made him very keen to attempt to bag the beast that was the talk of the neighbourhood, and as he had a rifle he made his way to Bellundur, which was only about seven miles from the railway track, on the few days' leave during which he hoped to succeed. And this is where old Buddiah, the necromancer, comes into my story.

Hearing that a white man had arrived and was making inquiries about the tiger, Buddiah donned his ceremonial saffron robe, plaited the long roll of filthy false hair that he kept for such occasions in a coil around the crown of his head, smeared ashes liberally across his forehead, which he further decorated with vermilion marks of a religious significance, hung his chain of large amber wooden beads around his neck, and holding his gnarled walking-stick, blackened by being soaked in oil, in his hand, presented himself before Johnson, offering his services, claiming that they were absolutely indispensable if the white man wished to succeed in shooting the tiger.

Now the situation was really very simple. To anyone of moderate experience, it was obvious that old Buddiah was endeavouring to earn a few rupees but more than that he was taking the opportunity to impress his fellow villagers with his greatness as a magician. He wanted them to feel that even a white man had to come to him for help. If Johnson had used a little psychology and common sense, he would have recognized these things and given the old man a boost with a few rupees to humour him. Instead, Johnson lost his temper, told the magician to get out of his presence, and when Buddiah began to remonstrate indignantly, made matters worse by threatening to break his neck!

So, the necromancer stalked away in fury: his prestige with the villagers, which he had been endeavouring to enhance, had been severely lessened by the white man's words. He felt his companions would laugh at him secretly, although he was still confident that they feared him too much to do so openly.

The villagers, on the other hand, felt abashed. Although none of them had any liking for Buddiah who had exploited them systematically since childhood, he was, nevertheless, their own magician. One of themselves. To be spoken to in such a fashion by the white man, and to be threatened with a beating, reflected scant respect for their magician and incidentally for themselves and the village as a whole. Thus by his hasty words, Johnson had made enemies all around instead of friends. The villagers left him where he stood and refused to have anything more do with him. Nor would anyone sell or hire him a bait to tie out for the tiger.

Being of a determined nature, Johnson made up his mind to succeed in spite of the local noncooperation. He made his way back to Tagarthy where, by exercising the tact he should have displayed at Bellundur, he was able to buy two ancient bulls. Engaging herdsmen, he had these two animals driven back to the outskirts of Bellundur, where he tied each up in a *nullah* said to be frequented by the tiger, or so he was told by the herdsmen he had engaged; but as these men were from Tagarthy and not from Bellundur, they did not know very much about the tiger's movements.

The following morning Johnson and his herdsmen visited the baits. One had disappeared. It certainly had not been taken by the tiger, for there were no pug-marks to be seen in the sandy bed of the *nullah,* which bore a number of human footprints instead. Had these been made by his own men the previous day, or by others? The other bait had not been touched.

Johnson rightly came to the conclusion that the villagers of Bellundur had stolen his first bait. He stalked into the village with a loaded rifle, demanded the return of the bull, and then threatened to inform the police. To all of which the villagers assumed an air of injured innocence. They maintained that the human footprints he had seen in the sandy ravine were those of his own men when they had tied the bait and asked him to prove otherwise. To Johnson's dire threats to shoot the thieves, the yokels turned a deaf ear and smiled.

Fearing the second bait would also disappear, Johnson ordered his two men to construct a *machan* over it, in which he sat that same afternoon, perhaps more to protect his bait from being robbed than in the serious hope of bagging the tiger. But the unexpected happened. I am told the tiger turned up while it was still daylight. Johnson fired, succeeding only in wounding the animal, which got away.

Throughout the next week, Johnson, with commendable determination, scoured the jungles in search of the tiger. No one came forward to assist him; even his two henchmen refused to accompany him on the plea that it was too dangerous. Unaided, the white man lost his way on one occasion and was compelled to spend the night in the forest. In the end, bitterly disappointed, Johnson had to return to duty without bagging his tiger.

Everything was quiet for some time after that. The Ogre did not show up and the villagers of Bellundur had to admit that, in spite of their best efforts at noncooperation, the *sahib* had rid them of the pest that had been exacting such a heavy toll of their cattle. Buddiah, the magician, was more aggrieved than ever. He saw his pride and reputation at a still lower ebb, for he had announced boastfully that the *sahib* would not or could not shoot the tiger; he had done so nevertheless and had rid Bellundur of the hated cattle-lifter.

So the cattle were driven out to the jungles once again each day for grazing. That is, until the inevitable happened!

Early one afternoon a herd rushed pell-mell back to the village minus one of its members—and minus the nineteen-year-old youth who had gone out with the animals that morning to graze them. Nobody worried about the matter till nightfall. Then the relatives of the boy grew a little anxious about him, while the owner of the missing cow grew far more anxious about his valuable animal. A search the next morning revealed the cow lying dead: her neck had been neatly broken by a large tiger whose pug-marks were clearly to be seen in the field where she had been struck down. A hundred yards away, hidden under a bush, was the body of the missing youth.

There was, however, this difference between the two carcases: the cow had not been eaten, while rather more than half of the youth's body had been devoured by the tiger. The familiar pattern had appeared once more: an innocent tiger had been turned into a man-eater through being wounded and left to fend for itself.

Tragedy succeeded tragedy after that and the pattern of events was repeated. The people of Bellundur locked themselves in their huts at sundown while the cattle were kept starving in their pens. Old Buddiah's prestige was at its lowest ebb.

Lack of human prey drove the tiger into extending his operations towards Tagarthy and more distant villages, and that was when the beast began to be referred to as 'The Ogre,' a name that was whispered with bated breath behind locked doors and only during daylight hours. Otherwise it would surely hear and bring dreadful vengeance upon the man who dared refer to the creature as a tiger.

After darkness the Ogre was about! It roamed everywhere and a man was not safe even in a locked room. The Ogre, or one of its spies, an evil spirit of the air in the form of a bat or an owl, or one of the many devils that lived in the jungle, might hear what was being said and carry words to the dreaded man-eater.

Then the man who had spoken against it was indeed undone! It would be only a matter of time before the Ogre exacted a terrible revenge. His fate was sealed and there was no means of escape. That was the universal opinion.

At this stage my old friend, Doctor Stanley, the medical officer of Tagarthy village, wrote a long letter to me and related this story, inviting me to join him in an attempt to end the Ogre's career. This doctor, who owned only a .12 bore shotgun and no rifle, had shot many tigers himself in his younger days, parelleling Dick Bird, the Postmaster of

Santaveri, whom I have mentioned in another story. Now that he had grown older, he felt that his rather antiquated gun, although still a trusty weapon, might not be quite up to the mark for a man-eater.

I met him three days later in the front room of his dispensary-cum-hospital, after motoring to Tagarthy in my Studebaker. The first thing he insisted upon was a tremendous meal, with gallons of tea, after which, over clouds of pipe-smoke, we discussed 'old times' for about three hours. Generally long-suffering by nature, at times I become impatient; finally I reminded the good doctor that there was a job of work to be done. Obviously the first step was to visit Bellundur and pick up the trail from there.

The Studebaker had a hard time to reach this village. The track, which was always bad, had become really terrible after the last rains. The doctor, who sat next to me, said we should have walked. Having reached Bellundur at last, I set about undoing, as far as possible, some of the mischief that had been done by the tactless Johnson. I called upon Buddiah, who was sulking in his hut, asked him to don his ceremonial robes and make *pooja* for me and repeat all the mantras he knew, to enable me to succeed in shooting the man-eater, presenting him with ten rupees to cover incidental expenses.

He brightened up at once. In no time at all he stalked out into the marketplace, all dressed up for the occasion, where the first thing he did was to demand another five rupees from me to cover the cost of a black fowl and a bottle of the local spirit called '*arrack*.' The fowl was to be killed, cooked and eaten by him, presumably to placate the spirits of the jungle, and the *arrack* was to be drunk, also by Buddiah, presumably for the same purpose. The old man declared that only thereafter would he be in a proper condition to utter the mantras that would lead to the downfall of the man-eater. Dr Stanley and I, knowing what state that would be, pretended hearty agreement.

I handed over the money and resigned myself to a further delay of another hour at least, which would be the shortest possible time for the cock to be half-cooked while Buddiah had conditioned himself with *arrack* for saying his mantras. But the old man, and the villagers of Bellundur especially, had to be humoured if the damage done by Johnson was to be repaired.

The doctor and I chatted while the unfortunate black cock was procured, slaughtered before our eyes, parboiled into a curry and then devoured by the greedy old necromancer. With scarcely an interval he proceeded to empty the bottle of *arrack* by the simple process of applying the neck to his mouth and pouring the contents down his throat. Why he did not choke in the process amazed me.

This done, the magician staggered to his feet. He was dead drunk and could hardly stand erect. With bloodshot eyes and an inane smile, he produced what looked like a bracelet of twisted and dried jungle vines from a filthy cloth-bag that he brought out from somewhere on his person. Asking for my rifle, he proceeded to pass this bracelet over the end of the muzzle and down the length of the barrel three or four times. He was so drunk that he missed his aim once or twice, but I was able to rectify the error unostentatiously by quickly guiding the end of the barrel so as to allow it to be encircled by the bracelet.

That was the end of the mantra. The tiger's doom was sealed! It would fall to my rifle! The spirits of the jungle, in the person of old Buddiah, had eaten and drunk well. The crowd of villagers, who had been watching every detail while they stood around us in a circle, breathed this assurance loudly. In any case the mantra, together with their assurances, ended just in time, for the next moment old Buddiah fell to earth as if pole-axed.

The important thing was that good feeling had been restored. Buddiah's prestige was up again, as was that of the villagers and of Bellundur village itself. Dr Stanley and I were smiled upon as 'good fellows,' while the activities of the Ogre were momentarily eclipsed. Just then it was no more than an ordinary tiger, waiting to be shot.

It was now dark, and the trip back to Tagarthy in the Studebaker was a nightmare. We made it, however, without any broken axles or springs, but resolved that henceforth we would walk there and back rather than risk a breakdown, which would be inevitable if we tempted fate too much.

Stanley procured two baits at Tagarthy, which we duly tied out the next day at suitable points near the track to Bellundur, for you will remember that I told you that the tiger was by this time, operating throughout the area. After lunch we walked the seven miles to that village, and we were able there, without any difficulty, to procure another three animals as additional baits. Obviously the little show we had organized with Buddiah the previous evening had had its good effects. These baits were tied out at points which the villagers informed us were often visited by the Ogre.

Time was against us, however, and we were in too much of a hurry to be able to set up a *machan* above any one of the five baits we had laid that day. This is against my usual practice of constructing a *machan* first and tying the bait in full view of it afterwards, which has two advantages. Firstly a 'kill,' if it occurs, is in proper view of the *machan* and does not have to be shifted. Secondly, no noise is made in building the *machan*, which would be inevitable if the 'kill' occurs first. Such sounds may arouse the suspicion of the tiger if it is lying up or otherwise lurking within hearing.

It was again pitch-dark when we walked back to Tagarthy, keeping a sharp lookout with our torches against a surprise attack by the man-eater, but the only animal we encountered was a pangolin foraging amongst the dead leaves, out much earlier than usual for these creatures.

None of the five baits we had tied out was touched that night, but late in the morning of the third day, a man came running to the doctor's dispensary to announce that his cousin had been taken by the tiger. The victim and his wife, together with our informant and his wife, lived in two huts constructed side by side and only a short mile away along the track to Bellundur. The sun was at meridian when this cousin, who was returning from a visit to Tagarthy for provisions, came into full view of the other three members of the little community, gathered before their huts and were chatting together. They had been about to call out to him when he had screamed loudly and then vanished into thin air.

Our informant stated he had then grabbed his axe and set out to see what was the matter, accompanied by his cousin's wife, wringing her hands and lamenting aloud. The thought of the man-eater had never occurred to them. Rather they suspected that an evil spirit from the forest had done away with their companion.

Reaching the spot where the man had disappeared, they were terrified to find the pug-marks of a tiger in the soft sand of the trail. Prevented by fear from going farther, they were about to turn back when the wails of the woman, which had now increased in volume, annoyed the man-eater who had just begun to taste his victim not far away. The tiger growled fiercely, whereupon both the man and the victim's wife fled. Stopping long enough to enable the two women to lock themselves into one of the huts, the man had come running to Tagarthy by a round-about route to inform the doctor and me of what had happened. The Ogre would be there still, he affirmed, feasting upon his cousin, if only we had the courage to come at once and shoot it.

Grabbing rifle, torch and warm coat, I set out at a jog trot with our informant, Stanley bringing with him the .12 bore gun and another torch. I was younger in those days than I am now, and the doctor younger still, so that we reached the two huts in fairly good shape, if a bit breathless. Minutes later, with the man in the middle, Stanley to the left of him and me to the right, we approached the place where the tragedy had taken place, determined to flush the man-eater on its kill.

The tiger sensed we were coming long before we knew where it was, for we heard no sounds of eating or the breaking of bones. As likely as not it had seen our arrival at the two huts, which were, as I have said, in full view of the spot where the Ogre had seized its victim.

When we were quite close, the man-eater began to growl, and its protests grew to hideous volume. Clearly, it was bent upon driving us away. If we beat a retreat now, while the going was good, all would be well. But if we continued to advance, it would either rush at us, or its courage might fail at the last moment, it would then run away.

We hesitated only a second before Stanley and I nodded to each other. With my left arm I thrust back the man who had called us, motioning to him with my hand to go away. Then we advanced, shoulder to shoulder. We could not see the tiger yet. Roar followed upon roar, and the bushes in front of us shook violently. We stopped, gun and rifle to respective shoulders, awaiting the onslaught that was inevitable.

It never came! At the last moment the man-eater shirked the encounter! It was accustomed to chasing and killing men. Never before had human beings deliberately followed and approached it. With a final shattering roar, the tiger sprang away from the spot and I was just able to catch a fleeting glimpse of a reddish-brown form hurtling into a bush; then it disappeared. I could have fired. Why I did not do so I just cannot say, but I was to regret my mistake.

The tiger must have been really hungry, for we discovered it had made the most of its opportunity by devouring over half its victim, leaving only the head, arms, legs and a few ribs uneaten. Stanley and I did not speak to each other. We were both experienced enough to know that the human voice carries a long way. Instead, I looked about to see if there were any possible places to conceal myself and await the man-eater's return should it decide to come back to finish what scraps were left.

But the Ogre put an end to my reflections by its next action, as unexpected as it was sudden. It might have been hunger or natural ill nature, or maybe the fact that as it fled it saw only two humans and not a crowd, had dared to follow. Anyway, this extraordinary animal stopped in its tracks, turned about and started to come for us, roaring louder as it approached. The ground literally shook with the intensity of the sound, while its ever-increasing volume indicated that the tiger was getting dangerously close. You must bear in mind that all this time we could not see the beast for it was hidden by the bushes. What we could see was the bushes shaking violently as it came closer and closer.

What was happening just goes to indicate the axiom I have so often repeated in my earlier stories. There are no fixed rules in the jungle and no two animals are alike. Like us they are individuals; they react differently under different circumstances and the unexpected often occurs.

Standing shoulder to shoulder once more, the doctor and I turned to face the man-eater, which was making things easy for us and solving the problem by attacking. In another minute the tiger would have to show itself and then all would be over.

But the minute never came! For the Ogre was wily beyond expectation. At the last moment it changed its mind once more and began to circle us and the remains of its meal without showing itself, still snarling and roaring for all it was worth. The animal's tactics were now clear. Again its courage failed when it had been about to press home its attack. Now its intention was to drive us away with the noise it was making.

Then I had an idea. Its success depended on just how observant the tiger had been, how persistent was its memory, and how alert its instinct. It had seen the two of us approaching. That much was evident. Now if one of us went away and the other hid in the grass somewhere near the remains of the victim, would the tiger be aware of the fact? Would it think the coast was clear and return to its meal? Would it be tempted to follow and attack the one who was retreating? Would it see through the trick we were trying to play by stalking whichever one of us had remained behind and leaping upon that one from the rear?

There were too many imponderables in the situation and I confess I did not like them at all. Moreover, the doctor was armed only with a shotgun. If I suggested that he should go back and leave me behind, it was possible the tiger might decide to stalk him, when Stanley would be at a decided disadvantage. Alternatively, if I left the doctor behind and walked away myself and the man-eater decided to attack him instead of me, the same disadvantage would be there. As a last resource, I could offer the doctor my rifle and take his gun.

Frankly, I did not relish that last solution. I was accustomed to my .405 in emergencies. No doubt Stanley had the same feelings for his shotgun. If we exchanged weapons we would both be unfamiliar with the firearm each of us was handling, and a shotgun, moreover, was hardly suitable for a meeting with a man-eater.

Evidently these very thoughts were passing through Stanley's mind and he solved the problem for me by whispering to me to hide while he would go away. Without speaking, I thrust my rifle towards him and reached for his shotgun, but Stanley turned it way from me, motioning impatiently towards the bushes for me to hide.

The tiger was creeping about now, circling our position and continuing to snarl and roar alternately. A single bush, not more than four feet high, grew about thirty feet or so away, its base hidden by the usual carpet of grass and greenery. There was no other large tree or rock that offered shelter. I tiptoed to the bush and took up my position behind it, crouching on the ground with my weapon ready. We waited till the tiger had reached a point that was opposite the direction in which the doctor would have to go to regain the track leading towards the two huts. Then I motioned to him to get away quickly.

With the purpose of letting the man-eater know that he was departing and that the coast would be clear to return to the meal, Stanley coughed slightly and began to talk to himself as he began to back slowly towards the track. I watched him looking intently in the direction where the man-eater was still demonstrating, his .12 bore gun ready for instant action should the animal charge.

But Stanley had made a mistake by talking. Instead of returning to its kill now that the coast was clear, as the doctor had hoped, this most unusual animal did the unexpected thing once again. Circling the scant clearing in which the remains of its victim reposed, and incidentally myself, the tiger began to follow the departing doctor. Worse still, it stopped roaring and snarling. Clearly, the man-eater now meant business. Whatever the Ogre was doing at that moment, or intended to do at the next, was to be done in silence. Stanley, already handicapped with only a shotgun, was going to be still further handicapped by not knowing from which direction the man-eater would attack him.

This thought worried me. It was hard to sit idly behind a bush while my friend's life might at that moment be in great danger. Without weighing the consequences I decided to creep after the tiger. No greater folly could have been committed than by my action at that moment, and I will tell you why.

Try to imagine the doctor stepping backward, a foot at a time with his shotgun loaded in both barrels ready for instant use pointed towards where he thinks the tiger is, creeping upon him unseen and in silence. He does not know that I have left my shelter in the bush and am following him and the tiger. Then put yourself in the tiger's place, your composure now regained after any exhibition of bad temper. You move softly and silently, bent upon putting an end to this interfering human being who has dared to follow you. At the same time, you are aware that you are close enough for a final spring, but instinct warns you that to do so will court disaster. And you do not know that a second human being is following you. Behind them both am I, creeping forward with equally great caution, my Winchester cocked and ready for use at the first glimpse of the tiger. But I cannot see it, nor Stanley. All I can hear is the faint rustle of a bush here and there before me, as either Stanley or the tiger brushes against it despite their caution. Finally, do not forget that the distance between the doctor and myself cannot be more than forty or fifty yards now, with the tiger somewhere in between.

If only that tiger had had a little reasoning power, what fun it could have had that day! All it had to do was to conceal itself and then mimic the sound of a charging tiger by roaring 'Wroof! Wroof! Wroof!' Stanley and I would have opened fire. One or the other would have shot his companion. Perhaps with a spot of luck—or bad luck—we might have shot each other. I would have made more tender eating in those days than now! So would the doctor, even if he smelled faintly of iodoform! And what headlines for the newspapers! '*Shikaries* after man-eater shoot each other! Man-eater eats both!'

So intent was I on following the tiger that all this did not dawn upon me at the time. The man-eater, unaware of being followed, kept steadfastly after Stanley; while the doctor, naturally worried by the silence that had succeeded the tiger's threatening roars, except for a faint and furtive rustling now and again as the tiger came after him, was wondering if he would reach the track to the huts before the attack came.

Then things happened! The doctor! The doctor reached the track. The tiger broke the silence with a shattering roar! Seeing nothing but hearing everything, I did not know right away whether the man-eater was launching its attack upon the doctor or myself. The doctor fired, and slugs from his gun spattered through the undergrowth uncomfortably close to me. The tiger, frightened by the sound, lost its nerve, turned, and dashed past me at full gallop. I saw the tiger coming, threw the rifle to my shoulder, and pressed the trigger at almost point-black range.

Stanley told me a few minutes later that my bullet whizzed past his head within inches. The only thing that kept it from parting his hair, he affirmed, was that he was bald! Inadvertently the Ogre had almost succeeded in accomplishing what it had been unable to do by the power of reasoning. The doctor and I had narrowly escaped shooting each other.

We still had hopes, however. We both had considerable hunting experience. Both had been ready to fire when we had actually pressed our triggers. Both had fired at point-blank range. The tiger must be lying mortally wounded close by, perhaps it was even dead. One of us must have wounded it at least. In the excitement, we overlooked the fact that I had heard the slugs from Stanley's gun, while he had heard my bullet.

So we searched far and wide, but not a speck of blood did we come across. Of dead or wounded tiger there was neither sight nor sound! Then it dawned upon us. Hard though it was to admit, the truth stuck out a mile. We had both missed, although the Ogre had met us almost face to face. Stanley looked woebegone. I do not know what I looked like; but I know what I felt like!

We made our way in silence back to the huts, where to the man and the two women still hiding there we confided all that had happened. We were half a furlong from Tagarthy before my mind, numbed with disappointment, started to function again.

Normally a tiger, after being fired upon, avoids the place where that had happened for a long time. This tiger, it should be remembered, had been fired upon not once, but twice! Therefore, by all the rules, it should leave the neighbourhood and not appear there again. But was there just a small chance to the contrary? The Ogre had already shown itself to be of a most unusual disposition on two occasions. It fled and then turned and crept back again. And it had deliberately followed Stanley when the way was clear to return to its kill. Would it once again display its singular nature by returning to a place where, at least instinct must tell it, it had suffered two narrow escapes? The chances were 99 per cent against. That left a one per cent chance that the tiger might return!

I halted in my tracks as the thought came to me. The doctor stopped also, wondering what was the matter. I told him. Stanley frowned and puckered his forehead in thought. Then he shook his head. But he was too much of a hunter himself not to realize the chance was one that could not, must not, be missed. So we retraced our steps to the huts.

The man and the two women, now all locked together in one of the huts for mutual safety, were surprised at our early return. When we told them why we had come, they were really pleased. But they were honest enough to say they did not think we had any chance of success. It was the man's opinion that the tiger would be many miles away by now.

Stanley and I retraced our steps to the place where the remains of the man-eater's victim lay strewn about, exercising extreme caution while negotiating the patch of jungle through which the doctor, the tiger and I had played our strange game of hide-and-seek. There was neither sight nor sound of our quarry.

A strange mixture of relief and disappointment filled us, relief that the Ogre had not launched another attack and disappointment at the feeling that it might never return.

My earlier survey of the possibilities of concealment, although made in such a hurry, had about summed up the chances accurately. Apart from the four-foot-high bush where I had stood while the doctor retreated there was no other place in which to conceal myself. Hiding behind that bush in daylight for a man-eater, as I had done already, was one thing; but remaining there after darkness was quite another. The tiger, with its ability to see at night, would spot me immediately as it approached what was left of its victim from any angle other than directly opposite the bush behind which I would be hiding, while for me to see it would be impossible. Further, should it indeed return in spite of being shot at twice only a few hours earlier, the man-eater would undoubtedly make an extremely cautious approach and I would not be able to hear it. Lastly, there was no possibility of erecting any sort of shelter behind that scanty bush that would not immediately betray my presence.

What could I do? I was reluctant to forgo that tiny possibility of the man-eater's return. To commit suicide, and that too in a most painful manner in the jaws of the tiger, I was still more reluctant.

There seemed no solution as we thought about the matter without speaking, till suddenly the doctor had a brainwave. Would it not be possible, with the help of the man and the two women in the near-by huts, to dig a narrow hole just where the human remains were scattered? He would hide in the hole which would be wide and deep enough to conceal him, wait until the tiger returned, and shoot it at point-black range.

Several obstacles to the execution of this plan presented themselves. Firstly, the tiger might discover the hole and shy away; worse still, the tiger might decide to investigate it. Secondly, admitting that the man-in-the-hole was hidden from the tiger, the tiger was equally hidden from the man-in-the-hole, who would necessarily have to stand erect to be able to shoot the beast, during which process the latter would surely spot him when he appeared, as it would seem, out of the very ground. When that happened, the tiger would be frightened, yes; but it would also be decidedly annoyed. What transpired after that would depend upon which of the aforementioned reflexes gained the upper hand.

Well, there was no use thinking further about it. The chance, and the risk would have to be taken or the whole plan dropped. Time was passing and it was now after 3 p.m. We would have to work fast. We hurried back to the huts, where the inmates gladly volunteered to help us, but stated they had no implements of any sort to dig with. The doctor, who in his capacity of village medico wielded much influence, solved this by returning to Tagarthy at the double, from whence he came back in an incredibly short time with six helpers, two with pickaxes, two with crowbars, and two with large baskets in which to remove all traces of the earth we dug out. With the three earlier helpers and ourselves, the eleven of us set to work, with the result that astonishingly soon the hole had been dug and all traces of loose earth removed and thrown far away.

I knew that as the father of the plan, Stanley had prepared the hole to sit in it himself. I also knew that no amount of persuasion would dissuade him. If I tried to tell him that his shotgun was not an effective weapon against so dangerous a quarry, he would reply that it was just the right thing at such close range. Nor would I be able to gainsay the truth of his assertions as, in reality, at point-blank range a .12 bore gun has its merits. So I resigned myself to inactivity for once by spending the night at Tagarthy.

Our helpers were just gathering their tools together, prior to departing with me, when Dame Fortune once again took a hand in this strange adventure. Two men burst upon us, having run all the way from Tagarthy in search of the doctor. One was the village *patel*, quite a young man for such a responsible post; the other was his servant. The *patel* annouced that his wife, who was ,heavily pregnant, had slipped and fallen while carrying her pot of water from the well. She had aborted and was bleeding profusely. The doctor must come at once.

While he was still speaking, the young man summed up the position and realized that Stanley was preparing to sit up for the tiger. So to make his summons more forceful, he started lamenting aloud that the doctor, as his best friend, must come to his aid at once to save his wife's life, while in the same breath he denounced the woman as a stubborn wench. How often had he told her not to carry weights, particularly the water pot from the well. Was he not the village *patel*? Did he not have servants enough for this task? Yet in her wilfulness she would never listen to him. Now this was the result. And never mind the tiger; was his wife's life not far more important?

Stanley looked at me, chagrin written large upon his face. Then he gripped my arm tightly, affectionately.

'Good luck, Andy,' he muttered, 'and be careful, please. Would you like to use my gun?'

'Thanks, doc,' I replied, 'you know how it is. Old Winny will do the trick.'

In another minute Stanley and the other members of the group, which had grown to twelve, were lost to sight. I was alone with the remains of the dead man.

Dusk was fast approaching and there was not a moment to be lost as I slipped into the hole we had prepared, to squat at the bottom and look upwards at a circle of sky above my head. By canting my Winchester, loaded and cocked, at an angle with the butt against my right thigh and the foresight-guard leaning against the wall of the hold opposite me, we had made sure, by means of measuring Stanley's .12 bore gun in just a position, that the end of the muzzle would not be visible above ground level.

In the excitement and hurry of forming and executing what I now began to realize was a rather insane plan, we had overlooked the fact that it would be terribly hot inside the hole. The earth around had been exposed to the sun's rays all day, no air could enter, and with my body in close proximity to the sides of the cavity, air could not circulate anywhere. I soon began to perspire profusely.

Fortunately in those days there were no wild elephants around Tagarthy or, for that matter, in any of the districts to the northwest of Mysore state. Those were the times when tigers roamed in hundreds, but things have now changed and carnivora are scarce, but 'jumbo' in his wild state has extended his wanderings into those jungles and herds of elephants have now made their home there, where once there were none.

I remember that it was almost deathly silent inside the hole and I could scarcely hear the roosting calls of peafowl, junglecocks and other birds as they settled down for the night. To hope to hear the man-eater's arrival by any faint sound that it might make was out of the question. I would only be able to hear it if it roared or snarled nearby, and the Ogre was hardly likely to do that—or so at least I thought till I recollected that the tiger had in fact done just that only a few hours earlier. How I hoped it would repeat its performance rather than decide upon a silent approach!

It was almost dark when the circle of sky above my head was crossed by an elongated black form that passed silently by. A nightjar, with wings outstretched, had flown low over the spot, evidently to investigate the possibility of devouring the insects that were already assembling to feed upon the exposed flesh that hung in shreds from the human bones and devoured portions of the carcase of the tiger's unfortunate victim. I could hear the bluebottles as they buzzed across the opening above my head to settle on the mess, while the stench of decaying flesh, increased by the sun's rays in which it had been baking all day, seemed to cling to the ground and flow into the hole as an invisible, nauseating liquid.

Would the tiger come? Would it start eating right away? Or would it know that something unusual was afoot? It might have been watching us from the cover of some distant bush. It might even know, at that very moment, that one of its hated foes, a man, had gone into hiding somewhere in the ground. Now would be an excellent opportunity for the tiger to unearth and devour that enemy. The thought was not a very bracing one!

Where there had been an oval of sky above, two stars now twinkled down upon me and I knew that night had fallen. They seemed so serene and peaceful up there, oblivious to my predicament down in the hole. My thoughts focused upon them and I wondered at what other tragedies, taking place at that moment in other remote corners of the earth, they also twinkled upon so impartially.

The next moment the two stars seemed to become endowed with a baleful significance. They turned into two cruel eyes that glowered down upon me in hostile anticipation. Of what?

I forced myself to cast off this depressing idea and to think of something else. It is amazing what strange and often irrelevant thoughts come to one when in danger, as I was then. Perhaps this is nature's way of providing protection from panic. I wondered if Stanley would be able to save the life of the *patel's* wife.

That was when I first heard the sound: faint but distinctly heavy breathing.

It must be the tiger! It had located me and was creeping upon its stomach to get close enough to pull me out of my hiding place. Involuntarily, my hand reached towards the rifle. The touch of metal and wood, warm like everything else in that wretched pit, was very comforting to my nerves.

The sound ceased for a while. Then I heard a sudden, loud hiss, followed by silence again. Could this be a passing panther?

I have already mentioned that panthers were scarce in this area as the tigers had driven them out simply by devouring them. Nevertheless, there were one or two to be found here and there, and it was possible that an odd member had happened to be passing and had stumbled upon the exposed kill, creeping forward to snatch a mouthful. The heavy breathing and the hissing sound could certainly have been made by a panther, bent upon stealing from the tiger's kill.

I did not hear anything more for quite a long time. Then came a dull, scraping sound, as of something gliding over the ground above my head. Could a large snake be the cause? A hamadryad? There were quite a number of them to be found in these forests, where the vegetation and jungles were of the 'wet' variety, unlike the forests farther south.

Silence followed, while I strained my ears to pick up the faintest of sounds, and my eyes stared upwards at the faint light of the hole above me till they ached. The two stars still twinkled down upon me, but whether in disdain or mockery I did not know. I saw that they had shifted farther towards the edge of the circle above me and would soon disappear from view, indicating that time had passed since I had first observed them. I would miss their company and then would really be alone. Would their place be taken by other stars, I wondered?

This thought was still in my mind when at last the heavy silence was broken. There was a loud crack and the man-eater began to gnaw the bone it had just broken.

The noise made by a feeding tiger indicates its mood. Generally it is one of great contentment, and the sounds of mastication, gnawing, chewing and the tearing and rending of flesh follow one another as the feast progresses. Should there be a second tiger present, or the killer be a tigress with cubs, there is a lot of growling and wrangling, accompanied by threatening snarls when the other tiger, or a cub, approaches too closely. For despite the ties of mother love, which are considerable—and instances have been known where a tigress has sacrificed her life for her cubs—when it comes to eating, instinct seems to tell a feasting tigress that food is something not to be shared too soon, and to urge her to eat her fill before

41

allowing her companion, mate or even her cubs to approach and eat what may be left.

The tiger above me began to growl. I knew then that it could not be alone. Perhaps there were cubs, perhaps another tiger, accompanying the man-eater. The situation was decidedly complicated and more than what I had bargained for. None of us had considered this possibility earlier in the evening, when this sitting-in-the-hole idea had occurred to Stanley.

I thought hard what to do next. Obviously, in order to take a shot at the tiger, I would have to locate it first by peeping over the edge of the hole and then by drawing the rifle right out of the hole and placing it on the ground outside so as to take aim. All this would entail considerable movement; I might even make a sound of some sort; the rifle might knock against the ground. The feeding animal would hear me and attack before I could free my weapon. There might be a slight hope of escaping the tiger's attention should he, or she, happen luckily to be facing the other way.

But there was a second tiger present. Even cubs could give the game away if they saw my head and shoulders, followed by my rifle, emerging from the ground. It was certainly straining imagination and luck too far to hope that all the animals above me would have their backs to me and be looking in the wrong direction. And if there should be two tigers above me, which of them was the man-eater? A silly question, that: obviously the one that was eating. But had both developed the man-eating habit, or only one? I must not kill the wrong tiger. Therefore, I must shoot both to take no chances.

The alternative course of action was to sit in silence in the hole, allow the animals to finish their meal and afterwards go about their business, then call it a day. But I had come here to shoot the man-eater; not to hide from it. I thought of the man it had killed and was now eating. What would Stanley and the villagers say of me when they came in the morning to find the ground covered with tiger pug-marks, the scraps of the man otherwise completely devoured, and me hiding in the hole?

Well, here goes, I said to myself, and a millimetre at a time, if such slow movement can in truth be possible, I began to position my feet so as to support me. Then slowly, very, very slowly, I started to raise myself, to bring my head to ground level. This in itself, took a long time, for I had to avoid making the slightest sound, and my thighs and legs were cramped from squatting so long on my haunches. The tiger continued feeding, growling and snarling now and again to keep the other tiger, or perhaps the cubs, away.

At last I was on my knees and toes and I stretched my two hands downwards to help support my weight on my outstretched fingers. Then very slowly, I began to raise myself.

Time had passed, and the strain on my hands and legs began to tell. But I must not hurry. Even now, as my ears came closer to the surface above, the tiger's growls grew stronger. I began to be frightened.

My hands were beginning to tremble with the sustained strain of supporting my weight, when I sensed that the top of my head must have reached about ground level. I could not delay longer, for the tiger or tigers would be able to see me should they be looking in my direction, whilst I would not be able to see them. I therefore quickly raised my head, until my eyes were level with the earth.

A terrifying sight confronted me. Luckily, through sitting in the darkness of the hole for so long, my eyes had grown accustomed to the gloom, so that I could see, only a few feet away, and lying broadside on, the enormous form of a tiger extended on its belly, chewing some part of the victim which it was holding between its front paws. Worse still, there was another form, also at full stretch, slightly farther away from me and a few feet from the feasting tiger, but facing it, and watching anxiously as the latter swallowed mouthful after mouthful. This second tiger, facing the first, was also facing me, and could not fail to see the top of my head popping out of the earth.

It let a snarl of surprise and scrambled to its feet. I ducked into my hole like a jack-in-the-box, grabbed my rifle, and looked upwards, expecting to find one or both tigers attacking the opening. I was wondering whether to sit tight, or to raise myself and the rifle quickly to ground level and risk a shot, but I remembered there were two tigers, not one outside. So I funked it and decided to sit tight.

All this occupied only a few seconds, but in that time the feasting tiger had not been idle. Hearing its companion snarl, and seeing it spring to its feet, this animal, not knowing that the sight of me was the cause of the excitement, concluded that its companion had decided to fight for a share of the kill. There was a second loud roar, followed by a fearful din, as the feaster, who was obviously the man-eater, attacked the tiger that had spotted me.

Now is my chance, I said to myself, for their attention was so distracted that they would not notice me.

I quickly raised myself. First the rifle, then head and shoulders, reached ground level. For a moment I could see nothing and do nothing because of the dust that was raised by the fighting animals. But neither tiger was anyway in sight, nor was there any growling or snarling to be heard.

I could not understand it. Perhaps the second tiger had fled with the first in pursuit. But if that was so, I should have heard some sounds at least, snarls and growls as one animal chased the other away. Perhaps they saw the rifle, or even the top of my head emerging from the hole, and fled at such an unexpected apparition. Then, too, there should have been growling and snarling; at least some sounds of departure.

As it was, the jungle was silent. I could not fathom it; it was eerie. The thought then occured to me that, if the man-eater had chased its companion away, it would undoubtedly return to finish what was left of the kill. So I ducked back into the hole to await its return and the renewed sounds of eating.

I waited in vain. Maybe half an hour had passed when I heard a loud, sustained human scream. It shattered the silence, rose to a crescendo, and then faded into choking sobs and was still. Then I heard other yells and shouts, and could make out a deeper voice and a more shrill one. These were the voices of the man and one of the two women from the two huts not far away. They were screaming for help.

That was when I grasped what had happened. The second woman had been taken by the man-eater! In chasing its companion away from the feast, or perhaps in its headlong flight after seeing my rifle and myself appear out of the ground, the man-eater must have passed the two huts where the man and his wife, and the widow of the late victim, were sheltering. But how did the Ogre get its second victim? Perhaps it was in such a towering rage that it just dragged her out of the hut in which she was sleeping. This tiger certainly was not hungry enough to justify such an action as it had been feasting all this while.

I wondered what to do. Should I remain where I was, or hasten to the huts? In either event, there was not much that I could do. There was little chance that the man-eater would return to the bones of its first victim when it had a fresh one at its disposal. And I would not be able to follow it up with the second kill, because of the darkness. That could be done only after daybreak.

I decided to remain where I was. It was just possible that the second tiger—the one that had been chased away—might return to the scant remains lying above me. If it did so, I would shoot; even if it were not the Ogre itself, this second tiger would undoubtedly become a man-eater in time. I remembered how, a short while ago, it lay anxiously waiting for a chance to eat the human remains, though held at bay by the feasting man-eater.

I spent a sleepless night after that, uncomfortably hot and stung by tiny ants and other insects that had decided to share my shelter. Nothing came, and no sound disturbed the silence till about four o'clock. Then a hyena discovered the bones above me and a great commotion began. The hyena smelt the tigers and knew it was about to commit the unpardonable crime of robbery. It also knew that to be caught by the owner or owners would mean death. It was undecided, therefore, between satisfying its hunger and its fear of being killed, and in this state of indecision made a great noise, letting the whole jungle know that it was faced with a tremendous dilemma. I could hear the creature running rapidly round and round, uttering weird sounds of every conceivable dilemma. 'Chee-ah! Chee-ay! Chee-ay!' it chattered, then growled like faraway thunder. 'Goodoo-Goodoo-Grooo!' Then it decided to be mournful about the whole business: 'Mee-ay! Mee-ay! Mee-ay!' it pleaded piteously, like a cat begging for food.

But the problem remained unsolved: the tiger did not show itself, but might come at any moment, and that would be the hyena's last if it lingered. All this amused me and served to distract my thoughts from the fearful tragedy that must have been enacted so close to me while I was powerless to intervene.

The opening above me grew a little brighter with the coming of the false dawn before the hyena, who had remained noisily persistent all this time, finally summoned up enough courage to start eating. I heard the crunch of a few bones for a short while, then fear must have returned to its craven heart, for I heard the pattering sound of its departure. I could picture the poor beast slinking quickly away, a human bone between its jaws, for gnawing later in the safety of its shelter among the rocks, or in a hole in the ground, far from this place of danger and lurking death.

I awaited the advent of the true dawn before raising the Winchester and myself very cautiously above ground level. The coast was clear and I dragged my cramped legs out of that awful hole, stamped about for a few minutes to restore the circulation, and set off for the huts to see what had happened. There I came upon a dreadful sight.

The terrified man and his wife, still hiding in a corner of one of the huts, told me a very harrowing tale. Along with the widow of the man-eater's victim, they had decided to sleep in one of the huts, the one they felt was the more secure of the two. The man had taken good care to sleep in the centre of the floor, equidistant from all the walls while his wife had slept to the left of him. The second woman had been forced to sleep somewhere by herself. So she had laid down a little distance away. Naturally she must have felt a little nervous, but as modesty forbade her to lie down to the right of the man, she had been compelled to sleep as far away as possible from the couple. So she lay down near the wall of the hut and opposite their feet.

The hut was comparatively small. It was roughly a square, about twelve feet by twelve. Allowing six feet for the man and his wife who were sleeping in the centre of the hut, and another three feet in order to be clear of their legs, the second woman was, therefore, lying at the most not more that a yard from the wall. The foot of the walls of such huts, in the damper parts of India, are kept a few inches from the ground

47

so that termites cannot climb them overnight and destroy a large part of the structure by daylight. This practice leaves a slight opening around all four sides at ground level.

The man-eater who had passed very close to the hut, either in pursuit of its companion or in flight from me, was probably in great rage. It must have caught a glimpse of the sleeping woman, or sensed her presence, through this small opening, and had decided to drag her out. It had inserted one of its paws under the opening, grabbed the woman and had begun to pull her out.

Her screams and wails, which I had heard, had awakened her two companions, who in turn had started to yell and call for help. Meanwhile the man-eater had succeeded in dragging the woman's head and neck outside the hut, and had killed her by tearing out her gullet. But the rest of her body was stuck inside, for in dying, the woman clung to two of the bamboos supporting the wall of the hut. These had broken, and the end of one of them, piercing her saree and jacket, had gone right into the flesh of her side, thus wedging her body against the bamboo wall.

The pandemonium caused by her wails, and the shouts of her companions, seemed to have acted as a deterrent; the tiger changed its mind and abandoned the victim. The carcase of the woman as it lay before me was a dreadful sight. The tiger's claws had pierced the chest and torn one breast to ribbons. Then the Ogre had bitten right through her gullet and had wrenched out her windpipe, leaving the bones of her neck and the skin behind to keep her head from being totally severed. She lay in a pool of her own blood most of which had soaked into the dry earth, except for some that coagulated here and there.

The two survivors, man and wife, crouched wide-eyed and paralysed with fear in a far corner of the hut, expecting the man-eater to return at any moment. In fact, they were so terrified as to be oblivious of the fact that it was already daylight outside. Hearing my approaching footsteps, and thinking they heard the tiger returning they started to gibber in fear.

I called aloud to reassure them. The man and the woman then hurled themselves at the door of the hut, opened it, and rushed outside, to fall on the ground trembling and crying in terror and relief at the same time. They were quite hysterical and took a long while to calm down enough to tell their story.

I had entered the hut and was reviewing the dreadful sight inside when Stanley and some of the men who had helped us the previous evening arrived upon the scene. Stanley had been awake all night but had not heard any report from my rifle, the sound of which would have carried to Tagarthy village. He therefore concluded that the tiger had not returned—or that I had been killed—and was hurrying to find out what had happened.

I fear my first question took the good doctor aback: 'How is the *Patel's* wife?'

He looked rather pained at my irrelevance, then muttered, 'She's safe. But what has happened?' I told the story. Our plans were soon laid.

We bundled the two survivors and their belongings out of the hut, an action that did not require much persuasion, and advised them to return, with the rest of our party, to the village. Stanley would hide in the other hut, while I would conceal myself in the one with the corpse of the slain woman. Ordinarily, the man-eater might be expected to return to its kill, but as there was a second tiger which was potentially a man-eater, if not already one, the doctor would be available to deal with it.

We laid our plans carefully. To begin with, neither of us would fire in the direction where the other was hiding. Secondly, should Stanley see one of the tigers, or both of them first, he was to hold his fire till the actual man-eater approached the carcase of its victim in order to give me the chance of a shot at the real culprit. As soon as I had fired, the doctor was to shoot the second tiger if it was still within sight. These precautions were necessary to avoid a mistake at the last moment for should the doctor fire first, he might shoot the wrong tiger and the man-eater would escape. We had to account for the Ogre primarily, although for reasons I have already given the second tiger had to be shot too. But the man-eater must die first and we could not risk its escape.

As I was tired after a sleepless night, while Stanley was less so, even though he had spent a good part of the night attending to the *patel's* wife, it was agreed that I should go back to Tagarthy for a meal and some sleep, returning by three o'clock, bringing the doctor's lunch and some food for both of us to eat later on besides drinking water, tea and the torch that Stanley fitted to the barrels of his shotgun. It was wise that one of us should remain on guard, just in case either of the tigers took the unusual step of returning to the kill by day.

Another idea then occurred to me. I told Stanley and he agreed to it. We took a gunny sack from one of the huts and walked down to the remains of the earlier kill. My plan was to remove all that was left of it, so that should either of the tigers, or both of them, think of revisiting the old spot, they would find nothing. That would urge them to come to the huts, where we would be in hiding.

A slight hitch arose when we asked our men to do this job. Being of high caste, they recoiled with horror and flatly refused. There was nothing but for Stanley and myself to do the job ourselves. Stanley did not mind, for he was a doctor, but it was an unpleasant undertaking for me. What little remained of the meat was two days old and stank abominably. Further, bluebottles had laid their eggs in the remains, and in the hot sun maggots had already hatched in myriads. The flesh was covered with a seething mass of them.

We gathered all the bits and pieces and put them into the sack. Since none of our followers would touch it, I had the unhappy task of conveying this nasty burden on my shoulder all the way to the village. It was surprising how heavy those bits and pieces turned out to be, although they represented so very little of their owner.

I smelled dreadfully and was in a bath of perspiration; some sticky fluid had oozed through the sacking from the putrefying flesh and bones within. It was on my hands, shoulders and neck when I dumped my grisly burden at the entrance to the local police *chowki*. The constable on sentry gazed at me goggle-eyed. For once in his life he was too taken aback to ask for a statement. I remembered about the statement well enough, but did not care to remind him. Why should I? There was going to be a hell of a row in any case, when the sub-inspector and other busybodies from headquarters arrived at Tagarthy. Whey had we removed the remains from the scene of the tragedy? How were the police to know the man had been killed by a tiger? He might have been murdered? Perhaps he had committed suicide? Time enough to answer these questions later. What I wanted was a bath, tea and plenty of it, a hot meal and some sleep.

I hastened to the little quarters occupied by the doctor, which he had invited me to share with him, and yelled to his servant-boy to prepare a gallon of tea. Then I divested myself of my stinking clothes and washed my shirt. Next I had a bath, and what a bath!

Emerging at least two pounds lighter in weight, I set about the tea and had consumed maybe two quarts when the doctor's servant seriously suggested I leave some room for lunch. But there was no lunch left when I stood up from the table. I observed the servant had conceived a new respect for me as a glutton of great capacity.

I told the boy to put the doctor's lunch aside and to make dinner for both of us, saying that I would take the three meals with me to the two huts at three o'clock. In sadness, the youngster shook his head and replied aggrievedly that there was no lunch left. I had eaten it all. So I gave him money to make some lunch; also the two dinners. And I told him to awaken me at 2.30 sharp.

When he awakened me it was nearly three o'clock, but as the meals were ready and packed, together with two flasks of tea and two canteens of water, I had only to pick up the doctor's torch and place it in a large bag with the food and flasks, sling the canteens and my rifle over my shoulders, and set out for the huts.

Walking fast, I soon arrived to find a very hungry doctor who had no news of the tigers. He swallowed his lunch while we reviewed our plans in whispers and drank some water. The flasks of tea we decided to keep for the night.

At four o'clock we separated; I went to the neighbouring hut where the woman's body lay, taking my rifle, torch, dinner and a flask of tea with half a canteen of water, leaving Stanley in the other hut with his share of the tea, water and food. Taking up my position at the farther end, as far away as possible from the spot where the corpse was lying half in and half out of the little structure, I made myself comfortable in preparation for the long vigil of fourteen hours till dawn.

I have cultivated the habit of sitting cross-legged for hours on end, practically motionless and without sound, a habit essential if ever you have to sit up for game. The slightest movement, or the faintest sound, will betray your presence to any wild creature, animal or bird. If your quarry is an animal possessed of a keen sense of smell, the direction in which the prevailing breeze happens to be blowing has also to be taken into account, and the stronger the breeze, the farther your scent is carried. For this reason, poachers of deer in India seldom go out on a windy night. Falling rain prevents scent being carried far, but equally so all animals, except tigers, take shelter from the elements, and if the rain is really bad, even tigers and elephants restrict their movements.

Now, as tigers have only a very poor sense of smell, that factor did not trouble me. What I had to be careful about was that the man-eater should not discover my presence by sight or sound. After the adventure of the previous night, and the scare it had received, we could expect both tigers to be very cautious. It is remarkable how instinct enables a man-eater to differentiate between a possible victim, helpless and defenceless, and a would-be hunter capable of taking its life.

Having been sheltered from the sun, the corpse was not smelling yet, and it was otherwise pleasant inside the hut, offering a great relief from the conditions of the previous night, in the hot and tight-fitting hole. Everything about me was quiet, for, in fear of the man-eater, the herdsmen of Tagarthy and the neighbouring villages for miles around had abandoned their usual habit of driving their herds out to the jungles to graze.

The afternoon passed in silence except for the buzzing of flies that had discovered the dead body and were busy laying their eggs in the raw flesh. The darkness of evening was accentuated within the hut and it soon became difficult to see, although I could perceive the lingering daylight outside, visible right around me through the few inches of space between the base of the walls of the hut and the floor.

Because of the scarcity of panthers and the larger species of wild cats, jungle fowl, which are the normal prey of these animals, swarmed in this area and their calls, together with those of spur-fowl and peafowl, told me the sun was about to set. Silently, I munched the food I had brought with me for dinner, and drank some tea.

In due course the cries of the birds died away, to be replaced by the calls of a nearby herd of spotted deer and the belling of a more distant sambar stag. This told me the sun had set, although by now it was already quite dark inside the hut where I was sitting.

Soon the nightjars began their teasing cries and a night-heron wailed in the little stream at the bottom of the valley. Then I knew that night had fallen indeed, and I could now see nothing in the interior of that hut. If the man-eater came and started to remove the cadaver of the woman, I would be compelled to use my torch.

This raised a problem. When I used the torch, its beam would necessarily strike against the inside of the wall of the hut and be reflected back into my eyes. I would not be able to see beyond, or to look through the gap between the wall and the floor. In other words, the man-eater would not be visible to me. The thought began to trouble me and I decided to change my position. I would lie prone on the floor, as close as possible to that part of the woman's body which remained inside. This would give me a great advantage. By keeping my rifle extended on the ground before me, all I would need to do, when the tiger came, would be to point the barrel in the animal's direction and press the trigger. The man-eater could not avoid making some noise when it began to pull the woman's carcase out of the hut, for, as you will remember, in the struggle of the previous night the end of one of the bamboos of the hut-wall had become embedded in her flesh. The tiger would have to tear the body free from this obstruction.

Gathering the flask of tea and my weapon, I crept quietly across the floor till I reached the woman's body, and then lay down beside it, the rifle on the ground before me with the butt under my armpit and the end of the barrel only a few inches from the opening. Accidentally my shoulder touched something that was cold and hard and very stiff. It was the corpse's leg and I drew a few inches away.

Three hours passed with no sign of any tiger. It was well after ten o'clock. Tigers generally return to their kills around eight; panthers very much earlier, and I was beginning to think our quarries had decided to keep clear of the huts when the leg which had touched my shoulder three hours ago touched it again.

What was far worse, that cold stiff leg was now moving very distinctly. It was not only rubbing against my shoulder now, but moving gently forwards.

Not a sound could I hear. But the leg moved again! The hair at the back of my neck stood on end. Panic seized me. I was on the verge of scrambling to my hands and knees and getting as far away as possible from that awful, mangled human thing that had come to life. Then reason returned. I could feel myself trembling and the perspiration was pouring down my face as I discovered the solution. The leg and its owner had not come back to life, nor did it move of its own volition. The man-eater was moving it!

I could see nothing. There was no sense in sticking the barrel of my rifle forward and firing blindly; that would only scare the tiger away, to continue its depredations elsewhere. At the most I might wound it. I had first to make certain what I was firing at.

Then it was that I heard a faint scratching sound, coming from somewhere very close to me and a little to my right. I could still see nothing. I was tempted to switch on my torch, but remembered in time that to do so might result in dazzling myself. Yet it was imperative that I should find out where the scratching sound came from and what was causing it.

I did an extremely stupid thing. Not being able to see, I thought I might be able to feel what was going on, and with this in mind, I stretched my right arm very slowly forwards in the direction of the scratching.

I did not have far to reach. My questing fingertips contacted something hairy, something sinewy, and the next instant all hell was let loose. The man-eater, perhaps remembering its difficulty of the night before to free the body of its victim, or maybe in an endeavour to secure a better grip on the corpse, had extended its paw into the gap below the wall and was groping for a hold on something solid. That movement of its paw was the cause of the scratching sound I had heard a moment before. When my fingertips touched its skin, not having heard of ghosts, the tiger knew there was something alive inside the hut.

An ordinary tiger would have bolted. But the Ogre who was no ordinary tiger and had always done the unexpected, lost its temper. It let out a terrific roar, then grasped the wall of the hut in its jaws and began to tear it apart.

My task after that was easy. A great hole appeared before me and the beam of my torch revealed a horrifying tiger with the matting of the wall still stuffed in its mouth. With only a few inches to find its target, the bullet of my .405 entered high into the throat; then I rolled over and over with my rifle to get out of range of what I knew would follow. I was near the far end of the hut when the Ogre hurled itself through the gap. But I had time to put two more shots straight into

56

its head. With the dying animal threshing about the floor, I rushed to the door of the hut, flung it open and leaped out, only to be confronted by yet another terrifying spectacle.

Another tiger was there, about twenty feet away and to one end of the farther hut! But it was lying on the ground, stretched on its side and still twitching. Stanley had killed the second tiger, almost at point-blank range, with lethal balls fired simultaneously from both barrels of his shotgun. Because of the noise made by my own rifle, and because of my own excitement, I had entirely failed to hear Stanley's shots.

The doctor related afterwards that he heard the man-eater's roar, followed by the report of my first shot. Then the sounds of the hut-wall being demolished. Disregarding our agreement, he had dashed out to my aid, to be confronted by the sight of the second tiger, standing broadside on to him a few yards away, watching its mate and obviously undecided what to do. He had fired both barrels of his shotgun, loaded with lethal balls, into the animal's heart, killing it instantly.

As we suspected, the man-eater turned out to be a tigress, the other animal her mate.

There was much tom-tomming and rejoicing at Tagarthy until dawn, and when the news reached Bellundur next day old Buddiah strutted about, filled with pride. Was he not the greatest of all magicians? Had not his mantras brought about the doom of the man-eater and also of her mate? Buddiah was happy indeed. With his fame as a necromancer soaring once again, he could look forward to many feasts of cock curry and many more bottles of that fire *arrack* for which the villagers of Bellundur were famed. He was dead drunk by midday, when I called to thank him.

57

Three

The Aristocrat of Amligola

THE TITLE OF THIS STORY WILL LEAD YOU TO EXPECT THAT THE creature I am going to tell you about had nobility and fearfulness, and that he came from a place named Amligola, but you might not guess that the story really concerns a very large tiger that had other characteristics which I am sure you will agree were far from noble. Very few of you will have heard of Amligola, for it is situated in the remoter jungles of the district of Shimoga in Mysore state, and was only a hamlet at the time of my story.

People called him 'Gowndnorai' in the Kanarese tongue, being a term approximately equivalent to 'aristocrat,' and he earned his title by his unexpected behaviour at the time he first appeared in the thick forests surrounding the hamlet. It was rumoured that he came from the jungles of Tagarthy, a place renowned for tigers and only eight miles away; while others said he had strayed from the Karadibetta Tiger

Sanctuary, which he had deserted in disgust because his kindred in the sanctuary were numerous and the quest for food had become more competitive.

The 'Gowndnorai,' apparently, did not like this sort of thing. It was bad enough to have to hobnob with the proletariat of the tiger species, but when it came to having one's quarry snatched from under one's nose, as frequently happened, by younger and fleeter tigers, or the whole hunt thwarted and the prey driven away by a fledgeling tigress, he felt it was time to shift to more select jungles, where there were fewer of its species and more game for him to hunt.

There is a small hillock in the forest about two miles from Amligola which borders the track leading from this village to Tagarthy, and it came about that around five o'clock one evening, woodcutters returning home along this *path* were surprised to see a tiger sprawled on a rocky promontory of the hillock, basking in the rays of the sun that had still an hour to go before it would sink behind the tops of the towering teak trees to the west.

They quickened their footsteps. Everyone knew that these dense jungles were the homes of tigers, although such animals rarely showed themselves in broad daylight. The tiger they were now watching although fortunately from an appreciable distance, was an enormous brute and, to judge by his attitude of lazy indifference, seemed to care little about their presence. They were talking loudly and he could see and hear them, but he continued to lie on the warm rock as he turned his huge head in their direction with the mildest curiosity.

Thus the woodcutters judged it better to get home while the going was good and before darkness overtook them. Against such a monster they would have no chance whatever, once the sun sank and the brief jungle twilight merged into gloom.

Quite often thereafter, the graziers, woodcutters and forest guards saw this tiger of an evening, at about the same time, sunning himself on the same promontory and looking at them quite unconcernedly, as they moved through the jungle or followed the footpath that wound around the base of the hill on its way to Amligola.

None of them remembered having seen a tiger do this sort of thing before. Panthers had been seen quite often, on the same rock, on other rocks, sunning themselves of an evening; but never a tiger. The larger carnivores are too cunning and too shy to expose themselves in this way to an easy shot from a rifle.

Nobody fired at the basking tiger, for the very good reason that nobody in Amligola at that time possessed a rifle, while the range was too great for the ordinary muzzle-loading gun, a couple of which, unlicensed of course, were owned by local villagers.

For the first few months this seemingly inoffensive tiger had been content to confine his attentions to the spotted deer and other wild fauna of the forest. Then, as rarely happened in this area that was so close to the Western Ghats and received a heavy rainfall, the southwest monsoon failed one year and the jungle became dry. The grass withered, the fields lay fallow, and the wild creatures that fed on the grass and the grain were compelled to move away to regions where a little water was still to be found and some grass for their bellies. The herds of cattle that had hitherto fed along with the deer and had not been molested by the tiger so far now found themselves alone.

Nevertheless, this tiger was choosy about his meals. He left the herds and wandered into the village postmaster-cum-schoolteacher's field, where he started by killing the owner's large white bull that used to draw his cart all the nineteen miles to Sagar town once a week, on shandy (market) day. Not only did the tiger slay the huge bull with one slap of his paw and a twist of its neck, but he slung the quarry across his back and walked off with it in broad daylight, neatly leaping the six-foot-wide *nullah* that divided the field from the forest.

The field was at the back of the postmaster's house, and the owner was in the backyard, washing his clothes at his little well, and saw the whole thing happen. He shouted at the top of his voice, hoping to frighten the tiger into releasing its prey, although this would have done no good anyway because the white bull was already dead. But, far from being alarmed, the tiger was not even perturbed. He walked majestically at the same pace towards the *nullah,* the dead bull across his back, jumped the obstruction, and disappeared into the forest beyond.

The tiger killed again, and quite often after that, but strange to relate, on each occasion his prey was a lone, large bull or a fat, sleek cow. Never did he attack the herds, as other tigers and panthers had done before him, to choose and kill the first animal within reach.

This tiger spent a long time in reconnoitring and selecting his victim, and it always had to be the biggest animal he could find, proportionate to his own colossal size, revealed by the immense pug-marks he left on the fields and in the wind-blown sands of the pathways leading into the forest.

At that time I happened to visit Tagarthy, a favourite haunt of mine, where I came to hear about the Gowndnorai and his colossal size. As this animal was killing normal prey I had no intention of interfering with him, but repeated stories of his extraordinary size made me curious to catch a glimpse of him if I could.

So I set out on foot one dark night along the jungle track that led through dense forest to Amligola, the rifle across my back in case of emergency, a three-cell spotlight torch in my hand and a set of spare cells in my pocket.

I remember that night well. On the way, the beam reflected the green light of the eyes of spotted deer and sambar, bobbing up and down as they tried to avoid the torch-beam; the single, red eye of wild boar that refused to face the light but rushed away; the wide-set blue light from the eyes of a bull-bison that stared morosely as I passed; the red-white light of a panther's eyes as they sank behind a small shrub and then peeped at me from over the top; and the pinkish-blue eyes of a sloth-bear as it sat on its haunches to watch me as I padded past in my rubber shoes, not ten feet away.

I had entered the fields bordering Amligola when I met the Gowndnorai and immediately recognized him, although I had never set eyes upon him before. Two great blobs of light blazed white-red like brilliant stars suspended just above the tops of the grasses that were swaying gently to the night breezes as they blew down from the small hillock. It might have been a hundred yards away.

This tiger was, indeed, of colossal proportions.

The Gowndnorai gazed back at me unflinchingly as I stopped to watch him with the beam of my torch directed at him steadily. We returned stare for stare, and thus we remained for what might have been the better part of ten minutes. Then the tiger did a strange thing. With a low grunt, and eyes still blazing into the bright rays that confronted him, the Gowndnorai started to walk towards me.

No ordinary tiger would have done that; it would have bounded away. No wounded tiger, or even potential man-eater, would have done so either; it would have charged towards me, roaring in furious attack, or have melted away into the jungle, refusing a direct encounter.

The Gowndnorai did neither. He advanced upon me slowly, inexorably, determinedly, a guttural grunt issuing from his slightly opened mouth as he came, no signs of anger or of fear upon his striped visage.

One fact soon became evident. This strange animal, whatever his reason, was obviously quite determined to come right up to the torch and find out what it was all about.

I must confess his attitude rather unnerved me. I had no wish to shoot the beast, for he had done no harm to the human race. But what he might do when he came right up to my torch and found a man behind it was anybody's guess.

The tiger was now less than fifty yards away and still approaching, pace by pace, when these thoughts rushed through my mind and the reason for its strange behaviour dawned upon me. There were just four days until Christmas and this was the middle of the mating season. Without doubt the tiger was a male, and a tigress was sitting on her haunches somewhere near by, regarding the scene with admiration, as to her adoring eyes the Gowndorai displayed his prowess and contempt for danger.

Tigers can be very dangerous if encountered in the mating-season in company with their newly-found spouses. Their desire to flaunt themselves and their natural aversion to any intruder who disturbs their lovemaking, together with a fear that some harm might come to their mates, combine to turn them into creatures of destruction that will wipe out the intruder, man or beast.

Then came the disquieting thought that the tigress might even be creeping up behind me in the darkness, in support of her mate. I did not want to remove my torchbeam from the Gowndnorai's eyes, in case such action might precipitate a charge; at the same time the possibility of the close presence of the tigress behind me left no alternative.

Taking a chance, I whipped around, allowing the torch-beam to flash through the jungle in a quick semicircle to my right, and then behind. Sure enough, that was exactly where the tigress was. She was seated on her haunches, like a great big cat, directly behind me, awaiting the oncoming of her mate.

The reason for the tiger's strange behaviour was evident enough after that. He had been approaching the tigress when I had happened to move between them, and the mating urge had been too strong to deflect him from his purpose. I had no illusions about what he would do when he found me standing between him and his girlfriend. It was time to get the hell out of there!

This I proceeded to do forthwith, and with dispatch, by stepping sideways as rapidly and as silently as possible, while still keeping the torch-beam directed upon the tiger. The Gowndnorai halted abruptly and his grunt turned into a loud growl. What was worse, I could hear the tigress growling behind me. It seemed that a concerted attack was imminent.

With my left arm I unslung the loaded rifle, slipped the butt into my shoulder, and pressed the button of the other torch that was clamped to the barrel of the weapon, using my thumb for the purpose. The two beams shone together for a moment as I prepared to slip the three-cell torch into my trouser-pocket prior to placing my right forefinger upon the trigger.

Perhaps it was the two torches, shining together, that averted disaster. Maybe the Gowndnorai did not like the sight, and the potential danger revealed by the presence of a second light appearing so suddenly where a moment before, there had been only one. With a series of snarls he bounced obliquely forward in the general direction of his mate, and understanding the situation, I followed his movements with both torches still alight. As soon as he had reached her, the two animals turned to face me. Now two pairs of white-red eyes glared back at me resentfully.

Then I began to pace backwards in order to escape. Easier said than done, indeed. Have you ever tried to walk backwards, in pitch darkness along a twisting footpath, through heavy grass and jungle, with a rifle balanced awkwardly against your shoulder in your left hand, your thumb pressing against a torch switch, and another torch held in your right hand which is also helping to keep the rifle in place, while a pair of mating and naturally resentful tigers confront you?

I succeeded in the manoeuvre for a short distance and then, as the two tigers had shown no inclination to follow me, I whisked around in order to hurry along the footpath for a few seconds and afterwards whisked back again to see what the tigers were doing. They were in the same positions, obviously glad that I was departing.

Soon I reached Amligola and the hut of the headman, who was my friend, where I related my adventure. Ramiah, the headman, was a widower and invited me to spend the rest of the night with him. Perhaps in daylight I could study the tigers under better conditions, he suggested.

Along with numerous mugs of milk, and some rather stale *vadais* (small pungent cakes) that he offered me, Ramiah and I began to chat, but it was not long before loud roaring and growling from the forest told us that the tigers had begun their mating in right earnest. The din continued for quite a while. Then there was a period of silence, after which the noises started all over again. This sort of thing continued till we fell asleep.

Next morning I was in no hurry to investigate, for I knew that both would be resting after their strenuous mating-sessions and my appearance too early might precipitate a showdown. Besides, I was feeling inordinately sleepy after the rather restless night I had spent in Ramiah's hut.

It was nearly ten in the morning when I awoke and, after another bout with Ramiah's now tough *vadais*, followed by at least three cups of coffee which (rather than the tea that I would have much preferred) is the normal beverage of the Kanarese villager, I prepared to investigate the scene of the previous night's noisy mating. Ramiah excused himself from accompanying me on the plea of urgent field work, so I set out alone.

The spot whence the noises had come, when at last I located it, may be a little over a furlong away, revealed the energy that the two tigers had put into their lovemaking. Although fairly hard at this time of the year, the earth was scored and dug up in clods, the smaller shrubs having been ripped from the soil, roots and all, by the antics of the gambolling beasts.

From this place the ground dropped into a densely vegetated ravine, where scratchings upon the bark of a tree, along with freshly-shed dung which—unlike the panther—a tiger leaves exposed rather than covered with earth, indicate the way the lovers had entered the ravine. Curiosity prompted me to follow, although I knew that what I was doing was rash; so with rifle at the ready and eyes that endeavoured to see through and behind every bush, I advanced in silence, taking care my rubber-soled shoes did not tread upon any dry leaf or twig.

No sooner was I in the shadow of the large trees that grew in this hollow than the sweetish stench of death was borne to my nostrils and I knew I was approaching an animal that had been killed. A few yards farther, and I found it. The partial remains of a huge wild sow that had been slain by the Gowndnorai and upon which the two tigers had feasted hungrily, for tigers love pork. Although a sow, the pig had put up a fight, as could be seen by her hoof-marks in the ground.

I did not examine the sow very carefully, for you may be sure I was watching all around me against being surprised by one or the other of the terrifying lovers, and it was while I was doing this that I caught a glimpse of something white that showed through the leaves of a jungle-plum bush, perhaps thirty yards away. I approached this object, and it turned out to be the pelvis bone of a sambar doe also half-eaten by the tigers during their spree the night before. There was no means of knowing which of the two animals—the sow or the sambar— had been killed first, but it was clear that the latter had been slain some distance away and then brought to the spot by the Gowndnorai for the benefit of his mate, for no wild animal would have come anywhere near a spot where a kill had already been made.

The presence of the three crows, flying down from a branch to the earth and up again, betrayed a third kill slightly farther away. The fact that the crows were flying to the ground indicated that neither of the tigers was near. This kill turned out to be a spotted stag which the Gowndnorai had also brought to the ravine after killing it elsewhere. Little of the stag had been devoured, for by this time the tigers were too stuffed with food to do more than sample the meat.

But I had not finished yet with finding kills. In fact, I tripped over the carcase of another sambar doe that lay most halfway between the carcase of the spotted deer and the sow. There was little left of this sambar, most of it having been devoured by the tigers. I was almost certain now that this sambar, and not the sow, as I had thought, had been the first of the four victims. The sow had followed next, her hoof-marks on the ground showing she had fought before she had been killed. She ought not to have come near the dead sambar. Perhaps one of the tigers had chased her there. The other sambar and the spotted stag had been carried to the spot later, for nowhere had I seen any traces of dragmarks upon the ground, which made clear that the tiger had carried his victims, one at a time, across his back. If I needed further proof of his size, here it was indeed.

There is a strange satisfaction in reasoning out the facts of apparent jungle mystery, and I felt this as I reached my conclusion. The ravine was, in fact, a veritable charnel-house; the stench of death hung heavy in the air, and suddenly I grew afraid.

Something warned me that I was being watched. I took a quick pace to the rear to bring my back against a tree and so shield myself against attack from behind. Then I began to scan every bush and tree-trunk in the immediate vicinity.

Not a breath of air stirred in the forest that grew hotter with the passing hours, as the sun climbed higher into a cloudless sky, although I could not see it at that moment because of the trees. Not a whisper of sound broke the stillness; even the two cicadas that had been calling from trees higher up the banks of the ravine were now silent. The crows had seen me and watched the scene with mute expectation, heads cocked slightly to one side, beaks partly open and panting with the heat. It was as if the jungle lay in breathless suspense, awaiting the next act in the drama that was about to be played at any instant.

Out of the corner of my eye I saw a tuft of grass, frail and feathery, suddenly sway for an instant and then become still. It had no business to sway on that breathless forenoon, unless something had pressed against the stem near to the ground.

The something must be one of the tigers!

Most tigers—even a man-eater—will hesitate to attack if it feels that a man has discovered its presence. It prefers to have the element of surprise on its side. I knew this from my own experience, so I opened my eyes as wide as possible and stared hard at the spot where the grass had just moved. This would tell the tiger I had discovered where it was hiding.

For a moment I could see nothing. Then two black protuberances, tipped white behind, seemed to rise slowly from beyond the grass, and I knew that I was looking at a tiger's ears. An instant later, the animal raised its head a fraction higher and I was gazing into the baleful eyes, of one of the tigers. I knew it was the female. Her head was too small to belong to a male of her mate's size. That left the tiger to be contended with. He was probably in hiding at the moment, I knew not where, gathering courage for a sudden onslaught, if for no other reason than to prove to the tigress, who was watching closely, what a great brave creature he was.

Nothing happened while the tigress continued to peep at me over the top of the grass, and after a while I began to hope that she was alone. Maybe her mate had gone to look for a fifth victim!

It must have been ten minutes later when the tigress began to make a peculiar sort of noise. I might say she was mewing, but it was too guttural and hoarse a sound for that word to convey. She was summoning her mate. As she had not attacked me all this while, it was clear that the tigress, by herself, lacked the courage. What would happen when the tiger arrived would be quite another thing.

I decided that discretion was the better part of valour and I slipped behind the tree-trunk that I had stood against all this while. Then I started to back away.

The next moment a loud roar from the top of the ravine behind me told me I was too late. The Gowndnorai had arrived. Something in his mate's mewing calls seemed to warn him that all was not well. I could hear him crashing through the dead leaves and undergrowth now, coming directly towards me at the gallop.

I am far from being a good climber, but sheer funk lent me agility and I dragged myself up the tree with commendable speed, the rifle hanging on my shoulder. The first fork was hardly eight feet from the ground. I reached it and tried to climb higher, when the rifle slipped awkwardly from my shoulder down to the crook of my arm. I hitched it up again, and just as fast it slipped down once more.

The Gowndnorai arrived at the base of my tree and my movements made him look upwards and see me. I decided I must face him and bring the rifle from the crook of my arm to my shoulder. I expected him to make a bound at me at once, but strangely enough he did nothing of the kind. He crouched on the ground instead, looked up, and snarled and snarled and snarled.

Rather foolishly, as I think of it now, I changed my mind and decided to try to climb higher, but in any case I could not go very far. I managed another seven feet perhaps when I found I had gone as high as the thinning branches would permit. At this juncture, the tigress, confident of the protection offered by her mate, emerged and advanced towards him in gambolling leaps till the two of them were together barely fifteen feet below.

I hoped that neither of the tigers would try to follow me, as the bough to which I was precariosly clinging was too frail to support any additional weight, while by my own foolishness in ascending higher I had put myself in a nasty plight. I was obliged to cling to the branch with both my hands and knees, and this prevented any possibility of using my rifle, which I could not unsling, since I would fall from the tree if let go my hold. Moreover, the strain on the muscles of my hands and legs was tremendous, and I could not possibly maintain the position for long.

It occurred to me that I might try to shoo the tigers away by shouting aloud. The ruse would probably succeed; but again it might not. The sound of my voice might irritate the animals, particularly the tiger, who till now had behaved like a gentleman.

The two tigers settled the matter after a few minutes, as if by mutual consent, when they calmly walked away side by side. Allowing another five minutes to pass, I descended cautiously, but there was no sign of either animal even after I climbed the bank of the *nullah* and started walking to the village. I really owe the Gowndnorai and his mate a debt for sparing my life.

Shortly afterwards I was trudging back to Tagarthy, thinking I had heard—and seen—the last of the tiger. But as I was soon to discover, that thought was entirely wrong.

Hardly had I been a month in Bangalore when the headman of Amligola, with whom I had spent the night listening to the Gowndnorai and his mate, wrote me a postcard which he had tramped all the way to Tagarthy to post, informing me that the big tiger was growing overbold and begging me to come and shoot him. It was only a matter of time, he said, before the Gowndnorai would turn man-eater.

I oppose hunting tigers that have not molested man, and I was not going to accept the headman's fear of something that had not yet happened; the Gowndnorai might never become a man-eater and I had certainly no justification for shooting an animal that had spared my life on two occasions.

It happened that I had a few days to spare and could think of no more pleasant occupation than trying to see my benefactor, the huge tiger, once again. But things had changed by the time I reached Amligola, although it was only a matter of a few days since Ramiah had written. The big tiger had grown bolder indeed, killing more of the villagers' choice cattle. Ramiah had already lost his best bull, and now the Gowndnorai saw it fit to slay his second best.

This was too much for the already exhausted patience of the headman. Disdaining to wait for my arrival, Ramiah journeyed to the town of Kumsi, about twenty miles away, borrowed his cousin's .12 bore shotgun, and sat up to ambush the tiger when he next visited the outskirts of Amligola in search of prize cattle. Having succeeded so many times before, the Gowndnorai walked into the trap all unsuspectingly, to receive a charge of slugs full in his face from Ramiah's borrowed weapon. The tiger then dashed away roaring terribly as he went. So great was his anger, caused by the wound, that he entirely demolished a bamboo platform erected by the villagers on a field from which to drive away the birds that fed upon their grain, and which stood in the tiger's *path* as he rushed back to the forest.

All that day and night, and throughout the two nights that followed, Ramiah and his companions were forced to listen to the pain-racked roars of the wounded tiger as he voiced his woe and anger to the jungle at large, while they cowered within their huts.

Unaware of what had happened, as nobody told me anything at Tagarthy, I arrived late in the evening of the fifth day at Amligola, having walked through the jungle in blissful ignorance for eight miles without hearing or seeing a thing. We did not hear the tiger that night, but the morning of the sixth day brought the first result of Ramiah's ill-timed shot.

It was just after nine o'clock and I was about to set out on my return journey to Tagarthy, when a man staggered into Amligola and fell exhausted in the one lane that formed the main village street. He said that he and another man had started out from the village of Chordi, which was some miles away, just before dawn, and had been travelling to Amligola when, about two miles from their destination, they had seen a tiger following. Accustomed to tigers and not knowing that the Gowndnorai had been wounded, they were not unduly perturbed, but decided to keep a sharp lookout behind them as they walked.

For the next two or three hundred yards they saw nothing. Then they glimpsed the tiger, and this time he was not more than thirty yards behind them. Sensing that the animal was bent upon mischief, the two men had broken into a run, whereupon the tiger roared and charged them.

The man who had staggered into Amligola had escaped merely because he happened to be the faster runner. He told how the tiger had quickly caught up with his companion, who was racing just a yard or so behind. His friend's dying scream had compelled him to look back over his shoulder and the lucky woodcutter affirmed that the sight he had seen would remain in his memory for ever. The tiger's countenance had been dreadful to behold. It was badly mangled and a mass of blood. He did not think the animal had any eyes left: its ferocity vented upon the victim it had just seized, was truly awful. Not daring to look back any longer, the man had raced to Amligola for all he was worth, to reach its shelter utterly exhausted.

The wounded Gowndnorai had killed its first victim. To judge by what we had heard, Ramiah's slugs had blinded the unfortunate beast.

Without delay, I hurried to the place where the attack had been launched, Ramiah and the surviving woodcutter reluctantly accompanying me. The tiger must have been ravenously hungry; he had eaten the most of his victim on the spot. Then he must have heard us coming, for he had carried away what remained as he dashed into the undergrowth, perhaps only a matter of minutes before our arrival. We knew the tiger had eaten well, for his victim's head, hands and feet lay scattered about, a sure sign of a hearty meal.

The trail was fresh, but the undergrowth was extremely lush. Ramiah and the woodcutter were Kanarese and not of the stuff of jungle-men and trackers. They flatly refused to come any farther. So I followed by way of the broken weeds and the bent branches of his victim. It was difficult to watch ahead and both sides against a surprise attack while moving fast at the same time.

The Gowndnorai, for all his size, did not stop to fight it out. Probably his recent wound, and the pain he was suffering, made him reluctant to risk an encounter with another armed man. It is uncanny how a wild animal is able to sense the presence of a human being who may spell danger and distinguish him from one who is helpless, unarmed, or bears no hostile thoughts.

The trail led through the belt of thick forest into lighter scrub, where it was more difficult to proceed, and then down a steep decline where the tiger had finally jumped into a narrow ravine, more a watercourse than anything else. Here I had to go down on hands and knees and within a few yards it became too dense to go farther. In any event, pursuit was fruitless as I could never hope to overtake my quarry under such conditions.

Disappointed as I was, two facts were now established beyond any doubt. Firstly, the Gowndnorai had not been totally blinded by Ramiah's pellets. Therefore he remained a very real danger to the human race and would continue to be so till he completely recovered from his wounds and went back again to killing cattle and wild game. That was extremely unlikely to happen, however, as once a tiger has tasted human flesh and comes to realize how easy it is to kill a man, it rarely abandons the habit. In other words, here was a man-eater at the beginning of his dreadful career. Secondly, despite his enormous size, this tiger did not have a fighting heart, so he was likely to prove more cowardly, cunning, elusive and much more difficult to bring to book

74

than most ordinary tigers, normally more daring and so liable to expose themselves.

How correct both my surmises were was revealed in a comparatively short time. My visit to Amligola could not be prolonged as I had to return to work to the aircraft plant in which I was employed at that time. So leaving instructions with Ramiah to keep me closely informed of events as they occurred, I returned to Bangalore the following morning.

It did not take long for Ramiah to write again. He related that the Gowndnorai had turned into a dangerous and elusive brute. No longer did he sun himself on the slopes of the small hillock, in full view of every passer-by. Now there was no sight of him, no sound to be heard. Only his huge, saucer-sized pug-marks betrayed his passing, and with each such visit some traveller, who had set out on a journey, failed to reach his destination.

Ramiah said that the tiger had taken to haunting the most lonely section of the footpath leading from Amligola to Tagarthy, from where he would snatch the last of a group of travellers. Apparently this had happened on three occasions, and now people shunned this track. They preferred to walk twenty-five miles by a circular route to Tagarthy.

Having covered the short cut many times myself, I knew exactly the spot to which Ramiah referred. It was a dip through a valley running between two low hills, where the vegetation consisted of tall bamboos and fairly heavy evergreen scrub that provided ideal cover in which a tiger could spring an ambush upon a group of passers-by.

I left for Tagarthy the next day, parked the car at the rest house of the forest department that stood in a beautifully wooded setting a mile away, and set out to cover the eight-mile footpath to Amligola, which would lead through what had become the valley of death, in which the Gowndnorai launched his attacks. It was exactly two in the afternoon when I started, and it was a cloudy, cool day. The conditions for a tiger to be early afoot were ideal.

I would have to progress slowly and carefully and timed my arrival at Amligola at about six o'clock or at most half an hour later, just as it was getting too dark to see. To stay out after that would force the use of my torch, and realizing I was dealing with a very shy and crafty animal, I felt he was less likely to show himself then, and would probably prefer to launch his ambush at a time when he thought the traveller was unprepared.

For the first mile or so, the pathway traverses beautiful park-like country, and here peacocks, which had just begun to grow their new plumage after dropping their tail-feathers subsequent to the mating season, grubbed under the bushes and flapped heavily skywards as I appeared around a corner.

Gradually the vegetation grew more dense, the trees higher and the undergrowth thicker. After the second mile, I could only see the track ahead and snatch a quick glance around at it behind me. To my left and right a wall of impenetrable green hid everything more than a yard away from sight.

The dangerous valley about which I have spoken, where the Gowndnorai had thrice launched his ambushes, still lay three miles ahead, beginning at about the fifth mile along the track I had come, with another three miles to my destination, Amligola.

The closer I approached this valley, the more dense became the vegetation. Actually, this sort of jungle is not favoured by tigers as a rule, who prefer the park-like country I had already come through. Bison, elephant, sambar and barking deer are at home here, the felines choosing the more open jungles where their main prey, such as spotted deer, wild pig, and of course village cattle, graze on the plentiful grass that grows there. It was another indication of the Gowndnorai's craftiness that had induced him to change from the habit of his species to haunt a place affording him the maximum cover for his ambushes.

At last I tipped down the foot of the hill, the base of which marks the start of the valley of death. It is three-quarters of a mile, or perhaps seven furlongs, to the point where the *path* starts climbing the next hill, and dense bamboos with lush undergrowth press heavily upon the narrow trail on both sides.

I halted for a moment to pick up a handful of sand, which I raised to shoulder level and then allowed to trickle slowly from my fingertips. There was little breeze, but what there was carried the sand earthwards slightly to my left. The wind was therefore blowing from right to left, and the tiger, if he attacked, would almost certainly do so from the left-hand side of the track and not from the right. My deduction was based upon a fundamental law of the jungle.

Felines prey upon deer and such creatures as have a keen sense of smell. To do so upwind would render their stalk abortive, for the currents of air would betray their presence and their quarry would escape. Carnivores have therefore learned by instinct always to approach downwind, that is against the wind, so that their own scent will not give them away before they can attack.

Unlike deer, the human being has practically no sense of smell so far as self-preservation is concerned, and the average person would not be able to scent a tiger or a panther, even in hiding a yard away, whatever the direction of the wind. But the feline does not know this and so applies the same rules to stalking a man as it would to stalking any other jungle creature. For this reason, I was almost sure that the Gowndnorai, if he came for me, would attack from the left;

and being the coward that he was, ten chances to one from behind me.

Having established all this by reasoning, I began to walk silently forwards along the track, alert for anything that might happen.

The first quarter-mile or so was fraught with apprehension. Every little while I glanced backwards to see if I was being followed. Once, as I looked back, I was in time to see a bush I had just passed sway violently, then come to rest.

I swung around. I knew that I could not see beneath the bush; it was far too thick. But I could watch the top of it. A tiger cannot spring out of the middle of a bush, it has to creep forwards to break clear of its branches before he makes its leap, and when it creeps the tops of the bushes will shake. If you keep watching the tops of the branches you will be able to see them move, then you will know it is coming.

Sure enough the top of one of the branches very near the edge of the pathway shook slightly as something brushed against its base. This is it, I said to myself, and raised the .405 to my shoulder.

A moment later the branch vibrated more noticeably and out walked a wild boar into full view. Seeing me suddenly, it swerved head-on, the bristles on its neck rising like spines, head bent low with tusks aimed at me, small red eyes looking upward angrily.

I felt like laughing, but sighed with relief. The fact of the boar appearing from my left indicated that the tiger was not in the immediate vicinity.

Noticing that I stood motionless and made no move towards him, the boar decided that I must be harmless after all, although something to be regarded with grave suspicion. With head still bent at an angle to keep me in view and charge if necessary, the pig crossed the track to plunge into the thickets on the right with a loud brushing of the leaves. The next instant it was gone.

This time I really sighed. I went on again, relief making me a trifle less cautious perhaps, and was soon within reach of the end of the valley. I saw nothing in front of me; I looked back, but nothing was there. I looked in front again, when something urged me to turn around.

And there was the Gowndnorai, or rather his head, emerging from a wall of green to my left that I had just passed. Not a sound had he made. My rifle came to my shoulder and I squinted down the barrel.

But the tiger was no longer there to aim at. Instinct and his inherent cowardliness warned him that here was no defenceless passer-by. He vanished as silently as he came.

Confidence made me bold and I stepped forward to catch a glimpse of him, if possible. A low growl, and then the rustle of leaves several yards away in the undergrowth, told me that the big tiger would not stay to fight. He was running away.

I arrived at Amligola shortly before dark to recount my adventure to an astonished Ramiah.

I did not know quite what to do the next day. Ramiah said it was useless to tie out cattle as bait, for the Gowndnorai would not look at them. In any case, there were very few cattle in Amligola, and none of their owners would sell for this purpose. I would have to wait to walk back to Tagarthy the following morning if I wanted to buy a bait.

That afternoon the Gowndnorai broke his own rule. Perhaps he was over-hungry. Maybe he thought the valley was too dangerous for him to haunt for a while, with me in it. So he killed a man in the park-like jungle I have told you about, a mile or so from the Tagarthy forest rest house where I had left my car. The victim's three companions came hurriedly through the valley to bring me the news. They knew it was safe enough to traverse while the tiger was engaged in eating this kill. It was nearly three in the afternoon when they arrived and I had seven miles to cover to reach the site of the incident. We found what was left of the man a little after four-thirty.

The Gowndnorai had attacked his victim in the expected fashion from behind a bush, out of the centre of which grew a wild-cashew tree, killed him and carried him back to the same bush, behind which he had set to work and eaten more than half the body. The three men who had been walking in front of the victim had practically run the rest of the way to Amligola.

The wild-cashew tree growing on the spot was a very lucky factor. Its many branches and large leaves made the construction of a *machan* a quick and easy matter. Although I made a bet with myself that the Gowndnorai would never show up, because he was far too cunning for one thing, while the noise the men made in building the *machan*, in spite of all their efforts to work silently, must have been heard by him where he lay, probably not very far away, there was always the slimmest chance that he might appear. By six o'clock I was in the *machan*, quite a snug affair considering the short time in which it had been made, and the three men hurried back the mile to Tagarthy which they had covered that morning in the company of the unfortunate man now lying mangled behind the bush.

This was the Indian spring and it soon began to grow dark. Within another hour the remains of the corpse on the ground beneath me was hidden from sight. There was no moonlight and I was relying upon the torch, clamped to the barrel of my rifle, to light the scene if the tiger returned.

All was silent for nearly an hour except for the calls of a few night-birds and the flapping of the large fruit bats around the tree. I glanced at the luminous dial of my watch. It was eight o'clock, the time when tigers generally return to their kills!

Almost punctually to the hour, a group of spotted deer began to call in alarm from the park-like jungle to the east. Their cries were dying away when an animal moved in the bush directly below me. The Gowndnorai had come. In another moment he could start to eat and then would be my chance.

This was precisely the moment when I heard a tiger growl, but it was at least a hundred yards or more away; certainly not below me. So the Gowndnorai had a companion!

This fact raised complications. Was this the man-eater after all? I remembered his cowardliness. Maybe another tiger was the true man-eater. Or perhaps both had the habit!

My thoughts were interrupted when the animal below me snarled; then dashed off at top speed. After that I heard neither of the tigers and thought they both had gone when, a few minutes before nine o'clock, a twig snapped and this was followed by the crunching of bones. One of the tigers had returned. So I slowly raised the rifle to my shoulder in preparation for a shot.

An instant later pandemonium broke out. A series of shattering roars came from the darkness a short distance behind me, a coughing snarl issued from directly below, and this was followed by the sound of a large body frantically clawing its way up the trunk of the tree upon which I was sitting. At about the same instant a second body crashed against the tree, which shook under the impact, and started tearing at the trunk.

The tree swayed as if struck by a hurricane and I felt I would be hurled out of the *machan*. Roars, growls and snarls from below my very feet threw me into panic. Hastily pointing the rifle-barrel downwards, I pressed the torch-button. The light cut through the night and fell upon a panther, only two feet below. But it was gazing downwards.

I moved the barrel slightly, and now, I looked into the blazing eyes of the Gowndnorai, who would never have had the courage to attack the tree on which I was hiding had not the panther, stealing from the kill, thought fit to take refuge in it. Neither animal knew the tree was already occupied by me.

The first was an easy shot—between the eyes. The Gowndnorai fell backwards as his roars came to an end. So was the second. The panther looked up in startled amazement to provide another easy shot, also between the eyes. I could not afford to spare him, though I would have liked to do so. He had been eating from a human kill and might turn into a man-eater himself.

The Gowndnorai was perhaps the largest tiger I have ever shot; and surely the most cowardly.

Four

The Assassin of Diguvametta

IF YOU WERE TO TRAVEL IN A SOUTHEASTERLY DIRECTION BY METRE-gauge railway from Guntakal junction in the state of Andhra Pradesh, you would pass the large town of Nandyal and shortly afterwards enter a delightful stretch of hilly country, heavily forested and intersected by numerous streams. Over these you would rattle, halting briefly at the jungle stations of Basavapuram and Chelama, and traversing two tunnels, one short and one extremely long. Finally you would cross a verdant valley by a picturesque high viaduct, with tree-tops far below. In a few miles you would probably observe a large stone water-column at the right-hand side of the line, always overflowing, next to which stands the 'outer' signal that heralds the advent of Diguvametta railway station, where the hills and the jungle end and the cultivated plains begin again.

The 'assassin's' operations extended from this station as far as the very long tunnel in the valley crossed by the long viaduct, but it was particularly active in the vicinity of the dripping water-column and the 'outer' signal beside it.

I have always had a sneaking fondness for the forests between Chelama and Diguvametta, not because they are particularly well stocked with game or carnivora, but for the utter peace and solitude of the area, and the friendly disposition of the wild Chenchu tribesmen who inhabit the extensive jungles in this section of the Eastern Ghats. I have found that even the ordinary villager of Andhra Pradesh is, on the whole, much more friendly than his counterpart in Mysore state, where I live, while the folk in Madras state reveal a disposition between the two.

Also, the nature of the vegetation here is quite different from that growing farther south, and while no elephants or bison occur, this area represents the southernmost limit where the nilgai or blue-bull, a large animal of the antelope species, looking like a sambar deer, is to be found.

So to Diguvametta I travelled by train one day, passing through the long tunnel and over the long bridge, both of which always held for me a childish fascination, skirting the signal and dripping water-column, to alight at Diguvametta with my small bedroll, campkit, and rifle. A couple of urchins grabbed the bedroll and campkit, and with my rifle slung over my shoulder, we began walking up the road that ran parallel to the railway track in the direction from which the train had just come.

It was perhaps half a mile to the forest bungalow, a wonderfully cosy structure for so old a building; a plantation of teak seedlings lay to the south of it, the jungle lay east and north, while to the west was the road leading to the railway station, and after that again the railway-line, as I have just said. The signal and water-column stood a bare half-furlong away. My old friend, Aleem Khan the caretaker of the forest bungalow, welcomed me at the gate with his expansive smile, at the same time shouting to the urchins to get a move-on with my *samaans*.

The bungalow had two suites of rooms, and as usual Aleem was good enough to put me into the better one, the one that faced the road and the railway. It was better because the bathroom attached to this suite was fitted with a shower, while that on the other side had none.

Aleem was a Muslim and had only two wives, while so many of his co-religionists had four, the maximum allowed to a Mohammedan legally. He had told me once before that he felt that two were just enough. Without further ado he summoned these two women and set them to operate the hand-pump together. This contrivance drew water from a large well and fed it to a zinc water-tank situated on the roof of my bathroom. For half an hour, while I unpacked and then drank tea, hastily prepared for me by the caretaker, I could hear the clank-clank-clank of the hand-pump, and the chatter of the two wives as they argued with each other and then started to quarrel, each accusing the other of shirking her bit of the pumping. The dispute was brought to an end by the sound of water pouring off the bathroom roof. The tank had been filled to capacity!

Then came the much anticipated pleasure of a shower bath, or rather a series of shower baths, one after the other, the cool water trickling over my body in fine jets. Outside the temperature was well over 100° F as the sun shone down with the merciless intensity usual to Andhra, but inside that bathroom it was so cool, so damp, so heavenly. I smiled maliciously to think I was so callously wasting the precious liquid those two women had worked so hard to pump for me.

Refreshed, and stretched at length in an armchair on the veranda, I drew placidly on my pipe and drank mug after mug of tea. A goods train clanked past heavily, an engine at either end, the one in the front blasting clouds of black smoke from its funnel and tugging for all it was worth, while the one at the back came along unconcernedly, as if there was nothing to bother about at all.

Aleem Khan squatted on his heels on the ground at the side of my armchair, telling me some of his family troubles. His only sister had lost her husband, a forest guard who had died suddenly of tuberculosis, leaving his wife and two children unprovided for. They had immediately come to Aleem for shelter and the problem was now a major one. Aleem's first wife had three children, the second had two; and now his sister with her two children and himself made a total of four adults and seven children to be fed on his meagre salary.

Could I do something about it? Aleem confided that, in spite of her two children, his sister was still a comely lass, good to look upon, with a fine figure, amiable disposition, and all the attributes required to make a very desirable wife. In a moment of temptation, I closed my eyes and let my thoughts run wild. What fun it would be for me to announce my conversion to Mohammedanism! I could then marry Aleem's sister and take two more wives into the bargain. With the one back in Bangalore, this would make the fully permissible four.

Then the expense side of the question hit me a sharp blow, and the troubles that would follow as a consequence hit me a sharper one. I opened my eyes in horror to think of what a predicament I was in, and then smiled when I remembered it was all in the realm of speculation.

Hastily I told Aleem I would inquire in Bangalore for a suitable candidate, and then, equally hastily, changed the topic. Were there any tigers or panthers about?

A tiger had been poached just ten days ago he confided, by some government official in a jeep, using a spotlight, on the forest department's fire-line two hundred yards from the rest house. This fire-line, I must tell you, extended from west to east. It began at the road to the northwest of the bungalow and a furlong away, and went on in an easterly direction to another road two miles distant that traversed the forest and connected Diguvametta to a hamlet named Gondacheruvu, some forty miles away.

Aleem also mentioned that there was a panther about, and this animal was beginning to prove troublesome. Its pug-marks could be seen early in the morning around the rest house, and it had taken his dog three weeks earlier from the place where it had been sleeping on the back veranda. He added that his sister had not only brought her two children but her dog as well, and this the panther had attacked immediately outside the door of the outhouse that Aleem had allowed his sister to occupy. But this animal, unusually big for a village cur, had also a big heart. He had turned on the panther with such ferocity that the latter had fled precipitately with the cur in hot pursuit. Both Aleem and his sister had witnessed the scene in the bright moonlight.

Nevertheless, the caretaker said he was not happy about matters and felt the panther would summon up enough courage to return and would eventually get the dog. But what really troubled him was the presence of the seven children, two of whom were mere toddlers. Should the panther become sufficiently bold—or hungry—he might be tempted to run off with one of them.

Many people have asked me why I do not leave India and go to England, Australia or even Canada. I have tried to answer that question, but I do not think I have convinced anybody. This thought returned to me as I lay in the armchair that afternoon at Diguvametta. Where in England, Australia or Canada, where anywhere else in the world, except perhaps

Africa or South America, would I find the conditions of India? A journey by train or road of a few hours separated my home in Bangalore from the cold climate to be found on any of the several mountain ranges that lay within two hundred miles, or from the swelteringly hot weather of the plains that lay even closer; from the dense forests to the west, with their very heavy rainfall, and the extremely arid, semi-desert areas to the east; from the teeming millions of one of the cities and the utter solitude of a jungle within fifty miles of home; from the varied languages and dialects of the towns and the almost incoherent vocabularies of the forest tribes; from the safety and comfort of home and the ever-present hazards of death from a sudden sickness, snakebite or some wild animal. Where in the world would time be of so little, if any consequence, as in India? Where in the world would consequences themselves be of so little importance? It matters not how you dress, or whether you dress at all! The bare requirements of existence are all that do matter. Everything else is thrown in along with that, sometimes in good measure and sometimes scarcely at all; but really it does not make much difference either way and there is never any hurry about anything. There is a time to be born and a time to die and each event is as inevitable as the other. Moreover, death follows life and life follows death, so it really does not matter where you start and where you end, as it all works out to the same thing.

My friends cannot understand when I tell them that these things are the reasons why I love India, why I do not think I shall ever leave it.

My reverie was broken by trouble in the form of the forest range officer, who arrived on a bicycle to inform Aleem Khan that word had just been received that the district forest officer (D.F.O.) was passing through Diguvametta and would spend the next night at the rest house. Did I have written permission to occupy the bungalow?

I had to reply in the negative, and the range officer looked aghast. I had committed the unpardonable crime of trespass. I was occupying a government building without permission. He swallowed hard and then told me I would have to get out forthwith.

Here was the same difficulty that I had experienced in so many forest bungalows in so many jungles. This is why I have purchased so many parcels of land in so many areas, in order to be able to camp in peace without being troubled by authority, that ever-present bogy that has stalked the length and breadth of the country from time immemorial, that stalked it during the days of the British Raj and that dominates it even more since Independence.

I flattered the range officer and in no time he was eating out of my hand. Certainly, sir, he agreed, these senior officers coming on tour were a damned nuisance. Why (and being the gentleman that he knew I was, he could tell me in confidence), they did not work at all when they came. It was he and his subordinates who were the workers. These visits were only a pretext for collecting *batta*, the colloquial name for a travelling allowance, when they were hard up. Witness the fact that these 'tours' invariably took place during the last week of a month. Certainly, I could remain for the night in the bungalow, but I must promise faithfully to go before noon the following day or he would be in grave trouble should the D.F.O. find me occupying the bungalow without permission.

I promised, and then inquired if there was a vacant room anywhere in the village. The range officer did not think so.

At this stage in the conversation I mentioned that I had suffered similarly in so many other areas that I had begun purchasing small plots of land in nearly every jungle I visited and had at that moment over twenty camp sites of my own. He brightened at this idea. He had a friend, he said, in the revenue department, who owned many acres of land just beyond the railway station. Upon his recommendation, the ranger was sure this friend, whose name was Ranga Reddy, would be glad to present me with a small plot of land all my own, big enough to pitch a tent upon, as a gift and free of all charges.

Within the hour we were at this friend's place. There we drank coffee and were forced to consume two *dosais** each. Then Ranga Reddy took us to his land, which was a quarter of a mile beyond the railway station and to the east of the line, and invited me to select any spot I fancied, anywhere I wished and to the extent required.

The field was good agricultural land, consisting of rich black soil, and we had to go to the far corner to find a vacant bit, lying fallow and with earth that was not quite so rich as the rest of the field. After all, I required only a camping site and did not want to deprive my new friend of anything of value. A stream flowed a short distance away, while the main road bordered the plot on one side. An ideal camping-site! Ten cents of land would be ample for my requirements.

I told the owner of my choice. He answered with an expansive smile that I could certainly have the land. He would take me in his jeep the following day to the town of Giddalur, twelve miles away, where the formal registration of my ownership would have to be made.

I asked the price. Free, of course, he replied. This would never do, I answered. Besides, it would not constitute a legal purchase; he must accept some price. With hesitation, Mr Reddy said 'Five rupees,' and I said,' 'No, take fifty.'

---

* A fried flat cake made from rice flour.

90

He recoiled in horror. 'Take fifty rupees from a friend for such a useless plot of land!' Eventually we agreed to thirty rupees, which is less than two pounds in English currency.

The next morning we were at the registrar's office at Giddalur when it opened for business. Half an hour later I was the proud owner of my own camp site of ten cents of land at Diguvametta!

However, I have anticipated events a little by telling you about the purchase of the site. I should have related, in proper sequence of events, what happened on the night after I had returned to the rest house from a short stroll along the fire-line where the tiger had been shot so recently. This fire-line traversed a deep *nullah* that formed the bed of a running stream where the flow of water, now that the dry season prevailed, was not more than a yard wide. Implanted in the mud on both sides were the pug-marks of a medium-sized panther. This animal, like all its kind, had been loath to walk in the water, and so it had jumped across.

I wondered if it could be the animal Aleem had told me about. The tracks led towards the forest lodge and had probably been made the previous night. Then I stooped to examine them more closely and changed my mind. The dark-green layer of surface fungus that borders old watercourses and streams in some places grew to the water's edge on both banks, and it had been pressed down by the weight of the panther both on the side from which the animal had jumped and, considerably more deeply, upon the bank where it had landed. The fact that the dark green fungus was still pressed down on both sides was very significant. Why had it not returned to the upright position of the fungus elsewhere? It would have done so had the panther made its leap the previous night, as I had first thought. There could be only one conclusion: the facts clearly showed that the panther had crossed not more than an hour or two earlier.

It was now after six in the evening, so the animal must have passed this way between four and five, long before sunset. In this case it would be in the vicinity of the bungalow right now, unless it had gone on to cross the railway track in the direction of the water-tank. I turned back from my walk, wondering if I would hear it calling during the night.

I had just sat down to an early dinner of cold roast beef that I had brought from home when it happened. The time was exactly 7.45 p.m.; I remember this because I had just wound my watch, a habit I follow as I sit down to dinner. Aleem's sister's dog had made itself friendly and was sitting on its haunches by my chair, gazing soulfully at me in anticipation of receiving scraps from my plate. I gave it a piece of dried chuppatty.

Most dogs would have gulped the morsel and looked for more, but this creature, in common with all village curs, decided to take the mouthful outside and enjoy it in solitude. It ran out on to the veranda, and then I heard a low snarl, followed by a loud yelp from the dog.

My rifle was in the bedroom that led off from the central dining-room, and there was no time to get it. Realizing that the panther had struck and that if I wanted to save the dog I would have to act fast, I rushed on to the veranda where I was just in time to see in the moonlight a spotted form leap down from the raised plinth on which the veranda stood, with the dog in its jaws, still alive and struggling.

Shouting loudly to frighten the attacker, I hurled the first missile that came to hand at the slouching form, one of the hard wooden chairs with which all government buildings are furnished. The departing leopard was only fifteen feet away when the chair descended squarely upon it, but the panther did not let the poor dog go. On the contrary it began to bound away with the dog still held firmly.

I rushed back into the bedroom for my rifle, hastily loaded it, and followed in the direction taken by the panther. Bright moonlight lit the compound, and so I had not waited to attach my torch-equipment to the weapon. That would have taken time, and not a second was to be wasted if I were to try to save the dog.

It was quite a different matter, however, when I reached the jungle that flanked the bungalow's grounds. Darkness, cast by the foliage of the trees, enveloped me, relieved here and there by shafts of moonlight. I soon realized that to crash about in the underbrush and darkness would only serve to frighten the panther and make it carry the victim farther away. In any case, it was too late for me to save the dog's life. So I sat down in the shadows at the foot of a tree, annoyed with myself for not having fixed my torch to the rifle. It would have taken time to do so, but at least I would have been able to see.

The panther, realizing I had stopped chasing it, must have thought I had gone away, for within ten minutes it began to eat. Nor was it very far away, for I could hear its low growl now and then, alternating with the sound of tearing flesh and the crack of a bone. I was undecided whether to try to creep up to the beast or go back to the bungalow for my torch, and as so often happens when one is undecided, I chose to do the wrong thing.

Rising to my feet slowly, and treading cautiously in the darkness for fear of making any sound, I tiptoed towards the noises that reached me now and then, adopting the old hunter's practice of only moving while the sounds lasted, and stopping as soon as they ceased. For when an animal you are trying to stalk is eating or making a noise of any kind there is less chance of his being able to hear the sounds that you might make, however slight they may be, in your approach, but it would be much more likely to hear you if it were silent.

I came quite near the panther that night. I do not think it could have been more than five yards away when luck, that had helped me so far, decided to put a spoke in the wheel. Incidentally, it sealed the fate of three innocent people. A bear, pig or pangolin had dug a hole in the ground. In the darkness I did not see it and put my left foot right into that hole, bringing me down with a jerk. I stumbled forward, and the panther knew I was there. With a coughing snarl he was away, and I heard him bounding through the bushes.

Extricating myself, I went on till I found the body of the dog which the panther had started to feed upon. I could make out its form as a light blur against the darkness of the ground. When I returned to the rest house, Aleem and his family had come out, searching for the dog and wondering where I had gone.

I fixed my torch on to the barrel of the .405 then, and returned with the caretaker. Only a fourth of the dog had been eaten. Aleem carried the remains back to the bungalow, where he said he would bury them in the morning, while I decided to try to search for the panther.

It was easier now to wander in the jungle with the help of my torch, and I scoured the area right around the building within the radius of a furlong for over two hours. No sign of the panther did I see, while the presence of a small sounder of pigs showed that the spotted cat had moved away from this area completely. On the other side of the road and bordering the railway track close to the signal, a few spotted deer and a solitary nilgai cow grazed in peace, suddenly shattered by a shrill whistle of an engine and the heavy rumble of a goods train.

The panther had gone. There was considerable weeping on the part of the women and children when what was left of the dog was buried the next morning. A little later, as agreed, I moved out of the rest house, stopping at the ranger's quarters to borrow an old tent that he had promised to lend me.

Within two hours the tent had been pitched and a camp made on my new site. Two mud-pots, purchased in the market-place and stored in a corner of the tent, served for drinking and washing water. Two fireplaces, built with stones and placed outside the tent, were ample for my needs, one for brewing tea and the other for cooking food. The earth was my bed; the stream not far away was my source of water, both for drinking and bathing; a small lantern was my illumination at night. What more did I need? Free to come and go as and when I liked! At least, as far as Diguvametta was concerned, I was henceforth rid of officials and government rules and regulations for evermore. Happy was I and very contented.

There was just one thing that could go wrong. If it happened to rain, the black-cotton soil would be churned into a sticky quagmire. I had not brought a campcot as I had intended to stay at the forest bungalow. So I would, literally, be in a mess.

Early that afternoon, after I had returned from Giddalur, a jeep came tearing down the road, and as it flashed past my tent I read 'Andhra forest department' in large white lettering on boards both behind and in front. The dark face of the occupant next to the driver stared at me hard. The district forest officer had arrived!

Later in the evening I called at the rest house on a courtesy visit. As much as I dislike government officials, one has to keep in touch with them in India if one wants to move about freely.

The D.F.O. was a young man, practically new to the service, and had been recruited directly to the department after passing through college, followed by training and a departmental examination at one of the provincial centres. Very soon I discovered that he knew nothing whatever about the jungle fauna and that he harboured the usual vague ideas regarding the terrible ferocity of tigers and panthers.

Aleem had told him what had happened to the dog the previous night without disclosing my part in the story or, most important of all, the fact that I had been occupying the bungalow.

So the D.F.O. in his turn now related to me a highly embellished account of the incident, including how the panther had leapt upon Aleem's breast and carried away the dog that had been sleeping there, to all of which I listened with an innocent, not to say surprised, expression. Apparently it did not occur to him that people ordinarily do not sleep with great hefty dogs upon their chests.

However, the upshot was that the D.F.O. invited me to shoot the panther. He inquired where I was staying and was markedly surprised to hear I was the owner of ten tents and was camping on my own site. Very generously, he suggested I should occupy the other half of the bungalow and enjoy its comforts.

Hanging my head in shame, I reminded him that I did not have 'official permission to occupy the Government forest lodge,' and slyly added that the rules of his department were very strict on this point. Permission could only be granted by the conservator of forests or by the collector of the district.

My new friend was offended. Was not he the D.F.O.? Was his permission not good enough? To hell with the conservator and the collector! 'You come along to the bungalow right away,' he said; 'we'll have dinner together tonight.'

So I came back where I started, but now as a guest, having left rather in the fashion of a vagabond. Moreover, but this

I am sure was pure luck, I was installed once more in the western or shower-bath side of the building. And it was fortunate, indeed, that I returned to the shelter of the bungalow just in time, for that night we had a heavy downpour. Next morning, my campsite was a sea of black mud.

The D.F.O. made Aleem bring a dog from the village, at Aleem's own suggestion and much against my desire, and instructed the caretaker to chain it to a teak-sapling that grew about ten yards behind the building. He was keen that I should bag the marauder. I dislike using dogs as bait. They are far too sensitive and suffer an agony of apprehension when chained up, as they appear to realize the danger they are in.

The D.F.O. had no firearm, but sat with me on another chair inside the dining-room. By keeping the door half-open we could see every detail outside in the clear moonlight, while the panther might not be able to see us in the darkness of the dining-room.

You may be sure that I kept a sharp lookout, for I did not want the dog to be killed. The cur, on its part, realizing the danger and feeling the discomfort of the chill air, began to yelp and whine loudly. The panther, if it happened to be anywhere within half a mile or even more at this moment, would certainly hear it.

The D.F.O. began to doze shortly after 11 p.m., and retired to his bed before midnight. Soon after two o'clock in the morning, with the moon behind the trees, long shadows began to fall and hide the dog, which had resigned itself to its fate. It had stopped yelping and was curled up fast asleep, and out of my sight. Should the panther attack now, I certainly would not be able to save the mongrel from being killed. Yet I hesitated till the moon disappeared behind the jungle to the west and it became pitch-dark. Then I got up from my chair, untied the dog, who wagged its tail joyously on seeing me, brought it indoors, and went to sleep myself.

After lunch the next day the D.F.O. departed on his return journey to Nandyal, while I left by the midnight train after giving my Bangalore address to Aleem, along with a couple of stamped postal covers which I always carry about with me for just such a purpose, instructing the caretaker to write to me should any unusual event occur. I had a hunch that I had not heard the last of that panther. But I forgot all about the affair before I even reached my journey's end.

It came as a surprise when Aleem's letter reached me about four months later, stating that a railway ganger had been killed by a wild animal midway between the long bridge and the water-column with the 'outer' signal close beside it. The letter said that no tracks could be found and that the ganger's body had been partly devoured. Then it went on to explain that there was a division of opinion as to what kind of beast had perpetrated the crime. Some said the killer was a tiger; others said it was a sloth bear. A few supersititious people blamed an evil spirit, but Aleem himself thought it was the panther. Would I come and shoot the creature, whatever it might turn out to be?

I answered, saying that as the killing was an old one and might be merely the odd result of a chance meeting with an irate bear, my visit to Diguvametta would be of no use just then; but I impressed upon him to write again should anything further transpire.

The next letter came about a month later. This reported that the ganger in charge of the water-column had made a practice of returning to the railway station by sunset. Invariably he and another ganger, whose duty it was to light the oil-lamp serving the 'outer' signal at precisely six o'clock every evening would meet at the foot of the signal and return together. This had been their regular habit ever since the two had become friends.

On the evening before that on which the letter was written, however, this meeting had failed to materialize. The second ganger had lighted the lamp on the signal, came down the iron ladder and found no signs of his friend from the water-tank, who should have been waiting for him there. Thinking the fellow must have fallen asleep, he called his name loudly, 'Ram! Ram!'

No answer had come, so the second ganger, apprehending no danger, had gone in search of his companion. He came upon the body at the base of the stone structure that supported the cast-iron tank of the water-column. Not much of it had been eaten: just a little from the chest. And although it was after six o'clock, there was still light enough for him to see in the sodden earth, saturated by the overflow from the water tank, a number of pug-marks, crossing and re-crossing each other. They had been made by a panther.

The ganger took to his heels and did not stop running till he had reached the station.

'Come at once,' Aleem's letter concluded urgently. 'A man-eating panther is amongst us!'

Unfortunately, I had urgent engagements that day, so I decided to leave early next morning, travelling by car so as to avoid delay and in order to carry the tent, stores and all the other kit that I would require for living on my camp site. I did not want to risk again the nuisance of being ousted from the bungalow in the midst of my operations. Moreover, when hunting a man-eater, particularly a panther, one cannot possibly conform to government rules that limits one's stay in a travellers' bungalow or a forest rest house to not more than three days.

I had just returned that evening, completed my packing and was about to have dinner, when I heard a bicycle bell outside. Then Thangavelu, my servant, came in with a telegram and the messenger's delivery book for my signature.

Hastily I signed and tore open the cover of the telegram to get one of the most unpleasant shocks I have ever received: 'Panther killed sister's child. Come immediately. Aleem.'

Before dawn I was on my way.

If you ever go to the forest rest house at Diguvametta, at the southeastern corner of the building and within twenty yards of it, you will come across a little grave under a stone slab. Inscribed on the stone is the one word: 'Mischief.'

The story goes that many years ago, in the days of the British Raj, a visiting British forest officer, or it may have been a collector, was occupying the bungalow along with his little dog whose name was 'Mischief.' A panther had suddenly pounced upon the latter and was carrying it away when the Englishman fired, killing both the panther and his own dog with the spreading shot from his gun. In sorrow, and in memory of his pet, this officer had buried it where it had been killed and had later returned, bringing an engraved tombstone to place over the spot.

Aleem told me the story of the latest tragedy as I was getting out of my car. His sister's elder child, who was a girl, had been told the story of 'Mischief' and had formed the habit of placing a little bunch of jungle flowers early each morning on the grave. That morning, for some reason, she had forgotten to put the flowers she had gathered on the stone slab, but only remembered late in the evening when it was almost dark. Meanwhile, the little bunch of flowers had withered noticeably.

'Peearree,' which was the girl's name, had told her mother, Aleem's sister, about her omission and said she would put the flowers on the grave at once. Her mother had answered that it was growing dark and the man-eater would catch her.

Besides, the flowers were already withered; she could put fresh flowers on the grave the next morning.

Without heeding, Peearree had grabbed the dying flowers and dashed out. She must have reached her destination, for the little bunch was found there. Nobody had heard a sound; neither a scream, nor a whimper, nor a growl. The child did not come back.

Alarmed, her mother had called out to her, but receiving no answer summoned Aleem and his two wives from the adjoining room. The caretaker snatched up a stick and the four of them, carrying a couple of lanterns, went to the small grave, where they found the flowers, but of the little girl herself, no trace. A few feet away lay a scattered heap of glass beads, and the string on which they had been threaded. And, of course, a little farther on, a few drops of blood!

Aleem and the three women had hurried to the village, to return considerably later with the ranger, a couple of forest guards, and quite a number of people armed with hatchets, sticks, knives and lanterns. Nobody had a gun.

They searched the undergrowth rather haphazardly that night without result, because everyone feared the panther. Next morning, they had looked again. This time they found the killer's pug-marks, and the marks left by the child's body where it had been hauled through the thicker bushes. They even found some tattered remnants of clothing. After that, all signs of man-eater and victim had vanished.

Aleem said I should stay in the rest house and not expose myself to risk from attack by the panther while in my tent. This I resolutely refused to do till he tempted me with an idea, as brave as it was dangerous. He offered to sit on Mischief's tombstone all night as bait, if I agreed to lie prone upon the veranda with my rifle, hidden behind a pillar. He said he would call softly, as soon as he felt the panther's

101

presence. I could then switch on my torch, play the beam around, pick up the animal's eyes or form in the light and shoot it. There was no moon at this time, the nights were totally dark.

Aleem's was a magnificently brave, but an utterly absurd and foolish plan. As if he would ever feel the man-eater's presence in time to warn me before it attacked him! He would feel nothing till it was upon him, and then it would be too late. What was worse, I would not be able to fire, for if I did so, I would possibly hit him and not the panther. Even supposing Aleem sensed the panther coming and called to me, the man-eater would never show up.

'No!' I kept repeating, 'No, no, no!' But at the same time I was thinking that Aleem's scheme had possibilities and they gave me an idea: there was nothing to prevent me from dressing in Indian clothing and sitting on Mischief's grave! My usual attire might scare the man-eater away, as panthers are inordinately cunning and clever, but Indian garb would deceive him. No other party being endangered, no charge of manslaughter could be brought against me; nor could there be any idea of suicide. Should the man-eater come, and should I not be aware of it beforehand, the question of suicide could not arise, for the very simple reason that I would not be present to answer the charge. So I told Aleem of my scheme and now it was his turn to remonstrate.

I had my way, however, as I usually do in these matters, and sunset found me seated on Mischief's tombstone with crossed legs, dressed in Aleem's dirtiest clothing, my face and hands blackened with charcoal, and a filthy rag tied round my forehead to emulate a turban. The rifle lay inconspicuously on the ground close at hand, with the torch clamped to it, covered with a light layer of leaves so that the man-eater might not notice it. You may be certain I took good care to sit with my back towards the rest house so that I could watch the jungle on three sides.

The sunset hour and the corresponding break of day are the most delightful moments to be in a forest to anybody fascinated by the jungle and the wild creatures that inhabit it, for it is at these times that one hears the songs of the birds of the day at their best. The creatures and birds of the night seem to take the cue from their brethren of the day, and their calls of welcome to the hours of darkness that lie ahead mingle with those of their roosting fellows, to fade away correspondingly at break of day.

But I had no ears for such music at this moment, enchanting as it always is to me, for my ears, mind and nerves were attuned for the coming of the killer. Now was the hour, the sunset hour, when it would be afoot. It was at precisely this moment that it had taken poor little Peearree, and there was every likelihood that it would revisit the place where it had killed her in the hope of finding another victim. Thoughts such as these came into my mind and filled me with an ever-growing sense of danger.

It was soon quite dark. The rest house behind me, although so close, was a mere shapeless blur against the blacker background of the jungle behind it. Overhead, the stars twinkled here and there in the open spaces between the tree-tops that swayed slightly to the faint breeze. A short distance away a tall clump of bamboos reached heavenwards, the tops of their giant feathery culms drooping back to earth again in all directions like a graceful but huge bouquet.

Then I heard a faint rustle a little to my left. Very soon I heard it again, coming, it seemed, from a bush a few feet away. I strained my eyes but could see nothing but the blob of deeper blackness that was the bush against the blackness of the jungle beyond. My hand grasped the loaded rifle, kept ready at my feet, and in a lightning-swift motion the butt was at my shoulder and my left thumb was pressed hard upon the switch. A bright beam cut through the darkness to reflect tiny eyes that gazed back at me, brilliant as rubies, in innocent resentment. What I thought to be the man-eater turned out to be one of those huge black scorpions, common in India and particularly in Andhra state, rustling the dry leaves in its search for grubs.

These creatures grow to a length of eight inches, vary between jet black and very dark green in colour, are covered with short, bristly hairs, have a tremendous crab-like pair of pincerclaws before them and a long segmented tail, with a needlesharp point at its end. The sting of this creature brings with it intense agony for twenty-four hours and death to such of its victims as may suffer from a weak heart.

The scorpion halted in its tracks when the light fell upon it and hissed audibly with vexation. I picked up a handful of earth and tossed it at the scorpion, which hissed again before scurrying away. Then I switched off the torch, replaced the rifle carefully on the ground at my feet and, groping for the leaves I had displaced, lightly covered it once again, cursing under my breath.

The whole incident was most unfortunate. The scorpion had made me reveal my position by shining my torch. If the panther had been anywhere near by it would have seen the light, and with the uncanny instinct of man-eaters who can sense when they are being hunted, the beast would beat a hasty retreat and now be far away.

It is said that scorpions have more than two eyes. I began to wonder if this was so and which of its eyes could have caught and reflected my torch-beam, when I heard the whistle of an engine as it rounded the bend just before reaching the outer signal. The goods train rumbled to a grinding halt and the engine-driver started to whistle again, first in short, rapid bursts and then in a prolonged blast that disturbed the whole jungle. I could hear voices too, the driver and his firemen talking to each other. They seemed to be unduly excited and were making quite a lot of noise.

I began to wonder what it could be all about when what I thought to be the solution came to me. The 'outer' signal must be 'up,' against the train entering the station, because the down passenger on its way to Nandyal was coming in from the opposite direction. This meant it was midnight and time had passed much faster than I expected.

The sound of human voices continued while I heard the distant hooting of the passenger train's engine, followed by the sound of its arrival at the station. The goods train driver now whistled and started his train, which clanked slowly along. A few minutes later, the down passenger drummed by as it picked up speed on its journey to Nandyal.

The quiet that I had expected would follow did not materialize, however, for soon I heard voices again, which grew louder as a group of men carrying a couple of lanterns turned in at the gate of the rest house and approached the building. Annoyed because all hope of shooting the man-eater was now gone, I rose from Mischief's grave and approached the veranda, where I was joined by Aleem, who had been awake and listening. The party turned out to comprise the stationmaster, the ranger, and the driver, guard and one of the firemen of the goods train.

They were all worked up and told how, upon coming out of the long tunnel, the headlight on the engine had revealed what looked like a crumpled human body lying at the side of the track. Observing this, the driver had concluded that one of the earlier trains must have knocked over some man who had attempted to cross the line, and as his train was moving slowly at the time, he decided to stop and investigate, lest the blame of having killed the man be put on him later. To his dismay, however, the driver and his firemen discovered that the man had not been run over at all. On the other hand, he had been devoured by some animal, as was evident from the fact that his gnawed bones lay scattered around.

The train guard, who had joined them by this time, suggested the body might be that of some wandering Chenchu tribesman, as it was clothed only in a *loincloth*. Having heard of the depredations of the panther, the driver and his companions decided to inform the stationmaster at Diguvametta, who could report the incident by telegram to the authorities. This they had done when the stationmaster, knowing I was at hand and had come to shoot the man-eater, resolved to inform the ranger and me first, before sending out his message.

So I had been right! The panther was, indeed, far away. Perhaps it had never been near the bungalow that night. Perhaps it had come at just about the time when the big scorpion had given me a false alarm. Maybe it had seen my torchlight, scurried away, met the Chenchu near the tunnel and killed him. But this was hardly possible, considering the distance of the tunnel from where I was sitting. As likely as not the Chenchu was a traveller who had not heard about the man-eater, or perhaps he had heard and for that reason had decided to sleep inside the tunnel, thinking it a safe place where the panther would never come.

I thanked my informers and said I would do what I could. After they had departed, as there was no point in remaining any longer by the grave, I determined to snatch a little sleep, instructing Aleem to wake me after four o'clock.

He must have remained awake, for it was a few minutes to four when he called me. We brewed tea and munched a few biscuits, after which we set out in darkness, walking in single file along the railway track. Had the man-eater been a tiger, to have done this would have been extremely dangerous, for a man-eating tiger nearly always carries away the person last in line. With a panther the risk was less: the more timid, but also more cunning, it waits for the victim who is alone and helpless before launching its attack, avoiding showing itself when more than one person is present.

Dawn was just about to break when we reached the long bridge. Here we had to wait for about ten minutes before it became bright enough to attempt a crossing as this was a tricky business, involving stepping from sleeper to sleeper between the lines. One did not dare to look too much at the valley and the tree-tops far below as we glimpsed them through the open spaces between the sleepers.

It seemed an endless distance to the other end, but we made it eventually. Not far away was the yawning black hole that was the tunnel's entrance. Just before reaching it, on our left and close to the track, lay the mangled remains of what had been a Chenchu.

Examination showed that the man-eater must have returned to its meal, either after the goods train had passed or later perhaps, after the passenger train had gone in the opposite direction, for much more of the body had been eaten than had been reported to me. The head, feet and hands were now severed from the trunk and lay scattered about, leaving just a possibility, though not a strong one, that the man-eater might return.

Our thoughts were rudely disturbed just then by the rumbling sound as of distant thunder. It issued from the mouth of the tunnel, growing momentarily louder till it became a continuous roar. The up morning passenger train to Diguvametta was approaching. Making up my mind quickly and calling to Aleem to follow, I ran a few yards from the tunnel up the track to give the driver a chance to see me, stood between the rails and began to wave frantically as the front of the engine, in billows of smoke, dashed out of the tunnel.

The train was moving fast when the driver saw me. He applied his brakes while I skipped clear of the lines, but half the train had passed before it could be brought to a halt. I explained the situation briefly to the driver and guard who came running from both ends of the train, and asked them to take Aleem along and tell the stationmaster at Diguvametta to ask the ranger to issue orders through the local police, forbidding anybody to approach the bridge or tunnel that night. I intended to await the man-eater's possible return. To Aleem I gave hasty instructions, asking him to return with food, tea and blankets for both of us. A down passenger was due to pass shortly after 2 p.m., and he could safely come by it.

While I was speaking, a large number of passengers had crowded around, wanting to know what was going on. Some of these now insisted upon going to look at the corpse, so that it was over fifteen minutes before the driver could continue his journey. I watched the train as it clanked over the long bridge and disappeared around the curve.

In an incredibly short time the vultures discovered the remains. At first one appeared as a speck in the sky high above me, soon followed by other specks. Then came the loud rustle of air through their wing-feathers as they swooped to earth to alight heavily a few feet from their prospective feast, towards which they began to waddle in ungainly fashion.

Squatting at the mouth of the tunnel, I had an abundant supply of ammunition in the gravel ballast of the line. I hurled the stones at the venturesome vultures, and from such close range I managed to score a fair number of direct hits which

served to keep the unwelcome birds at bay. All this helped
to pass the time and an up goods train to Duguvametta roared
through the tunnel without the driver noticing me, squatting
to one side of the mouth, or the scattered remains of the
Chenchu, though he could not have failed to observe the
abnormal number of vultures that gathered on both sides of
the track.

The section is not a busy one and no other trains came
through till the arrival of the down passenger shortly after
two o'clock, bringing Aleem, the tea, my lunch and a blanket
for each of us for the night. The driver stopped his train for
Aleem to alight and then stepped down himself, with his
firemen and, of course, the guard and a crowd of passengers,
to view the cadaver which by now was smelling strongly.

Amidst cries of 'good luck' the train rumbled away again,
followed an hour later by a goods train, after which we were
left to our own devices. The vultures had by now abandoned
their task as hopeless and had flown dejectedly away, leaving
us to make our plans for the night.

There were two possible places in which to hide. The first
was the mouth of the tunnel itself; the second, somewhere
above the entrance. To determine which would be the less
likely of the two hiding places to be discovered, I put myself
in the man-eater's place. Instinct, and a long association with
the locality would have conditioned it to the fact that huge
monstrosities, rumbling and roaring and billowing smoke,
every now and then issued from the hole in the earth. So it
would certainly watch the hole very carefully and for a long
time before daring to show itself; in the course of this close
scrutiny it would very likely discover us, for I would have to
keep Aleem with me. There was nowhere to send him away
to, and it would be most dangerous to ask him to return
home unarmed.

The conclusion we reached therefore was obvious: we would hide somewhere on the hillside, as close as possible above the mouth of the tunnel, hoping that the panther would keep to the general rule of not looking upwards for an enemy. The ground above the entrance to the tunnel sloped gradually and was mostly covered with coarse grass and weeds with a stumpy tree here and there. It was quite rocky and boulders lay scattered around in profusion, varying in size from a football to the height of a man.

Grateful for the luck afforded by this cover, it did not take us long, working together, to construct a small buttress of boulders which we placed in line a little above the entrance to the tunnel-mouth in the form of a wall high enough to conceal us when lying prone behind it. Between these boulders we allowed enough space for two loopholes, one for Aleem and the other for myself, through which to keep close watch upon the remains at the side of the track below us, and a little of the terrain around it. For a wider view, and to take a shot, I would have to look over the top of the rough stone parapet we had constructed. If I were to try poking the rifle through the aperture, I might make some sound if the barrel struck against the stone. The panther would hear this, look up and spot us. The one disadvantage of our situation was that we were lying at a downward-sloping angle, with our heels at a higher level than our heads.

We were in place by four o'clock, with the sun still blazing down upon us and the ground fire-hot beneath. We lay on our blankets, but these soon became unbearably warm, while the disadvantage of the downward slope now began to make itself felt. I suppose, because of the steady accumulation of blood in my chest and head, rather than in equal distribution over my whole body, I began to experience an uncomfortably stuffy sensation, which grew more and more apparent as sunset approached. This caused me to squirm about, and I saw that Aleem was squirming too, from which I concluded that he, like me, was feeling uncomfortable. If in the short space of only two hours I could feel so suffocated, it was quite apparent that we would be compelled to change position before very long.

It was now beginning to get dark, and we could still make out the remains of the Chenchu, when a barking deer called sharply from the hill-top at the back of us. 'Kharr!' eh cried, 'Kharr! Kharr! Kharr!'

It kept barking hoarsely, but did not move away. Therefore, whatever it had seen was evidently at a safe distance, enabling it to hold its ground while continuing to give the alarm. A peacock honked loudly and left its perch on a tree, also behind us, and flapped heavily away. I caught sight of it out of the corner of my eyes as it sailed with spread wings into the valley beneath the long railway viaduct.

There was silence after that and darkness had almost fallen when a junglehen, also from somewhere on the hill behind us, fluttered from cover with a hysterical 'Kok! Kok! Kok! Kok!' I did not relish all this activity behind me. Without doubt, some animal that represented danger to the creatures that had given their alarms, was afoot somewhere behind us. It could be any tiger or panther, but far more likely it was the man-eater itself.

Within the next few minutes it became too dark to see the Chenchu any more, although I could observe the line of ballast beside the railway track, stretching away like a faint grey ribbon from the tunnel beneath me. While I was still looking, I heard a small stone roll somewhere behind me. The sound was faint, but my ears, attuned closely to any noise in the jungle, did not fail to register it.

From straining my eyes to see the ballast below, I turned my head to the left to glance uncomfortably backwards.

111

Aleem, next to me was doing the same. Then the thought occurred to me: perhaps the man-eater, in walking along the track, had dislodged one of the small granite stones down there. Maybe the beast had come through the tunnel itself and shifted one of the stones at the entrance. What a lucky thing we had decided not to sit at the mouth of the tunnel!

I was just congratulating myself in this way when a thought struck me with horrifying significance: perhaps the panther was not below us at all. Maybe it had seen us from the hill top above and was crawling down upon us that very moment from behind, waiting to get close enough before launching a final attack.

All further conjecture was interrupted at that moment as the earth beneath me appeared to quake and tremble. As deep rumbling increased to a prolonged roar, and a moment later a shower of sparks and black smoke shot out of the earth before me as a light engine, travelling backwards, rushed out of the tunnel-mouth. Because this engine was moving in reverse, the driver could not use his headlight, and we had no warning of his approach. All other sounds were shut out as the black silhouette of the engine disappeared into the darkness.

That was when the panther decided to attack, and it came from behind us, not from down below. Maybe it could see only one of us and therefore failed to realize that there were actually two people present, for it came bounding along in true man-eater style, but without making a sound, unlike the normal panther that 'woofs' and coughs harshly and loudly when it attacks.

We heard only the muffled fall of its soft pads on the hard ground as it leapt towards us, a faintly-scraping, hollow, bumping sound, which puzzled us. A moment more and it would have been upon us but it then discovered that it was attacking two people where it expected only one. The panther checked itself two yards away, snarling and growling in baffled rage. Then, and only then, did we know that the man-eater had indeed arrived.

I can hardly remember what happened next. I know Aleem sprang up, yelling and I know I rolled violently over and over away from where instinct told me there was danger. But I do remember switching on my light and firing into the face of the panther at point-blank range. It sprang forward then, passing between us and over the edge of the tunnel above which we were seated, to fall with a loud thud upon the railway track below.

The driver of the midnight down passenger was amazed at the sight revealed by his headlight some time later. Two men were drinking tea. Between them lay a dead panther, and but a short distance away the mangled remains and bones of a man. I wager he will remember the sight long after he retires from service. Being a good fellow, he gave Aleem and me, along with the dead panther, a lift to Diguvametta.

113

Five

Tales of the Supernatural

MANY PEOPLE HAVE ASKED ME IF I HAVE HAD OCCULT EXPERIENCES during the years I have spent in the jungles, and for my views on whether such things are true or fictitious, or perhaps the product of an overwrought imagination.

I have really no idea why the occult should be associated with hunting experiences and forest lore, but somehow it is so. Other hunters, far more experienced than I am, have related some interesting happenings of this sort and we have little reason to doubt them. I have had a few curious experiences myself and have told them already, like that of the dead watchman of the Kalhatti forest bungalow.* Fortunately I was not alone at that time; my son Donald was with me. We both saw the watchman as clearly as I can see this sheet of paper; yet he had been shot dead and buried long before!

* See: *The Call of the Man-Eater.*

114

Then there was the case of Captain Neide, who removed an old lamp from an ancient temple. He almost died of fever shortly afterwards and only recovered when he returned the lamp to its resting place. Practically in the same locality lived the girl who was possessed by an evil spirit or spirits, that made her vomit stones each time she attempted to eat her evening meal. I saw this for myself and I saw her cured by a religious healer. Details of both these happenings have been related by me in an earlier book.*

I am no authority on the occult and I think it is very foolish for anyone to express an opinion on a matter he knows nothing about. So I propose only to record some of the beliefs of the people of South India. Of course, this is no answer to the questions of those who have asked me for a personal opinion. In fact, I have no answer.

Perhaps the most common belief in the south of the peninsula is in a pair of evil spirits that exist as man and wife. The female is referred to in the Tamil language as a *minnispuram* and in Malayalam as a *Yakshi*. It is universally agreed that the female is very hostile and dangerous to human beings, particularly to other women, while the males are generally quite harmless, at least according to Tamil ideas. Such a view corresponds closely to our own as regards the males and females of the human race. But the Malayalees think differently: they say both *Yakshis* (female spirits) and *Gandharwas* (male spirits) are highly dangerous to humans.

The Tamils believe that *minnispurams* (female) can adopt any shape or form, animal or human, and frequently appear as tall pillars of nebulous whiteness or blackness. Malayalees say that *Yakshis* generally show themselves in a more comely

---

* See: *Tiger Roars.*

way, as graceful bare-breasted women, clad below the waist in semi-transparent lungis, their hair long and flowing down their backs, thus concealing the hollow backs that are characteristic of these spirits. Tales are rife of how a man or youth, returning home at night, had met one of these nebulous creatures and was tempted to her side; he was then struck across the head or back, began to vomit blood and died within twenty-four hours. Others have been tempted to the edges of wells or tanks and then pushed in.

There is a story of two *Namboodries* (west coast Brahmin priests) who encountered two *Yakshis* in the form of beautiful girls. They spoke to the women and were invited to their home. The priests were tempted, and the house where the two girls lived turned out to be a very nice place indeed. Each of the *Namboodries* went into a room with one of the girls. But for some unaccountable reason one of them became nervous: instead of making love he clutched in his hand his personal talisman, a palm leaf with the sacred word *Nghrie* inscribed on it.

From the next room came the sound of giggling, which stopped suddenly and was followed by the sound of crunching bones. The girl did not touch the priest, but besought him earnestly to throw away the palm leaf and make love, emphasizing the temptation by exposing to him her naked body. But the priest, by now thoroughly suspicious, clung tenaciously to his leaf.

Suddenly the crunching sound in the next room ceased, whereupon the girl grew angry, abused the priest loudly, slapped him across the face and vanished from sight. So did the house! And he found himself alone in the darkness with the mangled body of his friend.

Belief in vampirism, but in a special form, is common. Instead of sucking blood, as do the European counterparts, the Indian vampire, which also appears only at night and sleeps in the earth all day, specializes in dogging the steps of a solitary man at night, stopping when he stops and walking when he walks. This continues to within a hundred yards of the man's destination, and then the vampire strikes! It attacks from behind, then tears its victim to pieces to devour his flesh. The only way of escape is to utter a very sacred word and turn upon the vampire with a drawn knife. The vampire will scream like a stricken animal. It must be stabbed repeatedly till it falls, when it will certainly disappear in a pool of blood. Or so it is said!

Great success in business and much prosperous trading, together with the amassing of several fortunes, can occur when a man agrees to hand over his wife to a spirit of a certain genus who confers great wealth on the family in exchange for the favour. The earthly husband must live apart from his wife and have no sexual intercourse with her, although he is allowed to speak to her and even feed with her occasionally.

The wife must live in a house apart; at nine each night the doors must be locked and the earthly wife must retire to a windowless bedroom. Soon a nebulous mist appears which takes the form of the spirit-husband. He stays with her till three in the morning, which is when all respectable spirits must depart in wraithform, just as they came, while less respectable men sneak home with their shoes in their hands!

Years ago, I knew a Jewish family that came from Rangoon. The husband dealt in hardware. He had a wife and three children. They were long-married and business was not good. Then a pact was said to have been made with a spirit-husband who came to like the wife, the woman being still of comely appearance despite her three children. It is not clear whether she sought the arrangement or the business-minded husband wanted it.

According to the rules, she shifted to a house apart, closed the doors by nine o'clock and enjoyed her spirit-husband till three in the morning. The earthly husband and the three children slept in another house all night but visited her during the day. Business improved. Everything they touched flourished and turned to gold. The family became one of the most prosperous in Rangoon and fabulously rich.

Then, one afternoon, something happened. The earthly husband and earthly wife were together. The children had gone out. The wife was still a comely woman and old habits were too strong to resist. The couple were intimate.

That night there was a great commotion in the wife's house after nine o'clock. The spirit-husband appeared, and he was highly annoyed; jealous, too. He beat her soundly and said he would never come there again. He did not, and the fortunes of the family went down and down. Business failed completely. They had to sell out, and from being one of the richest, they became one of the poorest families in Rangoon.

There have been cases, too, of spirit-wives who come at night. But whether these bring material riches, or material poverty and trouble, as their earthly counterparts generally do, is not quite clear.

Very frequently I have been asked if there is any truth in black magic, and instances in the lives of close friends of mine are many. I have already related the case of Ossie Brown, to which I was a most reluctant witness.[*]

About twenty years ago I was guilty of having done something that I should have avoided; but it is not clear to me now whether I offended the party concerned or whether

---

[*] See: *The Call of the Man-Eater.*

I fell under the person's influence. Call it a subconscious fancy on my part if you like. But for more than a fortnight, at exactly 3 a.m., I would wake up with a frightening, choking sensation, as if something or someone were grasping me by the throat. Then I would hear heavy footsteps outside the window—the measured, slow tread of someone walking in army boots. I dashed out on more than one occasion with a stick—even with a gun! Yet in the bright moonlight nothing could be seen, while the footsteps ceased. No sooner did I return inside than the footsteps started once again. They would last for about ten minutes.

Things came to a head one night. I got up almost suffocated. I heard the footsteps. I dashed out with the gun as usual and searched everywhere. There was nothing to be seen. I came back and the footsteps started again. I closed and locked the window. It was all very strange, but I determined to ignore it. Switching off the electric light, I got into bed.

The next moment something soft struck against my mosquito curtain and fell to the floor. Leaping out of bed, I turned on the light. There on the ground, was a ball of wet mud as large as my fist. Where had it come from? The window was closed. My wife and children were in the next room, sound asleep.

At this stage I determined to do something about the matter—something I would normally never think of doing.

There is a seer living in Bangalore who has achieved considerable fame as a fortune-teller, a recoverer of stolen property and necromancer. His fee for consultation is one rupee (about one shilling and four-pence), to be presented to him on a betel leaf—nothing more; nothing less. I had heard a good deal about this man, and had thought him a clever rogue.

119

I went to see him. He had very large black eyes and a big moustache. Other than this, there was nothing outstanding about him. I came into his room and laid down my rupee on a betel leaf, feeling myself to be the biggest fool in town at that moment.

Looking at me, he calmly said: 'You are being troubled by hearing footsteps at night. Lately, a mud ball was thrown at you. You have been bewitched by'—(and here he described person concerned) 'because you refused to give the individual what was asked.'

That's easy to explain, you will say. Thought-reading is the answer; or some form of hypnotism; or both. You may be quite right. But listen to what happened next.

'Go home,' he told me. 'Measure six paces from your window in the direction in which the sun rises. Then dig a foot into the ground. You will find something. Destroy it. You will not be troubled again.'

I went home, feeling angry. I took a shovel in my hands, feeling more angry. I measured six paces from my window towards the east, and began to dig. Not only was I angry now, but also wondered how I had become such a fool. But I found something, and I had dug just about a foot deep. I found a doll made of clay buried in the earth. A crude affair with misshapen head and arms and legs. But human hair had been stuck to the head and a nail driven through it. At the pointed end of the nail was a dried lemon skin that had been sliced almost in half. The human hair looked remarkably like my own.

I was amazed; and I burned the damned thing! I did not hear the footsteps at three next morning, or ever again!

Now, how had the seer known? It could not have been thought-reading, because I did not know about the doll myself. And he could not have prepared the stage beforehand, for how did he know I would consult him?

Years later, I related the incident to a person who dabbled in such matters. He told me the clay doll with human hair was made to represent me. The nail driven through the head signified that the mantra had been made against my mind, my powers of reason. If the curse had not been removed by the seer telling me where to find the doll, I would assuredly have become insane within a short time!

This occurrence interested me so much that I made up my mind to investigate these matters more fully. As this friend was known to be a black magician, a necromancer, I began worrying him to tell me more; in fact, to initiate me into his brotherhood. But he flatly refused!

I have a trait about which some people who do not like me complain bitterly. It is stubbornness, coupled with persistence. The more my friend refused, the more I pestered him. So, at length, he initiated me as a member of the brotherhood of the Silver Armlet!

I have my silver armlet which I wear on certain occasions, and nobody else is allowed to touch it. Nor can I tell you all the mystic rites of the society as I am under oath not to reveal them; but I can give you the outline of the initiation ceremonies.

The first entails a visit to any old cemetery—the older it is the better—on the night of the *amavasa*, which is the night before the new moon. The neophyte must go alone, after midnight, carrying either a live black cock and a knife with which to cut its throat, or if he feels squeamish about cutting the creature's throat, a couple of pounds of pig's entrails and liver instead.

He must enter the cemetery, and after a brief *pooja* by lighting camphor, etc., he should cut the cock's throat and then proceed to cut up the whole bird, feather and all, into finger-long pieces. Or, if he has brought pig's liver and entrails

121

instead, cut that up into pieces. Next he must walk through the cemetery without looking back, throwing these pieces over his left and right shoulders one by one while using the most foul language he can think of, in whichever dialect he wishes. 'Take this, you—and eat it,' and so forth. This attracts the spirit or the disembodied entity, to him.

The neophyte then goes home and performs another ceremony which makes this spirit a servant to him.

You may have heard and read of miracles performed by holy men in India who can produce from the air articles like fruit of any kind, money, sweetmeats and even certain medicines. These things are made possible by the services of a species of small genii known as *kutty shaitan*, one of which becomes attached to the individual on a sort of fifty-fifty contract basis. They each become a servant of the other and are bound together for life. The word *kutty* in Tamil and Malayalam signifies 'small;' while the word *shaitan* in Urdu and Hindi means 'devil'—a curious combination of four languages. This spirit belongs to the category of 'elementals,' but assumes the form of a miniature negro, not more than three to four inches tall, in order to make itself visible.

After midnight on any night, but particularly on *amavasa* night, when it becomes perceptible, a curious movement can be seen by a watcher concealed in a pen with a herd of buffaloes. He notices something flicking from the back of one animal to another. It looks like a large moth, or maybe a small bat, but apparently has no wings! It dances on one back, leaps to another, sways, disappears and reappears on the back of another buffalo. But the animals do not appear to see it, or notice or feel its presence.

This is a *kutty shaitan* in its natural habitat and condition. If the watcher sees this much and is satisfied, all is still well.

But if he wants to become like the other great men who can pick up anything they want 'out of the air,' so to speak, he is playing with fire! For to do this, he has to get the *kutty shaitan* into himself. He has to make a 'deal,' a bargain, with the elemental spirit: a promise that they will serve each other for life. To make the deal is simple; but to get out of it is practically impossible.

What he has to do, to make the deal, is to approach the buffaloes and go through the motions of trying to snatch and capture the little sprite—although of course he can never do this in fact—while in his mind he concentrates on the thought that he desires the services of the *kutty shaitan*. He will receive a message, sometimes at the first attempt and sometimes after two or three failures—which is generally a telepathic message to his subconscious and thence to his conscious mind—as to what to do next. Generally the message instructs him to carve, (or even purchase) a small black doll, of wood, ivory, bone or any substance, which he must keep on a table or shelf in his house, and perform a daily *pooja* to it with lighted candles, incense, camphor and other things. This little image represents the *kutty shaitan*, and this ceremony seals the bond whereby the sprite agrees to serve him.

The man can then ask for and get anything he wants, *provided he agrees to return it within a fixed time*, say a month or two. *But he cannot get something for nothing.* The little sprite will bring him money, an apple, balm for a headache, a cooked meal, even petrol for a stalled car. *But everything has to be returned at the time promised.* Otherwise, the individual, whoever he may be, has had it!

The sprite does only one free service for its patron. It warns him of approaching danger and contrives to get him out of it. But the wages demanded by this sprite are costly.

The life-span of its patron is shortened; he can have no dealings with a woman; he is hardly allowed to sleep at night; he can never accumulate wealth, although he is permitted enough for his actual needs; he will not be on good terms with his family; he will always be a wanderer, restless, unable ever to settle down.

As a member of the brotherhood of the Silver Armlet, I can assure you that black magic is a fascinating subject to study—but a hard and ruthless taskmaster if embraced!

I have another good friend, a retired army doctor who was a colonel in the India Medical Service during World War II. He told me a story which he assures me is perfectly true. While stationed at Madras, he happened to meet two brothers, Mohammed Bey and Ali Bey, who were Egyptians. He became friendly with the former, but did not know for a long time that both brothers were necromancers who had been trained in Egypt under an adept.

When he learned this, the colonel jokingly told his friend. 'Oh, then you will be able to show me a spirit. I am longing to see one and have been trying for years, without success.'

'Not only will I show you a spirit,' replied Mohammed Bey gravely, 'but I will make him your servant for your lifetime, to help you in anything you want and to bring good fortune to you. But there is one firm condition. Never, at any time, must your employ this spirit servant to do harm to another, or for any sort of evil purpose whatever. If you do, he will turn upon you and you will surely die, and most painfully too. Do you agree?'

'You have my word,' the doctor said with a laugh. 'The proposition is very attractive and I'm extremely interested.'

Mohammed Bey then asked for a writingpad and a pencil, and when he had been given these materials was busy for a while. The colonel has very kindly lent me the sheet of paper on which the Egyptian made his drawing more than twenty years ago, and I have faithfully copied it and reproduced it on pages 125 and 126.

The mantra, or words for summoning spirits, as told by the Egyptian necromancer

Ah, Ah, Sharheel wa burrhoode wa noodaju wa askeerah if alue aywhel kadhamu ma amuro bi hi min shain hathal kagadi bi hyqi sharheel us Fur Ya rooh (three times) *Tha-al* (three times) *bill amruho* (seven times).

Begin by facing the north. Then turn to the right or east, and read the above words seven times. Then turn back again to the north. Then turn to the left or west side and read the words seven times. Then turn back to the north. Next turn right around to face in the opposite or southern direction, and read the words seven times. Then turn back again to the north, where the words should be read once more seven times. After having finished the four points of the compass, turn in the direction of the cemetery you have selected for your visit and read the words twenty-one times. Lastly, breathe in slowly, hold your breath a little and then exhale slowly three times, each time concentrating upon a good manifestation of the spirit desired by the person teaching this, or that you would like to see yourself.

This procedure is to be followed for twenty-two days, beginning in such a fashion that the twenty-third day falls on a Tuesday or a Friday. That twenty-third day is the day on which to go to the cemetery. In other words, carry out the directions for twenty-two days, ending on a Monday or a Thursday. The next day (Tuesday or Friday) is the day on which to visit the cemetery.

125

The following drawing may be traced on a piece of paper, folded and kept in a locket or wallet for good luck:

'I have written in Roman-Arabic so that you may be able to read it,' Mohammed Bey explained (Roman-Arabic is Arabic written phonetically in Roman characters). 'Next come the instructions in English. Carry these out faithfully and to the letter.'

'Order a large garland of roses to be prepared by the evening of the final day, and ninety minutes before midnight that day have a bath and dress in a clean white shirt and suit. I will call for you at 11.30 and show you what to do next. One more thing. You must fast on that last day, but you may drink a cup of milk in the morning and another in the evening. Nothing more.'

'Now let us start calculating which is the twenty-third day.'

Thereupon the Egyptian turned to a large calendar hanging on the wall, made some calculations while counting the days on the calendar with the tip of a pencil, and finally named a day and a date.

'Be ready,' he added cryptically, and the doctor agreed.

The instructions were carried out to the letter, but during the interval the colonel never met Mohammed Bey. At the end of the third week he had the feeling that his friend was deliberately avoiding him. He wondered if it was all a joke.

The final day came. The garland of roses which the colonel had ordered was ready by evening. At 10.30 p.m. he had a bath and then dressed in clean white clothes. He tells me he felt himself a fool.

At exactly 11.30 p.m., a car drew up beneath the portico of his old-fashioned residence and the Egyptian alighted. He, too, was dressed in white clothes.

'Bring the garland, doctor,' he said in a matter-of-fact voice, 'we must be there by midnight.'

Wondering where they were going, the doctor did as he was told. They reached the cemetery in fifteen minutes and, carrying the garland of roses, the doctor followed his companion through the wicket-gate. It was pitch-dark, except for a faint glow cast by the stars. Indside the cemetery the Egyptian stopped for a moment. Then he moved among the graves for some distance, as if in search of a particular one, while the doctor followed him. They found it at last. A grave with a granite slab and a rounded headstone. It was too dark to see more.

'Place the garland around the headstone, doctor,' Mohammed Bey directed, 'and stand at the foot of the grave with your arms folded across your chest. I will stand at the side. Now, whatever happens, do not be afraid. I am here; have confidence in me. We must wait for midnight.'

A few minutes later a distant clock chimed and then struck the hour of twelve. But Mohammed Bey did nothing for a few minutes more. Then he started intoning something in a language the doctor could not understand, but thought to be

Arabic. The words came in a singsong voice and the Egyptian appeared to be in a trance.

This continued for a while, and then something seemed to go wrong with the proceedings. The chanting came to an end abruptly, and was followed by angry words from the Egyptian, with an interval, and then more angry words followed. It seemed as if he was having a heated argument with some invisible person, whose voice could not be heard.

The Egyptian grew more excited. He waved his arms. He appeared to be using abusive language. Then he spat upon the grave. The next instant he fell as if pole-axed across the granite slab. His body twitched in the faint gloom, while horrible, gurgling sounds came from his throat. The doctor panicked and was on the verge of bolting, his only thought being to save himself by running for dear life.

At that moment his professional training came to his aid. He was a doctor after all. The Egyptian might be having an epileptic fit, a heart attack or a seizure of some kind. It was his medical duty to stay. Also came the paralysing thought that the Egyptain might die if left alone. When his body was found, if it was ever discovered that the doctor had been with him in the cemetery, he might be accused of murder.

So he ran forward, grasped the body of his companion that was still thrashing about and from which came dreadful gasps and groans, and attempted to raise him.

The doctor swears he encountered a force stronger than his own that was keeping the man down. A struggle followed, then the Egyptian gasped: 'Roses—the garland—give it to me.'

The doctor let go of his companion, removed the garland from the tombstone, and threw it to the prostrate man. While he still grovelled on the granite slab as if in an epileptic fit, Mohammed Bey tore the garland to shreds. And as the garland disintegrated, the black magician appeared to be gaining mastery over the situation.

Eventually he stood up, dishevelled and breathing hard. Blood trickled down his face from a gash across his forehead, where he had struck it against the granite slab.

'It's all right now, doctor,' he gasped, 'but let's get out of here. I'll tell you in the car.'

The two men hurried out to the car and began to drive back to the doctor's house. The colonel waited till his companion regained his composure. At last the Egyptian spoke.

'The spirit came all right. In fact, there were several. But they were in grotesque forms, resembling strange animals. They all volunteered to serve you. But I insisted there should be only one, and that one should adopt a human form. They refused, and were adamant that all should attach themselves to you and in their present strange forms. I would not allow it. There was an argument and suddenly the leader struck me down and they all set upon me, choking me. If you had not thrown me the garland to break the spell, I would have been killed.'

A clever piece of acting by the Egyptian, put on to deceive the doctor, you will say. The cut across his forehead against the tombstone was, of course, an unforeseen accident. Perhaps it was not blood after all, but something surreptitiously applied!

Quite possible I do agree, and a reasonable explanation. But remember, the Egyptian never asked his friend for money, or a favour at any time. Then why did he go through all this trouble?

Many Indian families, particularly on the west coast of India, believe they are guarded by what they call 'deities.' These are not evil spirits or jinns or even gods. They are thought to be superior spiritual beings. Each is distinguished from the other by the scent of a particular fragrant flower which comes from nowhere. Some bring with them the scent of jasmine; this is very common and I have smelt it myself many times in rooms and in places where flowers of any kind certainly did not exist. Superior orders are said to bring the scent of roses, or other fragrances.

Amavasa night—the night before the new moon, the darkest night of the month—is the time generally chosen for practising all kinds of black magic, and it is on such nights that many Indian families feel and hear the presence of their guardian spirits. These evidence themselves by the sound of a heavy chain being dragged or jingled, or in the case of a female spirit, by the subtle clicking of bracelets against each other. The major guardian announces his presence by making a noise as if a man were walking around the house snapping his thumb against his fingers every once in a while, or by measured, heavy footsteps.

Belief in the existence of spirits and in the occult has found its way into all religions in India. In my own opinion, all creeds, as originally preached and believed, were of pure and divine origin: Hinduism, Buddhism, Mohammedanism and Christianity all pointed the way to the Supreme Being. But priestcraft on the one hand, and superstition and occultism on the other, have become so intermingled with these doctrines that many of their followers practise a religion very different, and in certain cases quite opposed, to the doctrines of the original parent order.

The beliefs and practices of many Christian converts in India, both Roman Catholic and Protestant, are indeed a queer mixture of religion, superstition and occultism. Very properly, these people are the despair of most right-thinking priests of all faiths, although unfortunately here and there are some who encourage distorted beliefs to the point of malpractice in order to drive home that fear of hellfire by which they hold their congregations in submission.

Saint Anthony, who is regarded everywhere as a most beneficent man while alive, has come to be looked upon by many in India as an infallible means of effecting revenge upon others as well as acquiring benefits by prayer. Horrible acts of revenge and the defeat of enemies by fair means or foul, including painful illness and lingering death, are sought through him. Saint Anthony is also regarded as the main means for the recovery of lost or stolen property and for inflicting punishment, by many kinds of violence, upon the thief responsible. Some of the forms of punishment which Saint Anthony is asked to inflict upon the culprit or the enemy are of a revolting character and out of all proportion to the crimes committed. For example, in retribution for stealing a pound of rice, Saint Anthony is asked to inflict upon the thief, known or unknown, such appalling diseases as cholera and plague.

My servant is a Roman Catholic convert, but here is her procedure for recovering lost property through Saint Anthony. To find the thief, the supplicant must first take a bath. Then he must wash the statue of the saint, or (if he does not possess a statue) the glass covering the saint's photograph. To bathe the saint's likeness in milk, rather than in water, is considered more efficacious. The ceremony should be performed at sunset on a Tuesday. After this, four candles are lighted at the foot of the statue or photograph, before which an offering of flowers is made and incense burned. A small coin is tied in a cloth to the top of the frame of the photograph or placed at the foot of the statue.

A prayer is then offered to the saint to grant the favour of finding the thief, restoring the money or property, or severely punishing the offender, as the case may be. This is accompanied by a vow that, if the petition be granted, charity

131

in some form or another will be given to thirteen beggars in the name of the saint. This charity may be in the shape of a small gift of money, or a garment, or a meal. Such prayers to the saint are offered every evening at sundown for thirteen days. It is thought certain favours of a minor kind will be granted within eight days, whereas major favours, in respect of articles of greater value, may take longer, but action by the saint will surely be evident within a month.

The recovery of lost property purchased by hard-earned money, or of stolen money, is assured by the lighting of a single candle, accompanied by incense, for thirteen consecutive evenings before the statue or picture of Saint Anthony.

In some parts of India, particularly old Hyderabad state, these supplications to Saint Anthony assume a more forceful character. The feet of the saint's statue are bound with cord, signifying that the supplicant is not prepared to release him until or unless the favour is granted. The most drastic—and amusing—instance that I have met is the procedure followed by an old Anglo-Indian living at a place called Kazipet. He was an old army man and possibly thought Saint Anthony needed a spot of disciplining now and again. For should the favour not be granted within the stipulated time, the statue of the saint was subjected to rough treatment. It was tied to a tamarind tree out in the garden and smeared with a mixture of chili-powder and other ingredients that are known to be extremely pungent. The idea was by torture to force the poor saint into granting the favour, and once that happened the old soldier brought the statue indoors again, washed it, bathed it in milk and restored it to its pedestal.

Statues and photographs of the Virgin Mary were similarly appealed to for general favours. Thursday was considered the right day for the first supplication, to be repeated for eight days in succession.

The old English method of tying up a pair of scissors, so that the two loops of the scissors rest on the fingertips of two persons and rotate at the mention of the name of the guilty party, is very widely practised in India. So is the custom of suspending a rosary over a pot of incense, so that the cross is immediately above the fire; it is then said to oscillate at the name of the guilty party.

In cemeteries in which Indian Christians are buried, it is common to see the relatives of the dead come to the grave on certain days with offerings of milk and food, presumably to sustain the departed spirit on its long journey to higher realms.

My purpose in mentioning these things is to emphasize the extent to which superstition and ancient customs have become inextricably involved with Christianity in India. Superstition and belief and fear of the unknown are rife in all walks of life in all communities and all religions. Among the upper-class Hindus it takes a higher form but is nevertheless powerful. From birth, a child's horoscope is all-important and plays a primary part in the arrangement of a marriage—the boy and girl rarely see each other before the ceremony—and the stars continue to have a major role throughout the man's life. Conspicuously marked on calendars, for every day of the month, are two lists of timings, headed respectively *rahukalam* and *guligaikalam*, meaning 'bad time' and 'good time', and no Hindu, and many who are not Hindus, will dream of leaving home at a time, or embarking on a business venture or journey at an hour which falls within the *rahukalam* or 'bad time' period. He will patiently wait till that time had passed and the *guligaikalam* or 'good time' has come. Then he will set out on his venture, very confident and assured of success.

A ring that has very magical properties in attracting the fair sex, sometimes to their great embarrassment, can be made

133

in the following way. I took great pains to write down the formula, or whatever you care to call it. The only snag is that the mantras involved have to be acquired and learned. The secret is so valuable, presumably because the reward is so great, that so far nobody seems willing to tell me these mantras, so that I may learn and repeat them. But I am still trying to find somebody who will part with the secret.

However, you must procure a live fresh-water turtle of the dark variety of medium size. This is not very difficult. For about a rupee someone will bring one to you. They abound in fresh-water wells throughout the countryside.

Having procured the live turtle, get some dried pumpkin seeds that will germinate easily. These may be obtained readily from any seedsmen, or from any pumpkin purchased in the market, though in the latter event they should be well dried.

Next, tempt the unfortunate turtle with some food such as earthworms or a small frog. When he sticks his neck out of his shell to eat, decapitate him with a deft stroke of a sharp knife, delivering the blow just behind the back of his head and high up the neck; that is, be sure to leave a good bit of stump protruding. After all movement has ceased insert about half a dozen of the dried pumpkin seeds well into the raw stump of the neck. Then bury the turtle in an upright position in the ground, so that the neck-stump, with the seeds in it, is rather less than a couple of inches below the surface of the ground. Then water the spot sparingly every day.

The pumpkin seeds, or some of them, will sprout. Select the best and healthiest. Wait till the second shoot appears, and then carefully pluck the whole seedling, along with its roots, from the decaying neck-stump of the turtle. Clean away the mess from the roots, and cram the seedling tightly, roots and all, through the groove on the underside into the hollow of a ring, which you should have prepared in advance.

Any ring will do, but one of silver or copper is best. A hollow groove, as deep as possible, should have been cut around the ring.

After you have pushed as much as is possible of the seedling with its roots into this hollow groove, seal up the same with sealing-wax or any form of lacquer or gummy substance that will dry and harden. The ring should not be sent to a jeweller for sealing, as the heat he will apply to melt the metal to seal the ring will burn up the seedling inside.

The ring, having thus been made ready and sealed, must not be used till the next new-moon day. At midnight on the night before, that is that night of *amavasa*, a mantra has to be repeated over the ring eleven times, and it is then ready for use. Its efficacy in attracting and embarrassing females is said to last for a lifetime.

This topic will not be complete unless I tell you of an adventure that befell me near a town called Chitaldroog, in a jungle once renowned for tigers, situated to the east of the district of Shimoga in Mysore state. The village of Sampigehalli, a few miles from Chitaldroog, is surrounded by thick forest. About four miles from this village, along a track leading to another village named Budhalli, in the midst of the jungle, stands a ruined temple with a very deep well. The temple and the well are reputed to be haunted, for which reason hardly a soul will approach within a furlong of them in broad daylight, while the area is of course absolutely taboo after sunset.

Because of its isolation, a sloth bear or two invariably lived in or close to the ruins, while quite frequently a panther could shelter in the old temple close to the bears, but without having anything to do with them. Now and again a tiger decided to take up residence there for a few weeks, and when that happened the bears and the panther temporarily took themselves off to safer abodes. For either of them to dare to share the same abode with the king of the jungle might prove a costly experiment. But eventually the tiger would move on, and then the bears and the panther would come back and things return to normal.

Some time ago a villager disappeared from Sampigehalli, and a month later another disappeared from Budhalli. Nobody knew what happened to them, nor was there any sign of the remains. As villagers in India rarely leave their birthplaces voluntarily, the disappearance of these men, one after the other, left food for thought. It suggested that a tragedy of some sort had taken place.

About this time an unusually large tiger, said by the villagers to be exceptionally fierce because of the manner in which it boldly attacked their herds of cattle and never failed to make a kill, took up its abode in the locality, or even in the old temple itself. This was established by its pug-marks, to be seen early in the morning returning to the temple, superimposed upon the pug-marks it had left in the dust of the trail when it had gone forth the previous evening. The villagers felt that this tiger had devoured their two companions, one after the other, so they appealed to the authorities for help against the man-eater that they were convinced dwelt in the ruins of the old temple.

Sampigehalli was at one time a favourite haunt of mine and several of my village friends wrote to me to come to their aid. When I reached the village a fortnight later I made painstaking inquiries regarding the last movements of the two missing men, but everything seemed to be shrouded in mystery. A village girl was mixed up in the affair and it was said that both the men were her suitors. The girl was poor, whereas both the men were comparatively well-to-do, owning land in their own villages. They were married and had families, but no member of either family had the least knowledge of the large sum of money each of these individuals was reported to be carrying on his person just prior to his disappearance, nor did they know why their relative had been carrying the money about with him. All this came to light only afterwards. For India is one of the few places left in the world today where wives do not dare to question their husbands' movements or authority.

The man's word is law and women are content to confine their activities to the kitchen.

Meanwhile, there was no evidence whatever to connect the tiger with the disappearance of the two men. Casually, in the course of inquiries, I spoke about the missing men to the girl concerned and came away feeling that she knew much more about the matter than she would say. To my mind, she was much more dangerous than any man-eating tiger and far more astute; but not being a policeman, I did not feel obliged to act as an informer or a detective. I was much more interested in the tiger than in the girl's motives and movements and what had happened to her suitors.

I therefore decided to go to the old temple immediately after lunch that day, select a suitable hiding place and remain there all night in the hope of seeing the suspected man-eater. I had not made up my mind whether to shoot the creature if I did happen to see it, for something told me that it was not the culprit. In any case it was summer time, far better known in India as the 'hot weather,' and it was only a day or two until the full moon. The moonlight and the open air would be much more pleasant than spending the night in some little mudhouse, where the heat would be intense, or even in the forest department's bungalow.

After a good lunch I got together the few things I would require for the night: my rifle, ammunition, flask of tea, water-bottle, electric torch and some biscuits in a cloth bag, that would not crackle as a paper wrapper would, and set out for the old temple. In a little over an hour I reached my destination. I knew the place well enough, although I had never spent a night there. It consisted of a small central structure built of solid, irregular blocks of granite, surrounded by what had once been a fairly high stone wall. The well, which was indeed very deep, still held water and was in the courtyard to the front of the temple.

I do not know how much water was in the well, but the surface glinted down below, far beneath the level of the ground. The well itself was not more than fifteen feet in diameter, ringed at the top by a low stone parapet about a yard high. Many of the granite blocks forming the main temple, the four walls of the courtyard and the parapet of the well, had become loose and had fallen away from their original positions, while gnarled or dwarfed trees, principally the jungle fig, had been able to take root wherever the lantana shrub had not already taken possession. The scene in general was bleak and dreary, and it was clear that with time the few remaining traces of the temple and its environs would be swallowed up by the advancing jungle.

But at the moment I was not interested in the temple as a structure, historical or otherwise. What I was interested in was the hiding place of the tiger, and that did not take me long to find. The only possible place was the main temple building itself. The earth was mostly hard, but here and there were sandy patches and clearly imprinted in the soft ground, both coming and going, were the pug-marks of a large tiger, leading to and from the old ruins.

I knew that if the animal were at home at that moment it would probably be sound asleep inside. I had never been inside this structure myself, but felt safe in conjecturing that it followed the general pattern of such buildings, with a sanctuary in the form of a small separate room at the farther end of what would be the one and only prayer-room of the temple proper. This small inner room would house a Nandi or two, stone images of varying sizes of the sacred bull that is universally respected by the Hindus in India, or perhaps an image or several images of one of the many gods and goddesses.

To approach this opening would, in the circumstances, be to invite disaster. If the tiger were at home, man-eater or not, it would definitely resent such blatant violation of its privacy and would probably decide to get rid of the invader with the utmost dispatch. It was one of those occasions when brain rather than brawn was indicated, so I stood still to take stock of the situation and decide upon a plan.

And the solution lay right there before me in the broken parapet of the old well. All I had to do was to sit comfortably behind it, facing the opening leading to the main temple. If the tiger were inside, as I felt sure it was, then sooner or later it would have to come out, and this it could only do by using the entrance. I would have this entrance covered in the sights of my rifle, so that it did not matter at what angle the tiger decided to emerge. The whole thing seemed 'a piece of cake.'

The sun blazed down upon me when I took up my position behind the parapet, directly facing the temple entrance. I realized my head was above the top of the parapet, so I picked up some of the fallen stone blocks and arranged them before me, leaving a space about six inches square through which to peer. If the tiger showed up, and if I had decided to shoot him by then, I could fire through this loophole.

The only other requirement was that I should sit absolutely still. Fortunately I am well practised in that sort of thing, so that neither the heat nor the winged insects that came as if from nowhere, not even the occasional slate-black lizard with its brilliant orange and yellow back worried me when the sweat trickled down my face and the insects settled on my lips and lizards crawled over my body.

Then came the evening. The calls of roosting birds preceded the squeaking of early bats and the buzz of a passing mosquito. It was almost dark when the moon, that was not yet at the full, began to rise. Soon its glow outlined the dark shadow that was the entrance to the temple through which the tiger might, at any moment now, if he was at home, be expected to emerge. What was left of daylight faded rapidly, but moonlight took its place, so that even before I appreciated the passage of time, it was night. I shivered a little, for in those few minutes it had become distinctly chill.

That was when I heard the sound for the first time. Three distinct, sharp whistles that seemed to come from the well right in front of me. The first whistle was low, the second higher, the third shorter, sharper, louder and pitched yet higher than its two predecessors.

Who the hell could be hiding in the old well? To say the least, I was very annoyed. After all the time I had spent sitting motionless in the sweltering heat of the sun, must this so-and-so start whistling at this critical moment and frighten away the tiger that might be expected to emerge from the temple? Was it worth hiding any longer? The tiger would have heard that whistling even more clearly than I had done, and it would never show up with a human being just outside its shelter. Or would it? If it really was a man-eater it might think some victim was within striking distance.

Quite ten to fifteen minutes must have elapsed when I heard the whistling again, loud and clear, in three sharp blasts. The first low and rather long-drawn; the second louder, shorter and higher pitched; the third loudest, shortest and on a yet higher note. Then there was complete silence.

I was in the act of getting up to peer down the well and curse the intruder when a slight movement in the oblong blackness of the temple entrance caught my eye. A greyish blur seemed to pass against that blackness. It vanished, came again, and disappeared once more. A moment later, clearly outlined, sideways on the moonlight, stood the tiger!

It was obvious that it never suspected my presence for a moment, as it never even glanced in my direction. It was looking directly ahead when I first saw it, but stopped at that moment to bend its neck and lick its right foreleg. I could clearly see the movement of its head, and hear the rasping of its rough tongue over its coat each time that it licked itself. And then, for the third time, came those three loud whistles in rising crescendo.

That has done it, I thought. The tiger must surely hear them now. It would crouch, growl, spring back into the shelter of the temple, or rush away, according to its disposition or the state of its nerves. But nothing happened! The tiger continued to lick itself, unperturbed. Evidently it had not heard the whistling, and for this there could be only two explanations. Either the tiger was stone deaf, or the whistling did not register upon its hearing.

The tiger stopped licking itself and began to move forward. At the same time I heard what appeared to be the flapping of wings from the depths of the well before me. The sound was heavy, slow and distinct. It must have been made by some large and heavy bird, I decided, or a bat not much smaller than the familiar Indian flying-fox or fruit-bat.

Then for the fourth time that evening came the whistle, louder and closer than ever before. My decision whether or not to shoot the tiger was quite forgotten in this mystery.

Indeed, I did not even watch it, but stared at the top of the old well, waiting for I know not what to come out.

The heavy, slow flapping was continuous now. The large bird or bat, or whatever it was, drew nearer every instant to the top and would show itself in a moment or two. A strange fascination came over me as I stared at the opening. Once again came the three whistles, and then what seemed a large, dark shadow of indefinite shape issued from the well.

The moonlight was bright and clear and I was staring at the spot. There was no mistaking that I saw something, but it had no real form or shape: a small cloud of what seemed to be dark smoke came out of the well. It might have been six feet in diameter by about the same height.

A great lassitude seemed to come over me; a sort of strange, morbid despair. Did it matter what came out of the well? Was life worth living with all its troubles? Why not jump into the well and forget about everything?

I shook myself and stared, and as I watched the cloud hovered for a moment above the mouth of the well and in the next second was gone. The moonlight shone clearly through the spot which, a moment before, had been clouded by the indefinable shape. I had started perspiring with excitement when the tiger made its appearance, which is something I still do to this day when I see a tiger in the wild. Now I felt cold and clammy.

Meanwhile the tiger, which at least was of flesh and bone, wandered away. I knew that in all likelihood it would not return till the early hours of the morning, unless it found something to kill and eat sooner. I would therefore, in all probability, have to wait for a long time if I still wanted to shoot it when it came back. But somehow I did not want to shoot this tiger; the strange whistling, and the still stranger shadow that had emerged from the well, interested me much more. In any case, it was far better to sit there in the moonlight and the open air, than to be in the stuffy shelter I was occupying four miles away at Sampigehalli.

I forgot everything but the whistling and the shadow, and fell to conjecturing what on earth could have been the cause of what I had seen. The whistling had not resembled the call of any bird with which I was familiar. Rather, it was distinctly human in timbre. The flapping of wings I had heard could have been caused by some large bird, or the Indian flying-fox that I have already mentioned. But neither bird nor bat had emerged from the well, and I had never for a moment removed my gaze from its mouth. What had come out had been something far different and quite unexpected: a smokey shape of indefinable nature. In plain words, a small cloud. And that cloud had vanished before my eyes!

So absorbed was I in the problem that I lost all count of time and became oblivious to my surroundings till a low growl, somewhere behind me, brought me back to earth with a jolt. The tiger was standing there! It had returned from another direction and had discovered my presence. It was reputed to be a man-eater that had killed and devoured two men already.

I swung around in alarm, instinctively raising the .405 to my shoulder. About forty yards away this tiger sat on his haunches in the moonlight, staring hard at me. Then it inclined its head slightly and snarled in mild protest. As clearly as if it had spoken the words, this animal was saying, 'Can't you get the hell out of here?' That satisfied me entirely. It had had me at its mercy and could have killed me before I was even aware of its presence. This tiger was no man-eater!

I try to be grateful when a good turn is done to me and I was definitely grateful to this animal. It had spared my life and I would return the courtesy. I got to my feet, whereupon the tiger disappeared from sight.

Keeping the rifle in the crook of my arm to guard against a sudden change of mind on the beast's part, I shone the beam of my torch down the well, expecting to discover the mysterious whistler who must be hiding there. But only the water, deep down, reflected the light. There was certainly nobody in hiding, for I searched every inch of the interior. Then I turned and started to walk away from the place, thinking furiously. The tiger was nowhere to be seen.

I decided to spend the rest of that night on the veranda of the forest rest house, so I walked to the little bungalow that stood about a mile from the village and called aloud to the watchman who should have been sleeping inside. Nobody answered, although I called again and again and again. Obviously, the watchman was not on watch, but snugly asleep in some hut in the village.

This was no surprise. Those who have lived in India will know that invariably watchmen do not watch. They sleep soundly instead; perhaps even more soundly than you or I, for their minds are quite clear that night is the time when people must sleep.

So I climbed the stone leading up to the veranda which stretched around three sides of the little rectangular bungalow. The caretaker had been careless enough to leave an armchair out on one of these extensions, knowing well enough that nobody would steal such a rickety article, even if there had been a thief in so desolate a place; so into the armchair I sank to snatch a few hours' sleep.

My intention was to tell my friends as Sampigehalli the next morning that I was convinced the tiger was no man-eater, and that if they really wanted to solve the mystery of the missing men, they should suggest to the police that they question the lissom lass who was so intimately connected with both of them; particularly as to what had become of their money. Then I would head for home in the Studebaker.

But sleep eluded me for the rest of that night. Those mysterious whistles, the sound of flapping wings, the peculiar lethargy that had come over me, and above all that strange cloudy shape that had come out of the well, demanded a sane explanation. Wrestling with the problem, tired, nature finally asserted herself and I fell asleep after dawn had broken. It was late when I awoke that morning, but the caretaker of the bungalow had not yet returned.

I went to the village, where I told my friends that I had seen the tiger and that it had seen me. I explained it was no man-eater. I did not tell them about the whistling sounds I had heard nor the cloudy form I had seen, for there appeared to be no point in complicating my story unnecessarily and making myself ridiculous.

Then one of my friends inquired where I had concealed myself, and I told him that I had hidden behind the parapet of the old well. At the mention of that word, he looked at me strangely.

'Did you see anything other than the tiger?' he inquired. 'Did you hear anything?'

I did not answer for a while. Then I countered. 'Why do you ask?'

'Did you see, or hear, a huge bat? The sound of beating wings?'

The sound of beating wings! Most certainly I had heard that sound: the sound of heavy, flapping wings issuing from the depths of the well. In fact I had heard that sound several times, each time coming higher and closer to the mouth of the well, and it had ceased only after that strange smoky shape had emerged. What a fool I had been not to shine the light of my torch down the well the first time I had heard it! I might have been able to see something. Then I remembered I had been waiting for the tiger and so had not wanted to show myself.

My friend had noticed the delay in my reply. His face took on a knowing smile. So I told him everything.

He appeared horrified when I mentioned the hazy form that had emerged from the well. Evidently others had heard the whistling and the sound of flapping wings, but nobody seemed to have seen anything, because no one had waited to see.

Then my friend came up with a strange tale. According to him, a couple of hundred or more years ago—he did not exactly know when—the temple flourished and was a centre of widespread veneration, while the surrounding area was ruled by a petty chieftain who had made himself independent of the rajah whose capital was far away. In the court of this petty chieftain was an individual who played the dual role of adviser and jester, and for whom the chieftain evidently had considerable regard.

The temple itself was in charge of a number of priests—all Brahmins—governed by a high priest who was of strong character. As always happens when people of strong minds come into contact with each other, there was a clash of interests between the chieftain, his adviser the jester, and the Brahmin high priest.

Of course, all the details had been long forgotten, but it appeared that the high priest had contrived to trump up charges against his rival, the jester, who had been accused of treachery towards the ruling house. The result was that the unfortunate adviser had been publicly tried, condemned to death for treason, and forthwith thrown down the well alive, but not before he had screamed threats of vengeance against the high priest and all the temple monks.

The sequel to this story was that within a week the high priest was missing, and a couple of days later his body was found floating in the well. The jester had claimed his first victim. Thereafter, at intervals, the other priests disappeared one by one, and their corpses would show up, floating face downwards in the well just like that of their high priest. Other priests came to the temple, but each and everyone of them met the same fate.

Elaborate ceremonies were held from time to time to exorcise the spirit of the avenging jester, but to no avail, as slowly but surely priest after priest vanished and his drowned body was later found floating on the surface of the water in the well. It took perhaps a hundred years for the avenging spirit of the jester to accomplish its task, but the time came when no priest, however holy he might be, or appear to be, would risk his life by volunteering to officiate in the temple. And that was how the temple and the well came to be deserted and eventually fell into ruin.

The narrator closed his strange tale with a very significant sentence: 'Consider yourself very lucky indeed, sir, that you are alive this morning. That evil spirit could easily have thrown you down the well, as easily as it has destroyed at least a hundred priests in the past!'

Because I'm not a Brahmin priest, I retorted sarcastically, adding, 'Stuff and nonsense. Damned rot!' The words came from me violently, explosively. To say the least, I was annoyed! Did this silly fellow think he could frighten me with such old wives' tales? I fear I was very rude to my unfortunate acquaintance for the next few minutes, for I told him exactly what I thought of his story, and of him for relating it.

The poor fellow's face fell and he walked away abashed. Unabashed, I scowled after him. Then I started packing the Studebaker preparatory to returning home, which did not take me long. I wished my friends goodbye, half-heartedly and rather abruptly, noticing that the man who had told me about the temple was not among them. In the usual hospitable Indian fashion, they pressed me even at that last moment to extend my stay. In answer I pressed the self-starter, shifted the car into gear, and drove away.

I had travelled quite six miles from Sampigehalli when I stopped the Studebaker, switched off the ignition and started to think clearly. I had behaved churlishly for no valid reason. After all, the man had only told me the story as he had heard it from others. It was I who had heard the whistling, had listened to the flapping of wings and seen the strange shadow. It was up to me to believe the tale, or reject it if I could find some better explanation. The sensible thing for me to do would be to try to make further investigation into the matter by talking to more people about it. Most sensible of all would be for me to spend another night at the well to see if the phenomenon was repeated. Instead of doing either of these things, I had acted like a child and cleared off in a huff.

So I turned the car and drove back to the village, where the first thing I did was to seek out my friend and apologize. He readily forgave me saying he understood how I had felt, and was all smiles again. In fact everybody smiled at my return till I told them that this time I had not come to hunt a tiger but a ghost—the evil spirit who lived down the well at the old temple.

At these words everybody stopped smiling. Then my friend said: 'Sir, I don't want to be rude, but please go back to Bangalore at once rather than do this foolish thing. You might escape from the tiger but not from the evil one.'

That evening, having nothing to fear from the tiger, I did not go to the old temple as early as I had done the previous afternoon. It was nearly six o'clock when I settled down in the place I had earlier occupied behind the parapet of the well. I had brought my rifle along with me in case the tiger should prove to be difficult, but as there was no particular need to keep silent on this occasion, I had allowed myself a large flask of tea, bread, butter and a tin of corned mutton and even some oranges to wind up with, not to mention my battered briar pipe.

There was no sign of the tiger as I settled myself, as quickly and as comfortably as possible, in my old position, arranging the torch, flask, water-bottle and other articles to right and left of me. He might have come out of his hiding place in the holy-of-holies of the temple before my arrival, although I did not think that was likely. In this conjecture I proved to be right. The time was a few minutes after seven and it was growing very cold. The nightjars had begun to call when a stone was dislodged inside the dark opening of the sanctuary and rolled loosely down the bank outside.

I knew the tiger was standing at the opening, looking out to see if it was safe enough to emerge. It might see me now, or might already have seen me; perhaps it remembered my presence at the parapet of the well the evening before. Precisely at that moment I heard the first whistle, loud, rather low and rather long-drawn-out, followed in quick succession by a louder, far higher and shorter whistle. After that there was absolute silence.

I remembered with a sense of shock that on the evening before, the whistling had begun just before the appearance of the tiger. The same thing had happened again. The thought came to me: could it be that the thing that whistled was trying to warn the tiger of my presence?

This notion was dispelled a moment later when the tiger emerged from the dark outline of the temple's entrance, first as an indistinct shape and then as an animal of immense proportions in the early light of the newly-risen moon.

As I had observed the evening before, for some unaccountable reason these loud whistles did not register on the tiger's hearing, although they were very clear to me. The fact was uncanny and was confirmed the next moment when the three successive whistles were repeated, more insistent and louder than ever. But the tiger took no notice of them. Then I began to hear the flapping of wings again, faintly and as from a distance. The source of the sound was at first difficult to place, till it was brought home to me, with an unpleasant shock, that it came from the bottom of the deep well in front of me.

Meanwhile the tiger was standing still, clearly visible in the early moonlight. It was staring fixedly in my direction. It was evident that the tiger now remembered having seen me there the previous night. I wanted to flash my torch down the well to discover the cause of the flapping sound, but this meant taking my eyes off the tiger, something I was rather reluctant to do. The rumour that this was a man-eater came to my mind once more with renewed force. Supposing this was a fact: I would be at its mercy if it should decide to attack me while I was looking down the well.

The three whistles, coming for the third time, with the closer approach of the flapping sound, got the better of my caution. A quick glance showed the tiger was still looking in my direction when I raised myself to my knees, thrust my head and shoulders over the parapet of the well, extended my right arm with the torch grasped in my hand as far as possible down the well and pressed the button. The bright beam cut into the inky depths, then lost itself in what looked to be a cloud of thick black smoke or vapour that was heaving some distance down the well.

Forgetful of the tiger I stared down the well, transfixed with curiosity, while the cloud that appeared to be issuing from the bottom, and was dense enough to prevent my torch-beam from penetrating it, rose inexorably towards me. It would not take long to reach the surface where I was crouching.

A loud snarl brought me back to an awareness of the danger I was in from the tiger. Quickly I shone the torch in the direction where it had been standing, while I groped for my rifle with the other. But the tiger was not there! Gratefully, I realized it had seen me and bounded away, the snarl I had heard being its protest at my intrusion. In a strange way I missed the tiger, for now I did not have a material antagonist to deal with, but something intangible with which I did not know how to cope. And I can tell you the thought was most unnerving.

The flapping came again; loud, heavy and near. The torchlight, which I directed into the well, showed that the eddying billows of the smoke-cloud were now scarcely five feet from the mouth of the well and that the rays of the torch could not penetrate them. They rose rapidly upwards and soon reached the face of my torch as I held it pointing downwards. My hand began to tremble violently so that the light danced crazily.

There seemed something indescribably evil about this vapour, and it brought a reaction I had never experienced before. Unlike normal smoke this mist eddied in dense, ribbon-like trails, resembling the coils of a giant snake of interminable length that twisted and wound around and around, in and out and about itself in a seething, restless, engulfing, devouring, never-ending movement.

Soon, it had reached my head and shoulders and engulfed me as I craned myself forward to look down the well. The cloud was far more dense than it had been the previous night, rather like a pea-soup fog that could almost be felt. I am by no means a squeamish person, but for the next few moments I did not know what was happening. The feeling is hard to describe. Perhaps to say that I was taken out of myself would be nearest to the mark, although I realize that such words hardly convey any meaning.

Once again I felt unutterably tired, forlorn, depressed, altogether without hope. A deep and urgent yearning came over me to jump over the parapet and into the well, once and for all to end my misery and unhappiness. It would be such an easy, such a pleasant ending, to the tortures and troubles and trials of living. Such an easy way out! So comfortable and soothing! So Soothing! So Soothing!

And then the gas, or smoke, or whatever it was, lifted. Rather, it cleared the parapet of the well and rose above my head as a dense, heavy, whirling cloud. With its lifting my mind cleared too and I was back to earth once more, remembering in amazement my recent dismal thoughts of throwing myself into the well. The cloud rose higher and higher and thinned out as it mixed with the air. I watched it in my torchlight for a full ten minutes, by which time it must have risen to perhaps fifty feet or more, when it dispersed and I could see it no more.

I put out the torch and sat back to ponder the strange phenomenon. The words of my friend and the story he had told me came back in forceful recollection. I pondered again upon the tale of evil and vengeance, and I remembered with dismay the odd feeling of careless lassitude that had overcome me as the vapour engulfed me and passed over my head: the feeling of despair, and the comforting temptation to end all my troubles merely by jumping down the well into oblivion. I had almost, in fact, fallen a victim to the age-old curse myself. It gave me quite a jolt, I can assure you, to realize that but a few moments earlier I was dispassionately contemplating suicide.

Then there were other aspects of the occurrence that defied explanation. The three strange whistles in quick succession; the unaccountable sound of flapping wings; the fact that the tiger could not hear these sounds; and strangest of all, that the weird thing, or whatever it was that came from the well, assumed the appearance of a dark cloud.

I walked back to the forest bungalow for the second time, to seek the solace of the battered old armchair, more puzzled, more vexed in mind, more dissatisfied with myself than I had ever been before.

It was in this frame of mind that I finally drove away from Sampigehalli the next morning, after recounting my latest adventure to my village friends. All of them, without exception, had nodded and wagged their heads and repeated in varying phrases the same words, 'We told you so.' The man who had annoyed me the day before said in exultation, 'You were angry with me yesterday. Today you are indeed lucky to be alive. Fate spared you a second time from joining the others who have been drowned in that well. That was because your time had not yet come. But do not sit there for a third night, Sir. For then it might be your time and you will surely jump into the well.'

I might have argued with him and pointed out that, if indeed it was my fate to throw myself into the well on the third night, I would have been compelled to remain at Sampigehalli, whether he or I or anybody else wanted me to leave or not.

Six

The Strange Case of
The Gerhetti Leopard

GERHETTI IS A TINY VILLAGE OF NOT EVEN A DOZEN HUTS, LYING A mile or so from the forest track that wandered in an almost southerly direction from Anchetty to the larger village of Pennagram in the Salem district of Madras state.

It is only seven miles from Anchetty, but to reach Gerhetti your car has to descend the winding track at an almost impossible angle, guaranteed to impose a severe strain upon the best of braking systems, bump across a couple of very rocky streambeds that hold no water for over nine months in the year, and then clamber up an equally winding and impossible gradient. In the old days of the Model T Ford, which were my young days, it would give me childish and utter delight to sit at the steering wheel of my beloved 'Lissom Lizzie', the name painted in large letters upon her rear, press hard upon the left of the three pedals that controlled her, and attain the summit in clouds of steam, billowing from a red-hot engine and a boiling radiator.

On one occasion Lissom Lizzie climbed half-way up that gradient but could not climb any more. I was bound for the forest lodges of Muttur, a dozen miles beyond Gerhetti, where I had arranged with Byra, my aboriginal poojaree friend, to help to catch a crocodile that had become stranded in the Forest department well situated upon the banks of the Chinnar river, and I had to keep that appointment. What was I to do? Praise be to Henry Ford and the wonderful adaptability of the Model T. I turned the car round, placed the hand-lever to my right in a neutral position, pressed upon the centre pedal of the three (which was the reverse pedal in the Model T) and climbed that fearful gradient backwards with ease! The car was strained and so was my neck, but we made it.

A mile or so after reaching the top of the gradient, a narrower track veers to the right, the jungle crowding in upon both sides. Another mile along this track brings one to a water hole on the right side, immediately opposite the driveway leading to the Gerhetti Forest Lodge on the left. This is a delightful little bungalow which, in those days, had but one snag. It was always locked, the reason being that the caretaker, who was also carefree and careless, and did not give a damn anyway, was away on holiday, sometimes at Anchetty but more generally at Pennagram which, although poor of soil, was rich in girls. And thereby hangs a tale.

In the old British days there was a district Forest Officer (D.F.O.) of the old school type in charge of this area. He had a double-barrelled name, was stickler for rules, and did not like me anyway. The cause of this dislike I could never fathom. Perhaps he disapproved of my wandering about the forests of which he had charge as if they were my own, and he showed his disdain, upon the few occasions I was unfortunate enough to have speak to him, by looking at me distantly, as if I were something the cat had left on the doorstep. This gentleman insisted that before occupying any of the Forest department bungalows in his area, I should apply for his permission and obtain the same in writing. As a matter of fact, this was the rule and still is. But ask anyone who has lived in India and he will agree with me that rules are made only to be broken. Everyone breaks them and enjoys the process. The stricter the rule, the more it has to be broken. At least, everyone seems to feel this way in India; and that being the case, why not I?

However, to avoid coming to grips unnecessarily with this man, I gave him on one occasion a full month's notice in advance, with my request for permission to occupy the Gerhetti Forest Lodge. As I possessed a shooting licence for the area, he could not very well refuse. Back came his written permission in due course, but along with it quite a substantial paragraph warning me not to try to break the rules and regulations in any way, not to cause a forest fire by throwing matches about, not to fail to pay the prescribed rent for the days I was in occupation and so forth.

The glad day dawned at last and I set forth in my Model T for Gerhetti. Fortunately, I had just reached the top of the ghat, when down came the rain in torrents. Model T's never worried about bad weather, and it took more than raindrops to stop a vehicle of that sturdy vintage. By the same standards they expected a passenger to care nothing too, for they were without adequate protection of the sides.

So I was soaking wet when I arrived at the front door of the Gerhetti lodge, to find it fast closed with a lock of outstanding size. And the carefree caretaker was away on his revels.

I had the written permission of the nasty D.F.O. to occupy the place. I had given him a month's notice. His office should have notified the caretaker to welcome me with open doors. Nevertheless, I was locked out. This old bounder, who was so hot upon other people keeping to the rules, had himself foundered! Besides, the rain was coming down in buckets, saturating me and my equipment.

So I staggered around the building and discovered that the bathroom door at the back was weak on its hinges. I put my shoulder to it and heaved it off its hinges. The door burst open, and that was how I got into the bungalow.

I camped at Gerhetti for the full week for which I had come, but in all that time the caretaker never showed up. Apparently his dates at Pennagram were more important. Then the time came for me to leave. The bathroom door, which had left its hinges 'by accident', could only be pulled to and closed. And there was no one present to receive the rent.

From Bangalore, I sent the rent by post to the D.F.O. and made out a strong case against his carefree caretaker. The storm, I claimed, had 'caused me, in seeking shelter, to slip and fall in the mud, whereupon in an effort to save myself my hand contacted the bathroom door. Unfortunately this mere pressure had caused the hinges, which were of ancient vintage, to give way and the door had opened'. The implication was that the security of this government building was not all it should be.

But the careless caretaker turned out to be less carefree than I had thought. He and his boss worked out as foul a plot as ever was hatched against an innocent, upright, law-abiding, Christian gentleman! The teak armchair from the bungalow and the zinc bathtub in the bathroom were missing. They had been stolen! Either I had stolen them, in which case I was liable under the rules to be prosecuted and jailed for breaking into a government building and stealing part of its furniture.

Or my irresponsible action in breaking into the building had rendered it insecure and unsafe, whereafter theft of government property had inevitably ensued, for which I was entirely responsible. I was called upon to reply within seven days, whereafter very severe action was proposed to be taken against me. Not a word was said about the caretaker's absence.

I thought fast. Had the D.F.O. been a less unpleasant individual I would have offered to pay for the missing articles. As matters stood, any such offer would be pounced upon as a clear admission of guilt. Furthermore, no thief in India would go to such a benighted spot to steal an ancient armchair and leaky bathtub, both of which would be of no value, either for his own use or for sale to any villager.

Obviously, the articles had been removed by the carefree but crafty caretaker, or by order of the D.F.O. himself, in order to 'fix' me. I could hardly believe that an English officer would do this kind of thing, however much he disliked me. So the culprit was obviously the caretaker himself. He had done this as a retaliatory act against me, when called upon to explain his absence, as reported by me. But where could the articles be? He would not have tried to sell them, because that would have left a trail. So he must have hidden them.

The obvious answer was that he had hidden them in his girlfriend's house. So off I went to Pennagram and arrived after midnight, when all were asleep. I aroused my henchaman Ranga, put the case to him and asked him where we should start searching. The question also arose as to how the caretaker could have brought the two cumbersome articles from Gerhetti to Pennagram, a distance of twelve miles. Ranga offered the answer without hesitation. In a bullock-cart, carrying felled bamboos!

From the forest around Gerhetti there was a constant flow of bamboos to Pennagaram, where the Forest department had a timber depot. As an official of the service, although a very minor one, it would be easy for this caretaker to persuade a cartman or two to convey the articles, concealed under the bamboos in a cart, to Pennagram.

More fortunately, Ranga, who had once been a cartman himself, was well acquainted with his confreres. Late though the hour was, he set out to question those that were in town and returned by 4 a.m. to give me the good news that not only had he succeeded in finding two cart-drivers, each of whom had brought one of the articles in his conveyance, but had also found out where they were hidden.

This was an ungodly hour to awaken any solitary sentry, snugly asleep in a police station, but that is exactly what we did soon after. The constable was very indignant. Moreover, claiming to be alone in charge, he declared that he could not leave his post. But when a certain exchange had been made his conscience was softened. Leaving us in charge of the station, he hastened to the police lines and shortly returned with a confederate, who had dressed himself in full uniform as befitted the occasion. This policeman accompanied Ranga and myself to the tiny house occupied, I do admit, by an exceedingly becoming lass. I was obliged to admire the taste in women of the careless but carefree caretaker. But, more important at that moment, there was the old teak armchair and the zinc bathtub, as large as life in a corner of her tiny abode.

The poor girl was arrested and the two articles removed to the police station. Later that morning the sub-inspector (S.I.) arrived, and to him I submitted two written documents. The first was a letter of complaint regarding the theft, back-dated by a few days. The second a letter of appreciation, commending and congratulating the S.I. He was delighted. I asked him, as a favour, to release the girl and capture the caretaker; but looking at me with disapproving eyes, he said he could not do that, for the girl was 'an accessory after the fact', even if she was a comely wench.

To the D.F.O. my lawyer sent a notice for defamation claiming a fabulous sum as damages, with a copy to the Chief Conservator of Forests at Madras. But time was kind to the poor fellow. He was on the verge of retirement anyhow and he disappeared overnight on furlough, from which he never returned. What gave me the greatest satisfaction, however, was the 'armchair' detection I had displayed in identifying the culprit.

You must forgive me for this digression, but my excuse is the need to let you know that even in the jungles we have our problems. India is a country that demands of its inhabitants a sharpness of wit. And this brings me to another tale.

Ticketless train-travel in India is rife. To try to combat it, the authorities institute many checks, so that in the course of even a short journey one my be required to show one's ticket to 'travelling ticket inspectors' a number of times. Now, an acquaintance of mine who emigrated from India to the U.K. was agreeably surprised to find that there were no ticket-checks on the suburban line on which he travelled to work daily. So he bought no ticket and travelled free for some months until one day he was caught.

All this, however, has nothing whatever to do with the strange leopard I meant to tell you about.

About two furlongs behind the forest lodge at Gerhetti is the small hamlet of the same name, consisting of half a dozen huts. The occupants are woodcutters, who earn a supplementary wage by working as coolies for the Forest department, repairing the road, stealing sandalwood and timber when they can, and poaching deer in the summer months when there is no water in the jungle and the animals come late at night to drink at the water hole which, I have already told you, stands a short distance in front of the lodge at the point where the 'driven-in' turns away from the main track.

The people in this hamlet had a few sheep—keeping goats in a forest area was strictly forbidden in British days, due to the destruction wrought by these animals upon seedlings—and a few fowl. There had been some cattle, but tigers and panthers had wiped them out.

The leopard in this story, being an animal of only average size, had begun its depredations by stealing a fowl here and there when they wandered from the huts to feed among the fallen leaves at the edge of the jungle. The next stage was reached when the leopard decided to go further, raiding the hut in which the fowls were kept by creeping through the wall of thorns and eating up as many as possible, killing or severely injuring the rest of the birds just for fun. It now had to turn to the sheep, there being nothing else to eat, and these it started killing one by one, whenever opportunity offered. I had been told about this leopard, but as it was reported to be quite a harmless beast—indeed, almost friendly in its habits—I had thought no more about it.

The first time I laid eyes on this animal was about 4-30 one evening. I was reclining in the armchair on the veranda of the lodge, sipping tea, when a movement at the water hole, the farther bank of which was visible from where I was sitting, caught my attention. The sun was shining brightly and the day had been a hot one. Normally, no wild animal would be afoot. The movement came again and some yellow object thrust itself out from the wall of reeds that bordered the pool. I could not make out what it was.

Perhaps a minute later, without perceptible further movement, the object turned into a panther as it emerged fully from behind the reeds. It was gazing fixedly towards the forest bungalow, knowing no doubt that if there was any danger about, it would be in this direction. I did not move in my chair. After a close scrutiny that lasted perhaps three minutes, the leopard decided all was safe. It stooped to drink, but stopped twice to look up at the bungalow to make sure that all was well.

The second time I saw this animal was when it chased a junglecock into a tree. I was returning from an early-morning prowl when the junglecock emitted its shrill alarm cry a few yards ahead and flapped heavily upwards.

'Cekh! Cekh! Cekh! Cekh!' screeched the cock, and I halted in my tracks. No doubt it had seen or heard me. But I was wrong, for an instant later a panther bounded out of the undergrowth and raced after the bird, to clamber quickly but futilely up the tree on which it had settled. The junglecock screeched again and this time flew far away, while the leopard, warned that all was not well, turned its head to look back sharply.

That was when it saw me. Releasing its hold, the panther fell back lightly to the ground, arched its back for a moment while curling its tail high above, for all the world like a friendly tabby, then turned and padded silently away, disappearing in the bushes.

The third time I saw this animal under peaceful circumstances was when I was chugging along in my Model T. I had passed the Gerhetti bungalow and the water hole, and was continuing along the track which, it will be remembered, branches off from the main route to Muttur and Pennagram.

No cars came that way in those days and bullockcarts were few. Cattle passed now and again, in the hot weather when the forest had dried up, on their way to the village of Natrapalayam and the Cauvery river, seven or eight miles away, where there was still some grazing to be had. The few people living in this area carried their loads on their heads or, when these were too heavy, on the backs of ponies or donkeys, the latter for preference because they were cheaper. The branches of the trees met above the narrow trail, for which reason the already tattered hood of the Model T had to be put down and the windshield lowered. Nevertheless, it was often needful to lie sideways on the front seat to allow a bough to scrape over the steering wheel.

Turning a sharp corner, I saw close ahead a fairly stout branch extending across the track, and lying along this bough was a panther that had evidently taken up this position in the hope of being able to ambush any animal passing beneath. It had not heard the car as I had been coursing downhill, semidepressing the left-hand pedal of Lissom Lizzie that served as gear-cum-clutch.

The panther rose on the branch when I was almost beneath it, then panicked and sprang clumsily, clearing the rear seat but landing on the back of the car, from where it took off again into the bushes, but not before the claws of its hind feet, in finding a purchase to make that second leap, tore a gaping hole in the already tattered upholstery.

There is a village along this track named Jungalpalayam. It is about half-way between Gerhetti and Natrapalayam, being two and a half miles from each. I knew it as the 'happy village', for the folks living in this hamlet, although far from civilization, medical help, schools, places of amusement and so-called cooperative centres that never seem to cooperate in anything, were always contented and laughing. It did one good to visit this little place and chat with its inhabitants. They seemed singularly free from the political consciousness that is such a dominating factor in India.

Each month, when the moon is at its full, and on two days before and two days after, the villagers would play games in the moonlight, commencing an hour or so after their evening meal, which might be at about eight o'clock, and continuing till midnight. Modesty forbade that the men and women should play together, so the women would form a circle in the centre of the village, while the men would go to the village threshing floor, a cleared space about fifty yards to one side of the hamlet. The women would mostly sing and dance, while the men played a variety of games, the most popular of which was *balchik* or *kabbaddee*, although in this particular hamlet it was known as *goddoogoddoo*, a form of the popular game of salts, played widely throughout India.

The rules of this game are simple. A straight line is drawn with charcoal on the ground, and two teams of from five to seven members each assemble on either side. Play starts when by a member from, let us say, Team A (although the villagers call the teams by such names as 'frogs', grasshoppers', or even less complimentary ones like 'illegitimates' or 'bastards') approaches the base line, muttering repeatedly and rapidly the word *kabbaddee* (or *goddoogoddoo*), crosses it while still muttering incessantly, audibly, and with his fingertips lightly touches a member of Team B (perhaps called the 'impotents' or 'eunuchs' or some other rude name), then springs back to the charcoal base line before any of the members of Team B can hold him down.

The point is that the man from Team A must keep on muttering *kabbaddee* (or *goddoogoddoo*) loudly and without ceasing. Should a member or more of Team B succeed in grabbing him and holding him down, so that he cannot get back to the charcoal base line, a point is lost to his team also.

After the man from Team A has scored a success or failure, as the case may be, the turn of approaching the line falls to a man from Team B, and so on. The winning side is that which first attains a predetermined number of points, usually

SKETCH MAP OF
GERHETTI

N

Anchetty

Rough

Stream

Stream

Motor

Pool
Forest
bungalow
Garage
Body   Gerhetti village
Heavy scrub
Scrub Jungle
Jungalpalayam   Low hill
Heavy scrub
Talvadi

Track

Track

Cart

Dense jungle
To Muttur and Pennagram
To Natrapalayam and the Cauvery
River

twenty-one. Sometimes a small bet is attached to the result, each member of a side ending up by winning—or losing—half a rupee in the course of the evening, somewhat less than a shilling.

On many a moonlight night have I joined the villagers of Jungalpalayam in a game of *goddoogoddoo*. I was a young man in those days and as hard as nails. Nevertheless, muttering *goddoogoddoo* aloud without stop, while dodging to avoid eager, agile, clutching village youths, would leave my lungs at bursting point. The women would cease their singing and dancing to gather around and witness the discomfiture of the *dorai*, which invariably happened, although the side on which I played would claim I was no liability to them, in order to make me feel at home. I would walk or motor back to Gerhetti in the early hours of the morning with the moon setting behind the jungleclad hills to the west, often horrified to find myself muttering '*goddoogoddoo—goddoogoddoo*' automatically.

It was then the leopard struck! Evidently the branch overhanging the track from Gerhetti to Jungalpalayam, on which I had surprised it, was a favourite ambush for this animal, for it launched itself one day from this very bough upon a donkey laden with tamarind-fruit packed into two sacks, one on each side, which the donkey's owner was taking to market at Pennagram. The man had stopped to pluck and munch a wild wood-apple nut and the donkey had turned the bend in the track fifty yards ahead, when the thud of a falling body and a hoarse gurgling sound were heard.

Not associating the noise with any calamity to his donkey, the man feared an elephant might be ahead of him. For this reason, he approached the corner slowly, while keeping a sharp lookout all round. But to his horror he saw his poor donkey dead and dragged to one side of the track, with the panther crouched against its belly, its fangs still buried in the donkey's throat, enjoying the warm blood that trickled from the severed vein.

Then the man, who ordinarily would have run away and indeed was already prepared to run from the elephant he expected to see, lost his temper and rushed at the panther whirling the stave he held in his hand. The leopard, excited by the kill it had just made, with the warmth of its victim against him and the warmer blood trickling through its jaws, was in no mood to relinquish his feast. In fact, I suppose it actually had no opportunity to do so before the angry man was upon him.

The stave thudded down across the panther's back and the panther leapt upon the man seeking for his throat, but being diverted by the long black beard this villager had grown, bit the man's chest instead. The man lost his balance, toppled backwards, and began to scream.

I happened to have come to Gerhetti at that time, but was far away at the moment, on the slopes of a hillside behind the hamlet, searching for a particular kind of beetle for my cousin who is an ardent collector. I heard those screams faintly, and thinking some man was being done to death by an elephant, ran in their direction. Most regrettably, I had left my rifle in the forest lodge. People who go catching beetles do not ordinarily carry firearms, and there was no danger to be envisaged in the area at the time from a man-eater or rogue elephant.

The screams I had heard so faintly had stopped by now, so that I was left guessing as to the point of their origin; but working on the belief that an elephant had attacked a man, I guessed that whatever had happened had taken place somewhere along the track to Jungalpalayam. So I ran in its general direction, stumbling through undergrowth and between bushes and trees till at last I reached the track.

There was nothing to be seen. Should I turn right or left? The sound had seemed so far away that I decided to turn towards Jungalpalayam and veered left, padding along as noiselessly as possible and expecting to come upon an enraged elephant at any moment.

Calling aloud but receiving no answer, I had traversed the better part of a furlong when I came upon the victim lying beside his dead donkey. The panther had left him; perhaps his screams had frightened the animal away, or may be at this, its first encounter with one of the human race, the leopard still felt some of its inherent fear of man. The man's eyes flickered open when I called to him and he managed to tell me his name was Subramaniam, that he had come from Pennagram for tamarind, and of how the panther had come to attack him. Then he lost consciousness. I lifted him over my shoulder with the intention of carrying him to the forest lodge, from whence I could take him in my car to hospital at Bangalore.

Alas, I had just reached the bungalow and laid him on the floor of the veranda, when he began to show signs of imminent death, while blood began to pour from his mouth and the terrible wounds in his chest. It was clear that his lungs had been punctured, and as I picked him up again to put him in my car he died. I will not dwell on the trouble I had in telling the authorities all that had happened, but while proceedings were still going on I returned to warn the people of Gerhetti, Jungalpalayam and Natrapalayam that the leopard might possibly turn dangerous.

Surprisingly enough, nothing happened for some months. Then the dreaded epidemic of cholera came to Pennagram and from there spread far and wide, even as far as Natrapalayam. Two or three persons died in this remote village, and because they had died of an infectious disease the villagers threw the bodies into the jungle to rot instead of burying or burning the corpses as in the normal way.

Perhaps the panther ate some of this flesh, although no one knew for certain, as no one would be bold enough to go near such a corpse. Otherwise the advent of the man-eater and the reason for the animal becoming one are shrouded in mystery.

The trouble began when a boy who had gone to the water hole at Gerhetti with his pitcher did not return. There was no reason for his absence other than supposed idleness, so his father went to look for him in the evening, carrying a stout stick to lay across the boy's back while he was still asleep. The father found his son's broken water-pot, dropped when it was full and therefore upon the return journey. He saw the boy's blood on the grass and the imprint of a panther's pugs where it had been walking down the main track before it saw the boy and pounced upon him from the wayside. A drag-mark indicated in which direction the body had been taken.

Panthers being far smaller, shorter and weaker than tiger, are unable to carry away their kills clear of the ground. They have to drag their dead victims along, for which reason they do not go far before starting to eat. Tigers, which are not only taller but immeasurably stronger, are able to lift a victim as heavy as a buffalo clear of the ground. Moreover, when a tiger intends to take its kill to some distant spot before starting to eat, it seizes its prey by the neck and, with a quick turn of its head, throws the dead body over its back, thereby supporting the weight evenly on all four legs. In this manner, tigers have been known to carry their kills for great distances, so that in the case of a man-eating tiger, their human kills, as often as not, cannot be found.

Returning to my story: the father hastened back to Gerhetti hamlet, called on its few inhabitants for help and, armed with sticks and stones, the small party followed the drag-mark. They had not far to go. What was left of the boy lay under a bush just on the other side of the water hole.

From that day nobody would move alone in the jungle. At least four men would form a party, arming themselves with wood-choppers, axes or stout staves. The news spread to Jungalpalayam, Natrapalayam, Pennagram and Anchetty. Everyone was on the lookout for the panther.

Strangely enough, the theft of an occasional fowl or sheep by a leopard still went on. Most of the people in the area had, at one time or the other, seen the harmless panther I had myself encountered upon three occasions, so nobody associated it with the animal that had struck the tamarind-merchant down and had later devoured the boy. The man-eater was thought to be some passing beast, or a leopard that had become inordinately hungry to the verge of starvation, due to sickness or wounds. A few even subscribed to the notion that the panther was mad, having eaten of the cholera corpses. For man-eaters in this region were practically unknown; there had been a couple of man-eating tigers in the past, but they had operated far away, in the region of Kempekerai. As for a man-eating panther, nobody could remember having heard of one.

A third victim followed the boy, this time a woman who was returning from the well after bathing her two-year-old child. The water in this well was very brackish and could not be used for drinking or cooking; it could be used only for washing purposes. Unaccountably the leopard did not touch the child, contenting itself with killing the mother and dragging her corpse into a *nullah* a few yards beyond the well. The wails of the infant attracted the villagers, who went to investigate.

With this tragedy, the alarm spread in right earnest far and wide. Woodcutting and all traffic in the jungle came to a dead stop, and the poachers who by night haunted the few water-holes in the forest put away their muskets and vintage muzzle-loaders until the advent of more propitious times.

My tenant at Anchetty, a young man named Narayan who cultivated the small plot of land I own there but has never bothered to pay rent, brought me the news, with a request from the *patel* of Anchetty, who was also nominally the head of the Gerhetti hamlet, to come and shoot the panther. I was tied up with urgent work at Bangalore just then and told Narayan I would come in a week, sending him back with a message to the *patel* to this effect, and an additional word of warning to the people of Gerhetti to move about only in groups and never alone. Man-eating panthers as a rule, being inherently cowardly, attack only under cover of darkness, unlike the man-eating tiger, which is braver and bolder and attacks at any time. In this respect the Gerhetti leopard was different; it had taken all its three victims in broad daylight.

On the day before I arrived at Gerhetti the panther struck for the fourth time, and the victim turned out to be the son of the bungalow-watcher, that carefree character who had tried to frame me with the armchair and bathtub. The panther took its victim in the early hours of the morning.

After the affair of the bathtub and armchair, the father had lost his job with the Forest department and had become a minor forest contractor, purchasing at public auction the right to gather fruit, various medicinal seeds and leaves, henna, honey, deers' horns that had been shed, and other lesser items. In this business the son played an active part, and at the time of his death the lad had come to Gerhetti to induce some of the poojarees living there to help him to raid the combs of the wild rock-bees that had hung their hives on the higher rock-faces of a low mountain named Periyamalai, some four miles from Gerhetti.

171

The lad, whose name was Nataraj, had successfully accomplished his mission and had succeeded in gathering some four or five kerosene tins of this wild honey. On an average, each of these tins held the equivalent of twenty-four bottles of honey, each of which in turn would sell for three rupees. The trip would thus earn him about three hundred rupees.

Well satisfied, he returned with the tins to Gerhetti, where he decided to spend the night, as rumours had reached the hamlet that a herd of wild elephants had recently come up from the Cauvery river and were roaming in the ravines of Talvadi, through which the road to the market at Pennagram passed. Nataraj had no intention of risking his precious honey by exposing it to wild elephants.

The forest lodge (the one from which his father had taken the furniture) was locked, but the garage was open: in fact, it had no doors! So Nataraj decided to spend the night in the garage, along with his tins of honey.

In the early hours of the morning, the people in the hamlet of Gerhetti said they heard his screams for help, but being few in number and moreover unarmed, they fastened the doorways of their huts more securely and waited for dawn. With daylight, a number of them eventually came to the garage to see what had happened. Nataraj was nowhere to be seen. Signs of a struggle were evident. There was blood on the earthen floor and one of the tins of honey had been overturned, attracting thousands of ants. There was also the impression of something heavy having been dragged across the ground and out of the open door into the jungle, which began ten yards behind.

The panther had not bothered to take him very far. His head, arms and legs, the portions that a panther, and even a man-eating tiger, is rather fastidious about and leaves for a later meal, lay scattered about in mute testimony of the panther's appetite. Rather small, as the pugs indicated the marauder to be, it had eaten a lot of meat.

I arrived at Gerhetti at ten that morning and was in time to see the remains before the police turned up from Anchetty and began their tedious and fruitless questioning. Why had I come? they asked. Had I an arms licence? A gun licence? A car licence? A driver's licence? Any question but those that concerned the panther.

I asked them to leave the remains where they were and go away as soon as possible, since this would give me a chance of sitting over what was left of Nataraj and perhaps shooting the man-eater. There was a possibility that it might return in the afternoon, and there was also the probability that it would return after dark.

The *daffedar* (head-constable or sergeant), who represented the party in the absence of his Sub-Inspector, flatly refused. He said the remains would have to stay where they were till his boss could see them for himself. And as he had to return to Anchetty, he would leave the two constables who had accompanied him to watch over these remains till the Sub-Inspector turned up, later in the evening perhaps, more probably the next morning.

At hearing the *daffedar's* words, there was unanimous disapproval of his scheme by his subordinates. One of them stated with some heat that he had not eaten his breakfast that morning, and certainly could not wait for it till next day. The other man pleaded that he was suffering from a servere cold. To this the *daffedar* rejoined that he had not heard him cough even once that day. Whereupon the constable coughed prolongedly!

Orders are orders, the *daffedar* affirmed sternly, and stalked away, to mount his bicycle and ride away to Anchetty. The two policemen stared at each other and at me, till I made them a sign in unspoken, but otherwise universally known language, that gave them the general idea; 'chins up, boys; every cloud has a silver lining'. At least this one did for them, and in a very literal sense, for with the *daffedar's* departure the two policemen were only too willing themselves to depart even if it was only as far as the nearby hamlet. Anything to get out of this dreadful place, away from those blank, staring eyes in the dead, accusing face. I was left to my own devices and the immediate problem of finding somewhere to hide and await the killer's possible return.

As so frequently happens there was no place that offered concealment. This is understandable as man-eaters—both tigers and panthers—carry or drag their kills into sheltered, dense undergrowth in order that they may enjoy their meal undisturbed. They do not leave their kills under some convenient tree from which they can be shot! There was a thick growth of lantana bushes and the panther had dragged the body of its victim between two of these bushes, where it had eaten most of it. Any attempt at constructing a hide in the vicinity would stick out like a sore thumb, and the panther would never put in an appearance. All said and done, my contemplated ambush seemed out of the question.

I thought and thought, and finally came up with an idea. It is rather difficult to describe, so I have produced a sketch which I hope may convey some notion of my scheme.

To the north of the spot where lay what was left of Nataraj was the forest lodge and the garage. To the east, not very far away, stood the hamlet and more or less open ground. To the west was light scrub, through which led the *path* from Gerhetti to Jungalpalayam. To the south was heavier scrub, flanked by a low hill. I had already walked along the *path* to the western side. No tracks of the panther coming or going showed on the sandy surface. So the man-eater had come from the hillock to the south and had returned that way.

My plan was to hide in the garage till I could hear it eating—at least I hoped I would be able to hear it. Then I would tiptoe out of the garage to the front of the bungalow, down the pathway to Jungalpalayam, and cut back from it to get between the panther and the hillock, in which direction I was sure the feline would beat its retreat.

Finally, when in a satisfactory position, I would throw some stones (previously gathered and kept ready in my pocket) as hard as possible in the direction of the garage, hoping the missile would sail over the feasting feline and fall beyond it. This would frighten it and cause it to come bounding blindly towards its only line of retreat, southwards towards the hillock, where I would be in hiding and awaiting it. Panthers have no sense of smell, so it would not be able to scent me while I tiptoed down the pathway. But they have acute hearing and it might hear me if I made the slightest sound. That was a risk I would have to take.

As an afterthought, I decided to tear up the khaki shirt I was wearing and hang strips of it on the bushes bordering the pathway, so that if the leopard did happen to break in that direction (towards the west), the sight of these strips of cloth fluttering in the breeze might turn it back again towards the south, the hillock—and me! It would not break towards the east because of the hamlet, or towards the north, as the bungalow stood there.

I do not usually tear up my shirts, particularly when wearing nothing underneath, but there was no alternative, as I was carrying no rags of any kind and the spare shirt I had brought in the car was a shade better than the one upon my back. So I removed my shirt and tore it into long narrow strips. In this way, I made some eight or ten lengths which I proceeded to tie to the lantana and other bushes bordering the pathway. They were out of sight of where the panther would be eating, but it would immediately spot them if it decided to break westwards towards the pathway, when I began throwing my stones from that direction. It would have been better if the strips had been of white or coloured material, rather than khaki, but one does not wear a white shirt when hunting.

Lastly, I went to the little hamlet to the east of the bungalow and cautioned its inhabitants, including the two constables, not to stir out for the rest of the day. I could hardly tell you my advice was unnecessary. With the killing and eating of Nataraj within a few yards of their huts, the inmates had already shut themselves up as securely as they could.

So that it should not be in the view of the panther, I pushed the Model T in which I had come to the front of the forest lodge. From there it was out of sight of the garage and any panther that might show itself from behind. And I took all the things I had in the car in the form of bedding, food, water, and the shotgun that I had brought as a spare weapon, into the garage. Here I would stay till daylight the following morning, hoping against hope that the leopard would return to what was left of its meal.

All this had taken up to half an hour to noon, and the sun blazed down mercilessly on the dry forest that throbbed to the sound of the cicadas, the cooing of the lesser speckled doves, and the calls of the black-bodied and orange-winged crow-pheasant that was diligently searching for birds' eggs, lizards and caterpillars by the edge of the jungle a few paces away.

The hours dragged by and the heat grew more intense, rising from the ground in shimmering waves. Even the crow-pheasant felt it and gave up his search, although the tireless cicadas continued to drone out their monotonous dirge.

The hours came and went while I strained my ears for the sound of crunching bones that would announce the killer's return. Not a sound did I hear other than the scream of a king vulture high in the sky. It must have spotted the remains long ago, but being those of a human being the 'king' had delayed its earthwards plunge that would be an invitation to all other vultures for miles around to foregather for a feast.

Five o'clock came, bringing a noticeable cooling of the atmosphere and a sharpening of the vulture's appetite. It delayed no longer, but plummeted to earth with the rattling rush of the wind through the tough feathers of its outstretched wings, to land with a faint thud in the vicinity of the kill. Soon other vultures would follow and nothing would be left of the panther's kill beyond cleanly-picked bones. The leopard, if it should come that night, would find nothing to eat and would wander away!

Four or five vultures joined the king at intervals, although the huge birds still hesitated to begin their meal. Nataraj's head, being left intact with its staring eyes, kept them away.

Time dragged by, and with the advent of evening the chorus of roosting birds began its tumultuous farewell to the day that is music to the ears of those who love the jungle. 'Kuck-kya-kya-khuckm!' crowed junglecocks from the foot of the hillock; 'Kee-kok! Kee-kok! Kee-kok!' challenged a partridge higher up, and 'Kee-kok-kok! Kee-kok-kok! Kee-kok-kok!' came his rival's reply from the summit of the hill. 'Wack! Wack! kuker-rawack!' growled spurfowl to each other, while far away a peacock joined the chorus 'Zank! Mia! Mia! Mia-oo-ow!'

There came a heavy flapping of wings as the 'king' and its equally cowardly companions rose ponderously from the ground to perch on some neighbouring tree. They would wait till morning and their appetites would certainly be sharpened.

Darkness began to fall; there was a deep silence that could almost be felt. Then 'Chuck! Chuck! Chuck! Chuck-ooooo!' trilled the nightjar and 'Whooo! Whooo! Whooo!' hooted a horned owl. I fixed the two clamps that held my torch firmly to the barrel of my rifle and adjusted the beam to form a spot. Soon after that it was night. The leopard had not put in an appearance and my deeply-laid scheme appeared to be coming to naught.

I will not weary you with a description of the half-dozen hours that followed. Indeed, there is nothing to tell you, for nothing happened. The moon, that was now on the wane, had risen late, and should the panther come to its kill I would not be able to follow my plan, for the night would not be bright enough to see it when it came bounding up the hillside after being frightened by the stones I was going to throw. I would either have to let it eat, or to try creeping up on it, something that would be very difficult to accomplish and was not at all to my liking.

With these reflections I must have dozed off. Then something awoke me with a start. I could not say what it was. It was not a sound I could hear, but a feeling of deadly peril seemed to close over me. It was oppressive and heavy; it could almost be felt.

For a moment I put it down to imagination, but the sense of danger remained and became very real. It seemed to close down upon me. Without doubt something, somewhere, was threatening me.

Then I realized what it was. The man-eater was close by! That strange sixth sense that I have felt in times of extreme peril, and was to save my life so may times thereafter, was telling me as if in spoken words that the leopard was about to attack.

I closed my hands over my .405 and, without moving, I strained my eyes to look in every direction. Moonlight framed

178

the rectangular doorway of the garage, with the rear of the forest bungalow in the centre of the scene. Then something moved ever so slightly at the bottom left-hand corner of this moonlit screen. Something black and slightly undulating. I could not quite see what it was, because it lay within the area of darkness thrown by the garage in which I was hiding and only the background of dim moonlight had drawn my attention to the faint movement near by.

The shadow moved ever so slightly and the faintest hissing sound reached my straining ears. A cobra? Or could it be the man-eater?

Luckily I had made not the least movement. Had I done so, the creature might have attacked when it realized that it had been discovered in its attempt to surprise me. But now movement—and very quick movement at that—was called for.

Springing to my feet I threw myself backwards, and was brought to an abrupt halt by the wall behind me. At the same time, I pointed the muzzle of my rifle forwards and pressed the switch of the torch. Although the beam blinded it, the man-eater launched its attack.

In describing the few moments that followed, I should write humbly and with a sense of gratitude. For it is not well to boast that 'with one shot I killed it', for any person even with a rudimentary experience of wild animals will tell you that a sambar can carry nine bullets in its body and move for miles, a bison fifteen, a wild elephant sometimes twenty-five, and a tiger or panther a great many before it falls dead. And it can tear you to pieces before it dies.

Then again the cartridge may be a dud, the cap may misfire, or the animal may turn aside just as you fire. Anything can happen. Suffice it to say that my bullet hit its mark by sheer luck and killed the leopard even while it was in midair, although to make certain I fired two more into the writhing body at my feet.

The sub-inspector arrived creditably early next morning. He was not happy to find that most of Nataraj's bones, including his head, had been taken away by the hyenas and jackals during the night.

Seven

The Lakkavalli Man-Eater

IF YOU WERE TO VISIT THE TOWNSHIP OF TARIKERE IN THE WESTERN parts of Mysore state, you would find two motorable roads open to you. On these, at a distance of not more than four or five miles from the town itself, if you had the time to stop and listen, you would hear many stories from the villagers about the depredations of tigers.

The first of these roads leads roughly southwestwards from Tarikere, passing in a curve through the village of Lingadhalli, to the south of the high horseshoe range of mountains known as the Baba Budans, crossing its lower slopes at the hamlet of Santaveri, and continuing to the town of Chikmagalur, about twenty miles away.

The second road leads northwestwards, passing the eastern and northeastern slopes of those same mountains, before curving through two hamlets, named Lakkavalli and Umblebyle, to the town of Bhadravati which itself is barely ten miles from Tarikere, by a third and more direct road.

The first and second roads in this way circumvent the southern and eastern slopes of the Baba Budan range, and the tigers that cross the hump of the mountains from the deep valley to the west and north, ringed in by these mountains, find themselves either in the vicinity of the hamlet of Santaveri on the southern road, or in the area known as the Laulbagh, west of the eastern road.

These should be kept well in mind: the hamlet of Santaveri and the area known as the Laulbagh. For it was at these places and in the area between them that the adventure with the tiger, about which you are now going to hear, took place. Santaveri, at the height of 4,500 feet above sea level, is a rocky, wild and thickly forested region, while the Laulbagh, perhaps thirty to thirty-five miles away as the crow flies, although more than a thousand feet lower and far less rocky, is correspondingly more thickly forested.

I happened to be visiting my old friend, Dick Bird, who was the postmaster at Santaveri and in private life one of the most famous tiger-hunters in the district, having shot all his tigers with a .12 bore shotgun, spurning the use of a rifle.

'Jock,' he asked me, 'have you heard about the tiger that has turned up around Kemangundi?'

I should explain that Kemangundi is about half-way between Santaveri and the Laulbagh area, and that Dick always calls me 'Jock'. For I have lived in so many places and hunted in so many forests and in so many different climates, with different fauna and flora, and have done so many different things, that I have become a sort of Jekyll and Hyde with a variety of names and nicknames. Very old friends call me 'Jock', 'Scotchie', or 'Scotch', while those met more recently address me as 'Andy', 'Kenneth', 'Ken' and 'KDS'.

At school they called me 'Snake Charmer', because of my fondness for producing these reptiles from inside my shirt and releasing them in such places as Sunday school, the school chapel, the classroom, the dining and study halls, and in cinemas and other congested spots. This was long ago, of course, and I have not been addressed as 'Snake Charmer' for some years, having dropped the habit of releasing the reptiles in public.

Most embarrassing of all, young Dudhwalla, my son's friend, insists upon calling me 'Dot'. Personally, I do not see the least resemblance or slightest connection between myself and 'any small mark with a pen or sharp point', which the dictionary gives as the meaning of 'dot'. So, because of the variety of names by which I am addressed, and being somewhat absentminded, I occasionally become confused and look around for the party addressed.

But to return to Dick's question.

'No,' I replied, 'I haven't been in the area for quite a while. I used to operate a lot in Salem district, as you know, but have had to extend my wanderings to the Nilgiris and into Andhra state. Tigers are still plentiful there.'

'Well, there are quite a few still,' Dick continued. 'But ordinary ones. You know, cattle-lifters. Snatch and grab beasts that haunt the cattle-herds. The animal I have mentioned appears to be a little different, though.'

He then went on to explain that reports from herdsmen stated a very large tiger had recently formed the habit of attacking their herds even while they were still on the roads and being driven to the grazing grounds. Before their very eyes it would seize and kill the fattest and choicest cow and carry her off, slung over its shoulders. This had happened several times and but a few miles from Santaveri itself, on the road I have told you about that led from Tarikere to Chikmagalur. The same sort of thing was reported to have taken place on another, smaller road, leading to a hillock named Kemangundi, which branched off the main Tarikere-Chikmagalur road shortly after passing through the village of Lingadhalli.

Dick went on to relate that two or three herdsmen had attempted to defend their charges by trying to frighten the tiger into relinquishing the carcase of the victim as it was carrying it away, by shouting and throwing stones.

They had soon desisted, however, when this tiger, instead of leaving the carcase and running away, had dropped the cow and charged in their direction—whereupon they had fled. Investigations later showed that the tiger had returned after chasing the herdsmen away, picked up the cow and made off with it. This tiger seemed to favour carrying its victim sluing across its shoulders rather than holding it by the neck or throat and dragging it along the ground.

We discussed this point and agreed that the indications were that either the tiger was an exceptionally bold animal—perhaps an old male—or that it intended carrying the carcase a long way before devouring it, perhaps to some distant cave, or other lair, should it happen to be a tigress with cubs. The animal was wise enough to realize that dragging its kill for a long distance would entail getting it caught in bushes and thorns; it therefore preferred to lift the carcase bodily.

'If only I would get some leave in this damned department,' Dick complained, 'I would bag it by hook or crook. But to get even two or three days' casual leave entails a hell of a fuss. A replacement for me has to be called from Tarikere or Chikmagalur, and the superintendent acts like mad. That's what comes of being a postmaster.'

My visit over, I returned to Bangalore and forgot all about the tiger. In any case, I was not interested in cattle-lifters.

Some months passed until, one morning, I happened to go to the district Magistrate's Court in Bangalore to purchase some government stamp paper, of which I was in need, when I met an Indian gentleman at the stamp vendor's booth. He was grumbling because the particular denomination of stamp paper he wanted was not available, nor were any smaller denominations that would add up to the total amount required.

I purchased the paper I needed, which was of a much higher denomination and was available.

'What name?' the vendor asked me, preparing to enter this on the back of the stamp paper, as required by rules.

'K.D.S. Anderson,' I replied slowly, spelling out the Anderson so that he could write it correctly.

The Indian gentleman with us was staring hard at me. After entering my name and receiving payment, the vendor handed me the stamp paper, and the gentleman spoke.

'Excuse me, sir,' he asked, 'but are you the Mr. Anderson who shoots tigers?'

'Well, I suppose so,' I answered with a smile. 'At least I don't know of any other Anderson who has the bad habit.' Then, as an afterthought I added, 'Perhaps you mean my son?'

'My name is Venkatasubbarao,' the man said. 'I'm the Assistant Chief Engineer working on the Lakkavalli Dam Project, near Tarikere. You see, when the vendor asked your name and you replied that it was Anderson, I pricked up my ears. I've heard of you shooting tigers all over the place. You must really come to Lakkavalli, sir. Come as my guest. I have large quarters and can put you up conveniently. You will be quite comfortable and I will make all the needful *bandobast* for you to shoot the man-eater.'

'What man-eater?' I asked in surprise.

'Haven't you heard?' he answered, evidently taken aback. 'Why, it came out in the newspaper three days ago. But come along and have a coffee with me and I'll tell you all about it.'

There is a restaurant, known as 'Tiffin Room', within a stones's throw of the Magistrate's Court, and there Venkatasubbarao and I went. Over not one, but several cups of coffee, he related the following story.

A large tiger had appeared on the road from Tarikere that led past the eastern slopes of the Baba Budan mountain range, and passed through Lakkavalli before going on in a circle to Bhadravati. It had begun by killing cattle belonging to the many herds that were taken to graze in the jungle bordering the roadside. The tiger was reputed to carry off its victims across its back, and if any of the herdsmen dared to interfere, this animal chased them off with loud growls. Invariably it would disappear in a western direction, into the jungles of the 'Laulbagh'.

Time passed. Nothing happened to any herdsmen, but the tiger continued to exact its toll. Naturally, the herdsmen grew more angry with the tiger and became correspondingly bolder. Equally naturally, the tiger grew more angry with them and grew bolder itself.

The day dawned when the anger of both sides came to a head. The tiger was moving off with a particularly fat cow across its shoulders when a herdsman, more plucky than any of his companions, rushed after it and hurled his stave. As was its custom, the tiger dropped the body of the victim and, roaring and growling horribly, charged the man, no doubt expecting him to bolt as so many others had done before.

But this man did not run away. Maybe he was braver than the others. Maybe he was stricken stiff with fear. Maybe, having cast his staff away, he thought it useless to run anyhow. Of course, not being present himself, Venkatasubbarao did not know what really happened. What he did know was that the tiger killed and ate the herdsman before walking off again with its fat victim, the cow.

Word got around and the herdsmen in the Lakkavalli area stopped interfering with the tiger. When it attacked a herd, the men in charge promptly fled, and the tiger, politely, did not bother to chase them any more. But other herdsmen, farther off, had not heard of what had transpired near Lakkavalli. They continued their old tactics of trying to drive the tiger off when it attacked their animals. The tiger, having come now to realize how helpless his human victim at Lakkavalli had proved to be, and emboldened by that experience, killed two herdsmen one after the other at Kemangundi, and one other not very far from Santaveri. These three victims it was reported to have completely devoured and, most significant feature of all, after eating them it had spurned the carcases of the cattle it had killed.

The tiger had returned to Lakkavalli after that. Once again the scene was set for tragedy. A herd of cattle was being taken out to graze by two men, a middle-aged man and his son of fifteen years. They were standing together, watching their charges, when the boy saw the head of a large tiger observing them from behind a rise in the ground. He drew his father's attention to it. Both had turned to flee, leaving their animals to the tender mercies of the tiger, when that beast, instead of attacking the cattle, had come after them.

The lad, being young and fleeter of foot, was running ahead when the father saw the tiger bound past him, overhaul the boy and pounce upon him. In heedless panic, the older man had swerved to the right and continued his headlong flight. When he reached the village he collapsed in a faint, and it was a long time before he could tell what had happened.

The villagers went to Venkatasubbarao's quarters to beg his assistance. My new friend, however, did not own a gun and so could not help them at that moment. He closely questioned the father and got from him all the details, just as he related them to me.

A runner was dispatched to Tarikere, some eleven miles away, for help. Meanwhile the herd of cattle came rushing back to the village. It was intact. Not one of them had been harmed.

The next morning a mixed posse of policemen and forest guards, nine in number and armed with lathis, arrived together with two constables with rifles and a police sub-inspector carrying a revolver. Thus a dozen men, led by the father, went to the spot where the tiger had attacked. The body of the boy was not to be seen and everybody returned.

Thereafter the problem of obtaining labour for working on the dam became insurmountable. Those who lived in huts in the village refused to go out, while many went back to Tarikere. Others—and quite a large number of them—had made a practice of cycling every morning the eleven miles from Tarikere to work at the dam, returning the same distance in the evening. These refused to undertake the journey any more. And those people who brought supplies of rice, grain, bread and vegetables from Tarikere to the technical staff working on the dam declined to travel on that dreadful road. So not only had work on the dam practically ceased, but the senior staff stationed at Lakkavalli were being starved out.

My new acquaintance had taken advantage of the inactivity to come to Bangalore on short leave, where we had met at the stamp vendor's counter. He earnestly begged me to return with him to Lakkavalli to try to rid the village of the menace that had beset it.

I had work to attend to, but yielded to my companion's pressing request and said I would come for five or six days only. I could not possibly stay longer.

Venkat, by which name I shall refer to him hereafter, was very pleased. I do not think he realized that it is practically

impossible to locate a man-eater in five days. It was arranged
that he should return to the hotel he was occupying, gather
the bedding and the few other things he had brought with
him, and be at my house by 3 p.m. the same day. We would
then travel in my car to Lakkavalli.

I hastened home to gather my own equipment, which is
always kept ready along with some tinned provisions, when
I had another surprise. The postman brought a short letter
from Dick Bird.

Dear Jock,

Hurry up and come. Be here by tomorrow. That
tiger I told you about has turned man-eater and
swallowed quite a few cattle-men. Yesterday, it carried
off my postman while he was taking the mail bag from
here to Hosoor village, three mils away. I had no time
to ask for leave, so reported sick and looked for the
remains of the postman to sit up over them. We
searched all day and only found the poor chap's cap
and slippers.

And, of course, the mail bag. (Couldn't the bloody
tiger have eaten that!)

Time's up and I have to return to duty tomorrow.
Now, no excuses man; I'm keeping lunch for you the
day after tomorrow (that is, the day after you receive
this letter), provided the tiger doesn't eat the reserve
postman who carries the mail today with this letter.
Poor beggar, he's in a blue funk and I can't blame him.

Your pal, Dick

Dick was surprised when he had two guests for dinner
that very night. Venkat and I had made the trip in record time.

189

We chatted till a late hour, but this did not get us anywhere. I remembered that, beginning the following morning, I had exactly five days in which to locate the man-eater and shoot it. Dick Bird could not leave his post. Venkat, with all the willingness he evinced, knew nothing about shooting and had no weapon anyway. There was no trace of the postman's body and it was not worth searching for it, as only bones would be left.

Venkat said that he had to be back at the dam by the following noon, so we decided to motor to his place that very night. By road, it was about fifty miles away, although much nearer as the crow flies. We downed a final rum and said goodbye to Dick well after midnight. I instructed Venkat how to operate the spotlight which with the headlights of the car enabled us to search the jungle as we drove along.

We were still about fifteen miles from Tarikere, at a place named Bagavadkatte, where a stream passes under the road by a small bridge with low parapets. Dark palms thickly fringed the road both to right and left of us, with heavy undergrowth and tiger-grass growing beneath the palms. It was there that we came upon a marvellous spectacle. Standing to one side, just beyond the parapet and evidently about to cross the road was a magnificent tiger!

It turned its head towards the car as the beams from the headlights, as well as the spotlight, caught it, and the reflection from its great orbs was brilliantly white-red, like two great stars shining by the wayside. By 'white-red' I mean more of white with a tinge of red. This is how I differentiate a tiger's eyes at night from those of a panther, which are smaller, closer together, and red-white in colour—that is, more of red and less of white.

We could see the tiger's striped coat, indeed its whole form, clearly in our bright lights.

I stopped the car. Both tigers and panthers, when a bright light falls upon them, often try to take cover by sinking to the ground, although they continue to stare back at the light, thus giving themselves away. This is just what our tiger did. It sank low and then started crawling forwards on its belly, seeking to hide behind the parapet of the bridge.

Venkat was beside himself with excitement. He trembled violently and the spotlight wavered. 'Shoot! Shoot! Shoot!' he hissed, louder and louder.

The tiger heard him. It scrambled forward the few remaining feet till the parapet hid it. Then it leapt down into the stream, passed under the bridge, and we heard it growl as it disappeared to our left in the long grass and undergrowth beneath the border of date palms. I could almost see tears in Venkat's eyes as he looked at me reproachfully. His lips trembled. For a moment I thought he was going to cry.

I explained to him at some length that all tigers are not man-eaters, that we were outside the man-eater's 'limit of beat' at the moment, and that Bagavadkatte was, and had always been, a well-known spot where tigers crossed the road, or passed under the bridge, from the low range of hillocks on the one side to the low range of hillocks on the other, and that the animal we had seen was undoubtedly a perfectly harmless-to-humans, innocent beast. Moreover, it was against rules to shoot tigers on the roadside with the aid of a spotlight, and unsporting besides.

I am not at all sure to this day whether Venkat was convinced by my arguments or considered me a fool. He certainly maintained an embarrassing silence till we reached our destination, his bungalow at about 2 a.m. There he brightened up a bit.

This happened when the watchman of the place informed him that the man-eater had carried away one of the few remaining coolies working on the dam when the man was returning to the village from work shortly after 5 p.m. the previous evening. As a result the coolies had told the watchman to inform his master when he returned that they would not come to work next day. Even if my arguments at the bridge at Bagavadkatte had not excused me in Venkat's eyes for not shooting the tiger we had seen there, he now had to be convinced that the animal that had crossed the road there could not have been the man-eater.

Venkat offered me food, but I declined and said we should snatch some sleep till five o'clock in order to be ready tò start our operations at 6 a.m. He thereupon conducted me to a little room with a comfortable bed, and in five minutes I was asleep.

Dawn had broken when we set forth, together with the watchman and three *coolies,* for the place where the tiger had claimed its latest prey. It appeared that these same three coolies had been with the victim when the tiger had taken him. The four men had been walking along the high bund—or wall— of the dam which was still under the process of construction. They had reached the end of it and were descending the steep slope where the sluice-gate was to be built, with the intention of climbing up the other side, when the man-eater struck. There was a piercing scream, and on looking around the fourth man was not to be seen by his mates.

A moment later they caught sight of him, held securely by the throat in the jaws of a tiger which bounded up the slope they had just come down. The beast crossed the top of the bund and disappeared from view. They delayed not a moment, but fled to report the news at the village. Next they went to the engineer's bungalow. Nobody had attempted a rescue of any kind.

We searched the cutting which was to form the sluice-gate, and there the tragedy of the evening before, in all its gruesome details, was made clear to us. The man-eater had not been lying in wait in the cuttings, as we had surmised. It had, in fact, been some distance away when it had seen the men and had deliberately followed them. The soft earth showed pug-marks where the tiger had clambered up the bund, bounded along the top, and then sprung upon the man who had been the last in line as he was descending the slope of the cutting.

The poor fellow had probably died soon after emitting his loud scream. There were no blood marks at the spot where he had been attacked, indicating the tiger had not delayed in picking up its victim and making off with him.

We found the pug-marks left by the killer as it was making off after crossing the top of the bund. Halfway down the steep slope it had skidded, and the piled-up earth showed the deep furrows left by its four feet when it had dug them into the ground to stop its slide. At this juncture it must have released his hold upon the dead man's throat, for when the tiger picked him up again, it left a trail of blood all the way down the rest of the incline and into the jungle beyond.

But for the blood trail it would have been impossible for us to follow the spoor, for the undergrowth, due to recent rain, was dense. But the vivid green of the carpet of weeds constrasted sharply with the bright red of the blood-drops which showed up clearly before us for some distance ahead.

The tiger had carried its victim westwards, and for a long distance. It had crossed the main road at a sharp curve about half a mile beyond Lakkavalli village and before the road had begun to circle back towards Umblebyle and Bhadravati. The animal was obviously making for the Laulbagh Forest Block, and I began to suspect that it must be living in some cave in this area.

A few minutes later we crossed the Forest department's 'fire-line' and were now officially inside the Laulbagh Forest

Block. Our quarry had not stopped for a moment, and it was becoming difficult to follow its trail. The blood in the body of its victim had coagulated and ceased to flow, so that the drops that had fallen were scarce and small. Our progress was consequently slow through having to search for them at long intervals, and I feared that very soon the trail would die out.

That was exactly what happened ten or fifteen minutes later. No further blood-drops could we find, nor was it possible to see the pug-marks of the man-eater. Twelve hours had elapsed since it had passed that way, and the freshening effect of the night breezes, together with the dew that had fallen, had again raised the bent stems of weeds, grass and undergrowth that had been trodden upon or brushed aside by the tiger and the body of its victim in passing. With stems and leaves standing stiffly erect, the weeds and undergrowth effectively hid from us any indication whatever as to the direction which the tiger and the victim had taken. The trail was dead.

Venkat and my other companions were bitterly disappointed. So was I. However, one piece of information had been gained from our work that morning. It was clear that the tiger lived in some cave or haunt within the Laulbagh area, as I had suspected from the beginning, and considering the distance it had already brought its victim, his hide-out could not be very far from the place where the trail had died out. I made inquiries as to the existence of a cave, but none of the villagers appeared to know about one.

As soon as we got back to the village I asked for the local forest guard. He would know the topography of the jungle within its jurisdiction. To my chagrin I was told that the guard had gone to departmental headquarters at Tarikere and would return only in the morning.

No time was to be lost, so I bundled Venkat into the car beside me and made for Tarikere without further delay. The bee that had got into my bonnet regarding the existence of a cave or other hiding place would have to be swatted before I was satisfied.

In half an hour we were at the district Forest Office, where we found not only the guard we were seeking but also his immediate superior, the forest ranger, and the divisional chief, the district officer, as well. With these people around us we related how we had followed and lost the trail of the man-eater in the Laulbagh jungle. Could they tell us if there was a cave or any other place of hiding in this block in which the tiger could have made its home?

The D.F.O. looked at the ranger, and the ranger at his guard. Then the guard looked back again, and so back and forth.

'There does not appear to be any cave in the area, Mr. Anderson,' the D.F.O announced at length.

The bee that had flown into my bonnet was dying an ignoble death. My theory was shattered! The guard, standing on one bare foot, scratched his shin with the toe of the other.

'I don't suppose the devil could be sheltering in the old Munneswara Temple, could he, *swami*?' he asked shamefacedly, addressing his immediate superior, the ranger.

'The Munneswara Temple!' ejaculated the ranger, thoughtfully; 'the Munneswara Temple!'

'The Munneswara Temple!' the D.F.O. exploded exultantly. Then, to the guard who was hanging his head in disgrace, 'You fool! Why didn't you say that before? That's it! That's where he is! The old Munneswara Temple!' The D.F.O. pranced about in the his excitement.

When emotions had died down I was informed that an ancient temple, almost in ruins, stood a short distance within the border of the Laulbagh Block. From the directions given by the guard, we must have been very near it when we had lost the trail that morning. The inner room, or sanctuary of the temple, was said to have partly caved in, but sufficient room was left for the tiger to live in, the guard thought.

Back we went to Lakkavalli, the D.F.O., the ranger and the guard following in government jeep. They said they wanted to be in at 'the kill', although they promised me they would remain in the village and not hamper me while the actual killing was taking place.

It was now past lunch-time, but with expectation at fever heat I decided to forgo the meal and set out with the forest guard on foot for the ruins of the old temple. We passed the spot where we had lost the blood trail and had gone another mile or more when there was a sudden dip in the ground. The centre of this little bowl or depression was an island of tangled undergrowth and bushes, and peeping through the varied foliage I could see the grey ruins of a small temple.

Instructing my companion to climb one of the taller trees and remain at the top, a suggestion that he did not delay a moment in executing, I picked my way on tiptoe towards the ruins, taking advantage of every intervening bush to cover my advance. The hot sun poured down on the scene and I was in no hurry.

In my excitement I discovered I had forgotten to ask the guard the direction the temple faced. This was important, if I hoped to take the man-eater by surprise. It would never do for me to be watching the rear of the temple while the tiger slipped out in front, circled around under cover of the undergrowth and attacked me from behind.

Eventually, on closer approach, I could make out the opening that led to the temple-sanctuary. It faced a little to my right and was partially blocked by debris. I was lucky. All I had to do now was creep up beside this opening, take cover, draw the man-eater out, and shoot it.

This is what I proceeded to do. Edging forwards, I reached the corner of the square that formed the outside of the temple. This struck me as being a very suitable place in which to hide and ambush my quarry. I would be safe from attack when the tiger rushed out. Naturally, it would charge straightforward and not think of looking for me to its right or left.

But there was a snag. If I hid behind one corner of the building, what was to prevent the tiger hiding behind the other corner at the back of me and pouncing upon me from the rear? It might not be in the temple at that moment, for all I knew. Perhaps it was watching me from the cover of some bush while It was searching for it.

I decided to creep up to within a couple of feet of the temple entrance and flatten myself against the wall. At least that would prevent me from being attacked from behind while I was peeping around the corner in front. This I did and was in position at last. Now it was a matter of drawing the tiger out. I had to avoid frightening it, and I should not anger it. It had to do itself out of curiosity.

So I moaned faintly, imitating the call of a tiger far away. Nothing happened! Perhaps the tiger had not heard me, although I could scarcely credit that. I moaned again, and still nothing happened. I moaned a third time, and much louder. That distant tiger had made a remarkably fast approach! Yet nothing transpired and I concluded that the tiger was not in the temple. I peeped around the corner very carefully; then I grew bolder and entered the broken opening, stooping double. A damp, mouldering smell greeted me. The dust at the entrance showed no pug-marks. Nor was there any trace of human remains. Not only was no tiger here, but no tiger had been here for months. Clearly the Munneswara Temple was not the man-eater's hiding place.

We were so disappointed that the huge lunch my friend Venkat had had prepared for himself and me was sufficient to feed the D.F.O. and the ranger also. Moreover, a little was left over, sufficient to give the forest guard a snack.

Sitting on the plinth of the veranda of Venkat's bungalow smoking, a short while later, I chafed at the delay while my friends continued to talk over events. Time meant everything to me, but nothing to them. It is the one thing in India that has never been rationed; and never will be.

In the afternoon sunlight, a Lambadi herdsman grazed his buffaloes outside. With the man-eater about, it was far too dangerous for him to take them into the forest, while the sparse grass in the compound of the engineer's quarters offered a meagre substitute. Attracted by the sight and smell of the assorted fumes from my pipe, Venkat's cigar and the cigarettes smoked by our two friends of the Forest department, this individual became sufficiently emboldened to approach us and beg for a cigarette. The D.F.O., threw him one and we forgot his existence, after seeing him move off to the rear of the bungalow where we heard him and the forest guard talking to each other.

A few minutes later the guard approached. He was excited, but also hesitated to interrupt the conversation of his exalted superiors.

'Well?' muttered the guard with great diffidence. 'I prey your honour not to get angry, but the outcaste Lambadi tells me there is an overhanging ridge of rock a mile beyond the Munneswara Temple under which there is sufficient space for a tiger to shelter. In fact, he says he saw one sunning itself on top of the rock one evening when he was returning with his buffaloes, and before the man-eater came amongst us. Of course, he ran away and his animals followed. He says he had not been there again.'

We summoned the Lambadi without delay and closely questioned him. His reply was exactly what the forest guard had just told us. The only new piece of information he offered was that he felt certain that the tiger he had seen and the man-eater were one and the same animal, bearing in mind the fact that the tiger had not turned man-eater at that time. Within a few minutes I was on my way again, the forest guard accompanying me rather reluctantly this time. But the Lambadi was in better spirits.

It was half-past four when we passed the temple, and close upon five before the Lambadi pointed out to me, about two hundred yards ahead, a slight rise in the ground above which peeped a sloping rock. He told me that, although we could not see it from where we stood, owing to the intervening jungle, when I came close enough I would find that the rock made a low overhanging cave, the entrance to which was not more than two feet in height. This, he thought, had been caused by the rush of rainwater during the monsoons, for the cave was not a very deep one. On his previous visit he had been at almost the same spot on which we were now standing and had noticed the tiger lying at full length and sunning itself on the top of the rock. He had run away as fast as he could.

Once again I told my companions to climb trees and to remain there till my return, and for the second time that day I crept forward on tiptoe as cautiously as possible.

This time my advance lay through fairly thick jungle, and not through open country like that which formed the depression in which the old Munneswara Temple mouldered. I looked to right and left and behind, to guard against flank and rear attacks. There was an oppresive silence and I glanced momentarily downwards at each pace that I made. On no account must I step on a leaf that might rustle or a twig that might crackle. Now and then, despite all my precautions, some part of my body brushed against a bush and made a faint rubbing sound.

I said to myself: 'I must not do that again: the tiger will hear me.'

I was now very near the rock, but the undergrowth in front still hid the ground level opening mentioned by the Lambadi. I halted for a few minutes. Maybe I could hear the tiger if I strained my ears. I did so, but I heard absolutely nothing.

'A few steps more,' I said to myself, 'and I will be able to see.'

I looked down. No leaf, or twig, no loose stone in front. It was safe for me to take another step forwards.

I took that step, but I overlooked an insignificant little shrub to my right. That shrub had thorns, and the thorns did the trick. They rasped audibly against my trousers, held for a moment, and then let go with another rasp.

Before I could guess whether the man-eater had heard me, it had in fact done so. Instinct warned it that this was no bird, no hare or other small creature that was approaching just out of sight. It knew full well that no living thing that could fly, walk or creep would dare to come so close to its dreadful presence. Therefore this must be an enemy, and more over, an enemy that was stalking it, the tiger, no doubt to kill it in turn.

Its reflexes gave it this message and there was no delay. The tiger charged, its shattering roars of 'Wroof! Wroof! Wroof!' rending the silence.

The bushes before me parted and its head and body catapulted through them before it caught sight of me. It halted for a moment prior to making the final spring. Perhaps it never expected to find a miserable human being confronting it instead of running away. Head and paws at ground level, hindquarters and tail sticking up, the tiger looked a bit ridiculous.

I fired twice into its head. Then I leaped quickly aside, for one must never forget to spring aside after firing at a tiger at close quarters, as the odds are ninety-nine to one that it will rush straightforward, even if it must die the next instant. A dying tiger can in fact do you an awful lot of harm.

The man-eater did as I expected, and I shot it twice more behind the shoulder. As it twitched and then began to stiffen, I saw that it was quite an old animal, past the age from hunting game.

The bones of the coolie for whose body we had been searching were strewn about the entrance to the shallow cave. They had been gnawed clean. Red ants were devouring what small strands of flesh adhered to them still.

The three of us returned in darkness, unafraid this time. There was another feast at the bungalow, and it gave me indigestion. Dreams of tigers rushing out of temples troubled me till the early hours. Then came a farewell to Venkat and my friends of the Forest department.

I was at Santaveri by nine in the morning. Dick offered me lunch, but I declined. My stomach was still rumbling in uncomfortable protest as I swallowed a quick rum. By four I was home, having accomplished my mission well within time.

Eight

What the Thunderstorm Brought

DONALD, MY SON, WAS IMMENSELY PLEASED WITH HIMSELF. HE HAD just tied for the first place in a clay-pigeon shooting competition held by the Rifle Association of Mysore state.

Now clay-pigeon shooting is something we in India do not normally indulge in, at least so far as I know, perhaps because there are so many wild pigeons that we cannot be bothered with the clay variety, or whatever substance it is that goes to make a clay pigeon. More likely, because up to this time nobody had the apparatus to eject these little things, these clay pigeons into the air. Certainly, I had never seen them before. I am sure I could not hit one myself. I am essentially a rifle shot and almost useless with a gun. My attempts years ago at snipe and duck convinced me of that.

Donald, however, is a natural good shot with both gun and rifle. Like me, he had never seen a clay-pigeon-shooting gadget, and therefore certainly had had no chance to practise.

But he entered for the competition and tied for the first prize. And now he suggested that we should make a trip to the jungles to celebrate the occasion.

To the jungles? What a strange place to go to celebrate! But the truth is we both love the jungles. In them we are at home; there we find peace. So it did not take much persuasion to get me to go.

This time we decided to try our hand at photographing tigers by night rather than shooting them. Donald had borrowed a wonderful camera with a flashlight apparatus from his old friend of schoolboy days, young Dudhwala, who was young no longer, and about whom I have told a tale in an earlier book.* For a long time Don had been wanting to try his hand at the most difficult and I might also add, most highly-skilled sport of night-photography and this was his chance.

I will not tell you to which jungle we went because it is one of the very few places remaining in southern India where tigers are yet to be found. Some enthusiasts have read my books and gone to places I have named, bent upon trying their luck, and it has become a matter of necessity, from the point of view of Indian conservation, no longer to name them. For tigers, panthers and bear are becoming very scarce in southern India. The heavy shooting which resulted from the influx of foreigners into India during World War II began their decimation. The Indian poacher particularly, of the kind that uses jeeps with spotlights, continued the process. Then came the deadly insecticide of which I have already spoken, which the government still supplies almost free of charge to protect the villagers' crops against various pests, but ryots whose cattle or goats have been killed by tigers and panthers have no compunction about smearing the flesh

---

* See: *Man-Eaters and Jungle Killers.*

203

of their slain animals with this stuff. Almost always, success crowns this dastardly deed by poisoning the marauder when he returns for a second meal.

The results have been so disastrous that, particularly in Mysore state, tigers, panthers, hyenas, and even jackals, and to some extent vultures, have been practically wiped out by the misuse of this chemical—without taking into account the high mortality among human beings all over the country by suicide, murder and accidental poisoning. The old-fashioned and far slower acting, less deadly posions like arsenic, strychnine and zinc salts, which can only be purchased in minute quantities, are discoverable, but the government will give anyone pounds of deadly insecticide almost for the asking. It is deplorable that the authorities cannot, do not, or will not see the truth of this matter.

So we went to 'tiger-land', to a lovely cabin of bamboo and grass that we had built on a small plot of land I had bought many years earlier for the sum of 120 rupees (about seven pounds sterling). Two hundred yards in front of our hut flowed a river, its presence plainly indicated by the heavy growth of giant *muthee*, tamarind, *jumlum* and wild mango trees that lined both banks. Here and there were areas where dense clumps of bamboo had ousted all other forms of vegetation, bringing their towering, feathery fronds to overhang the cascades and pools of the stream, while dark and silent glades, covered with a carpet of rotting leaves, reached down to the water's edge.

The crocodile loves such places, for the deer like them too. The dense cover afforded by the bamboos, their shade, and the flooring of decaying leaves permit a silent, sheltered and comparatively safe approach for the sambar, nilgai and spotted deer when they come in the heat of the day, and also at night, to slake their thirst with the cool water that has cascaded down so recently from the cold of the mountains above the forest.

In their anxiety to escape the great carnivores that may be lurking behind any tree, any clump of bamboo, or any bush, the deer lose no time in drinking as fast as they can, with their noses and ears alert for the scent or sound of a tiger, and their eyes on the watch for a panther or for the cruel wild dogs. Often enough, in the anxiety of scanning the landscape, they overlook the ugly crocodile, who is invisible anyhow, his head and body below the surface of the stream and very close to the bank.

And so a sambar lowers its head to drink, and as it does so the crocodile rises from the water. Cruel jaws, with long, saw-like teeth, close upon the sambar's snout while almost in the same instant the reptile's flat, scaly tail swings out of the water and whips across with irresistible force, striking the sambar's legs or flank and throwing it off-balance into the pool.

Never loosening its grip on the sambar's face, the crocodile swims backwards into deep water, dragging its struggling victim with it. Once in its element, the crocodile throws itself into a spin of incredible speed in order to break its victim's neck or otherwise render it unconscious, and the next moment both crocodile and sambar vanish beneath the dark surface of the pool and only a series of large bubbles disturb the placid flow of water over the scene of the tragedy.

But we know nothing of the grim drama being enacted in the slime and ooze at the bottom of the jungle river. From the comfortable cane chairs on the veranda of our hut we listen to the loud cracking of the stems of giant bamboos as they are broken by a herd of elephants grazing on the opposite bank of the stream. Now and again comes the faint squeak of an elephant-calf and the dull thunder-like rumble from the digestive organs of an adult, or a contented cow-like mooing from a feeding female. All is peaceful and the faraway call of a peafowl alternates with the shrill, cat-like meowing cries that come from above us, made by the pair of brown vultures in their never-ending quest for scraps of food left by the great jungle cats.

Although there was apparent peace in the jungle there was some discord in our hut. Trouble arose between the caretaker, whom we employ to look after the place in our absence, and his wife, who brings us water twice a day in an old kerosene tin from the river. There was muttering and grumbling, and an occasional high-pitched female screech that put even the vultures to shame.

'Some trouble between Boora and his wife,' observed Donald laconically. 'Better see what it is about. She hasn't brought water for my bath yet, although I've told her twice already.'

So I got up and went into the kitchen, which is a smaller grass hut about twelve feet square, situated behind our dwelling-place. There sat Boora on the ground, idly poking a wood fire with a stick while his spouse sat opposite him, chewing betel-nut vigorously and spitting red saliva all over the place. An interested spectator was my *shikari* Thangavelu, originally from faraway Closepet, who had promoted himself into Don's services as a camp-cook, table-boy, dressing-boy, and every other sort of boy except a boy who honestly did any work.

'What's the matter with you two?' I asked aggressively, glaring at Boora and his wife alternately. Then, addressing the woman. 'Your bad language is disgusting.'

There was silence for a while, then Boora explained in the local dialect: 'Sir, I married this harridan three years ago. She has had three children from me but doesn't look after them. Neither does she feed me properly. She won't work because she's lazy, All day long she keeps chewing betel-nut and demands money to buy more. Altogether, she's too expensive a proposition.

'As it stands when I married her I paid ten rupees to her father for her. Now, old Javanna had offered me his youngest daughter for fifteen rupees. She's a comely wench and will look after me well. What's more, Javanna is willing to take over this bag-of-bones from me for five rupees, half the price I paid for her, so that the deal will only cost me ten. She can keep the three children she had from me—I certainly don't want'em!'

Further plans on the part of Boora were interrupted by the screeching voice of Devi, his wife.

'You lecherous old pig!' she cried. 'What do you want with a young girl like Lakshmi? She's only fifteen years old, although she's a bitch at that! You're already half-dead, and after a week with her I'll have the trouble of burying your exhausted bones! As for that old sod, javanna! He's so old he hasn't any teeth! Also, he's fond of young boys! Who's going to satisfy me? I'm young and vigorous still!'

A knotty problem, indeed! But there was one redemptive factor. Considering the rate of exchange at one shilling and four pence to a rupee, the cost-factor involved in this mutual exchange, in whatever way you might look at it, was not very high. Thangavelu summed up the situation concisely with a wide grin, and in the butler-English which he had picked up, chimed in:

'Sar I like this place. Plenty very much damn good place. Plenty *shikar*, plenty tiger, plenty deer got-it. Plenty women, too, plenty damn cheap-rate. Here five rupees, ten rupees get-it wife. Then too, can pay next month. When no want, can change-it. Another wife get-it. Only ten rupees! Damn woman won't go 'way after. Want-it more money. Can't get 'nuther wife less than 'nuther hundred rupees. Sar, this very damn good place.'

Thangavelu ended with a meaning grin.

'Thangavelu, tell that bloody woman to fetch my bath-water,' Donald roared from the veranda. Kunmarie, the local *shikari*, turned up just then with the information we had asked him to bring us. He had been scouring the jungle since dawn and reported that a tiger as well as a panther, had walked up the bed of a dry *nullah* about half a mile away. The panther seemed an old resident as Kunmarie said his tracks, both old and fresh, appeared many times. The tiger was evidently on a casual walk and could not be expected to return that way for some time.

So the prospects were that if we tied a bait with the object of taking a photograph later, it would probably be a panther and not a tiger that would kill it. We were after tiger only; we reiterated this fact to Kunmarie, asking him to go out again to try to find a place frequented by a tiger rather than a panther.

That afternoon he returned with news of success. Across the river, he said, was a well-frequented game trail on which were tiger-pugs, both old and fresh. Further, there was a convenient tree, safe from interference by elephants, from which we could easily take our photographs when the time came. The tiger was sure to pass the same way that night or the next.

We had procured four buffaloes as bait and decided to tie out two of them—the larger on the tiger-frequented game-trail across the river, and the smaller in the *nullah* four furlongs away, where the panther was almost certain to get it. Thangavelu went with Kunmarie to help tether the two animals, while Don and I went for an evening walk along the river bank.

This particular jungle was still a veritable paradise for game and we saw large herds of spotted deer, with a fair number of sambar and individual nilgai, browsing by the water-side. Around a curve in the river we came upon a bull-elephant having his evening drink. As we were not on a *shikar* trip we carried no firearms. For a moment or two the bull looked nasty; no doubt he resented our intrusion on his privacy. Then he thought better of it, wheeled and lumbered away into the thicket of overhanging trees. It was extraordinary how so large an animal could move so quietly.

The following morning Kunmarie went to the game-trail and Thangavelu to the *nullah*, to see what had happened to our baits during the night. In the jungle the unexpected frequently happens, and the reports they brought us were as surprising as they were heartening from the photographic point of view. A tiger, and not a panther, had come along the *nullah* where we had tied the smaller bait, expecting the panther to kill it. It had easily broken the tethering-rope and had taken the buffalo-calf a little distance away to a ditch. There it had eaten every scrap except the head and four hooves. Because they were sheltered by undergrowth the vultures had not discovered the remains.

Strangely enough a panther, and not the tiger we had expected, had come along the game-trail across the river. It in turn had killed the large buffalo-calf we had tied for the tiger, evidently with some difficulty, for Kunmarie reported marks of a struggle. But the panther had not been strong enough to sever the tethering-rope. So it had eaten a small portion of the buffalo-calf, leaving the rest by the side of the game-trail where we should be able to photograph it easily if we wished, from the big tree bordering the trail when it returned that night.

Don was in high spirits. He would photograph his tiger at last. Naturally he decided to sit over the scant remains, consisting of the head and legs, of the smaller calf we had tied out in the *nullah*. To make sure the tiger put in an appearance, he proposed tying our third bait near by, just in case the tiger thought the remains of the first one too insignificant to merit a second visit.

Incidentally, I might remark that this is a plan I have found most successful with both tiger and panther. After all, they are individuals just as we are; they differ among themselves just as we differ and they suffer from some at least of our faults. The commonest of these is greed. Some panthers and tigers hardly ever return to their kills a second time. Others return only after they have spent a very long time reconnoitering the locality and feel it safe to show themselves. It is in this process of surveyance that they frequently discover the presence of the hunter, perched in his tree-*machan* or wherever he may have concealed himself. To exploit this greed, I have found it good to tie another live bait within sight of the partially eaten one, and if possible to sit at a spot between them; or if that is not practical, to sit over the new bait in preference to the old, partly-eaten one.

What happens is this. The tiger or panther returns to the scene of its first kill but does not approach the carcase straight away. It is suspicious and circles the spot several times to discover the presence of the man its instinct warns is in hiding somewhere. During this manoeuvre it comes upon the new live bait. One might conjecture that this would make the feline more suspicious than ever. How does a live animal come to be so close to the place where he had left a dead and almost completely devoured victim? But you must remember that tigers and panthers cannot reason as human beings do. They are creatures of instinct, even if such instinct is often uncanny in its efficiency.

The immediate result is that the prowling tiger or panther kills the live animal. No doubt the prospect of fresh meat is always more enticing than the decomposing flesh that has been exposed to the sun and vultures throughout the day, and so the tiger or panther brings about its own undoing.

I had no camera suitable for night photography, and as we were not on a shooting excursion and carried no firearms there seemed no point in my sitting on the big tree across the river merely to hear a panther tucking into a good meal. So I decided to spend the first part of the night in sitting in the comfort of a cane chair on the veranda of our bamboo hut, listening to the sounds of the jungle; and the rest of it in bed.

Showers of rain had been sporadic in the area, and for this reason each of us had brought along a tarpaulin sheet to sling as a roof over the *machan* in case of necessity. This is a practice I do not recommend at all. Firstly, it makes the *machan* very conspicuous and calls for extra camouflaging. Secondly, when the rain comes the noise of the water on the roof is so great that your cannot hear a thing. Worse still, any creature on the ground below at fifty yards cannot help but hear the pandemonium overhead. It looks up, discovers the *machan* and knows you are there. But it certainly is no joke to sit up in a tree all night in pouring rain, even if you are waring a greatcoat or waterproof cape. The rain has a strange knack of getting inside anything.

Don decided to use the tarpaulin and I went along with Kunmarie and Thangavelu, together with another man named Bunda, to help him with his *machan*.

A soap-nut tree grew to one side of the *nullah* and on this Don decided to sit. It was within about thirty yards of the ditch in which lay the head and legs of our first bait and it overlooked the course of the *nullah* in both directions. There was a third advantage to this tree. The tiger, in stalking our bait the night before, had come down by way of a third *nullah*, which was more a shallow ditch, and the soap-nut tree grew just opposite the point where this ditch met the main *nullah*. So it was strategically in an excellent position and, according to all the rules of the game, with ordinary luck the tiger should make itself visible somewhere, and Don should get the chance of a good photograph.

Our three henchmen made an excellent job of the *machan*, and as the sky was clouding over Don decided to stretch the tarpaulin above the platform of the *machan*, across a stick cut and placed in position so as to afford a slope on both sides to allow any water to flow off. The tarpaulin itself was cunningly concealed with leaves and branches that entirely hid it from view. The four of us went away about 5 p.m. leaving Don with the camera all set for an adventurous night.

I will tell you first what I heard from our bamboo cabin, and then let Don tell his part of the tale.

Thangavelu served dinner early, and then I sat on the cane chair on the veranda, smoking my pipe and sipping rum and lime-juice. Darkness had only just fallen and the jungle was silent for the moment. The 'Aiow! Aiow! Aiow!' came the cry of spotted deer from across the river while a sambar stag on the near bank hoarsely took up the warning with his strident 'Dhank! Dhank! Oo-onk!' and a doe sambar, farther away, heard the signal of danger and in a higher tone not quite so hoarse, answered 'Wonk! Wonk! Wonk!'

A bribe of langur monkeys on a banyan tree, the top of which was just visible to me in the darkness to my right, had all gone to sleep long ago. All except the watchman who, with a true sense of responsibility, had remained wide awake. Later, when he began to feel drowsy, he would awaken his relief, who would keep watch till the time came to awaken the next big male, and so on, throughout the night and all day long too, for the big male langurs have an uncanny sense of disicipline and responsibility. They take upon themselves, each in turn, the duties of a watchman, perched at the very top of the highest tree, to look for possible danger and guard the females and young from an unexpected attack.

The langur watchman heard the sambar and the spotted deer and echoed the alarm to awaken the members of his tribe: 'Harr! Ha-harr! Harr! Ha-harri!' I could picture the mother-langurs clutching their young to their breasts while peering down from their perches on the banyan tree into the blackness of the night below to try to discover the killer and reckon from where it might be creeping upon them.

I could plot the progress of the tiger's approach by the cries of the spotted deer and the sambar. He crossed the river and frightened a barking deer in the act of drinking. 'Khrr! Khrr!' the little animal cried. Its cry is quite unlike any other noise associated with the deer species. It sounds more like the hoarse bark of a dog and accounts for the colloquial name by which this small creature, otherwise called the muntjac is known.

The tiger was now disdainful. It knew it had been discovered and scorned to conceal its movements any longer. 'Oo-oongh!' it roared, and then modified its utterance to a softer but deeper 'Aungh! Ughh; Ughh-aa!' There was not anger in the sound, nor was it very hungry.

As if by magic, at the sound of its roars, deep silence descended upon the forest. The deer and monkeys were stilled. Even the frogs by the riverside stopped their croaking. All living creatures, large and small, knew that the king of the jungle was on the prowl and they trembled in fear. Only a solitary wood-circket, ensconced in cool comfort behind the water-pot in what goes for the bathroom of our bamboo-cabin, disdained the challenge of the striped terror. Maybe it had not even heard. Maybe it could not be bothered with such big clumsy creatures as tigers. Probably its problem was more mundane.

Then the silence was shattered down by the river: 'Haa-ah! Haa-ah! Haa-ah!'

The panther had returned long ago and had no doubt been eating its fill of our larger bait. All this fuss had upset it, while the roars of its bigger, irascible and bullying cousin, the tiger, had made it jittery and irritable. It resented the proximity of that majestic terror, but did not know what to do about it. Angrily it repeated: 'Haa-ha! Haa-ah! Haa-ah!' while deciding whether to remain or slink away.

I knew that Don must have heard all these sounds too, and that he would be getting ready to take his picture of the tiger, which by this time should be near the remain of the buffalo calf it had killed the night before, and the live bait we had tied near by.

Silence fell over the forest again. The frogs resumed their croaking by the river and the night seemed to grow black and yet blacker. I looked up at the sky and wondered why I could see no stars. A moment later knew the answer as thunder rumbled across the range of hills behind our cabin. Repeated flashes followed, and the artillery of heaven was loosed upon us, each crash preceded by vivid forked lightning that snaked across the sky like rivers on a giant map.

Then the wind started. I could hear it howling in the distance as it raged down the hillside with a prolonged banshee wail rising ever louder and louder until it hit our own jungle. I could hear the trees tossing wildly as their branches clashed in agony, although it was far too dark to see a thing, and the bamboo supports of our cabin swayed, straining, creaking and groaning. I thought that the thatched roof would be blown away.

Then suddenly as quickly as it came, the wind passed. I could hear it receding into the distance across the forest tops as far as the distant horizon. But the lightning increased in intensity, and the crashes of thunder drew ever nearer and more intense. All at once a giant tree was struck. It was cleft asunder as a vivid flash lit the forest as bright as day, so close to our hut that the thunderclap was instantaneous. I thought of Don in his soap-nut tree and was worried. It was not a very big tree or a high one, however, and hardly likely to attract the lightning that had so many loftier trees to choose from.

The rain reached the cabin and for a moment even approaching down the hillside, long before it reached the cabin. Donald must be really glad, I thought, that he decided to put the tarpaulin roof above his *machan*.

The rain reached the cabin and for a moment even the thunder was drowned in the uproar of falling water. The grass roof above me hissed, and streams of water from a hundred leaks dripped, pattered and flowed in all directions upon our possessions. What had been, only a moment earlier, a cosy cabin became a wet and muddy hole with pools of water on the floor and no dry spot within sight. I sat on, inwardly cursing the labourers who had made such a poor job of the roof.

Thangavelu, awakened at last by the hubbub, in which perhaps he was dreaming of wives for sale by the dozen at five rupees a head, dashed in, gazing in dismay at all the wet things around him, and then scuttled about aimlessly, trying hopelessly to find shelter for them.

The deluge continued for an hour and then settled down to a steady drizzle.

'Quak-ker! Quak-ker! Quak-ker! Quak-ker!' The frogs had now changed their note. This was the mating call of a thousand throats from the river and surrounding puddles, to salute the advent of the monsoon. I rose and prepared for sleep. The only dry spot seemed to be under the bamboo bed rather than upon it.

At that moment I heard the unmistakable scream of an enraged elephant. It came from the direction of the *nullah* and Don's *machan*. Thangavelu, who was still pottering about aimlessly, heard it too. He stopped and we looked at each other anxiously. Then we both went out on to the soaking veranda in order to hear better.

The elephant screamed again. There was no mistaking the fact that the scream came from the *nullah*. Then I heard distant shouting, muted by the continuous pattern of the rain, but there was no doubt that it was a human voice, shouting words I could not make out. The voice came from the same direction as the elephant's scream. Who but Donald was out there in the *nullah*?

Then the truth dawned upon me suddenly. My son was in danger: the elephant was trying to pull him out of the *machan*, and he was trying to drive it away. And he was unarmed.

The irony of the situation struck me and I cursed myself for my overconfident carelessness. I should have known better; they boy was not to blame. We were defenceless. For we had brought no firearms with us, leaving them behind because we had come on a photographic excursion and did not want to be tempted to shoot!

Grabbing the larger of the two lanterns in one hand and, for want of anything better, a walking-stick made from sandalwood in the other, I dashed out and began to stumble through the drenched jungle as fast as I could to cover the half-mile to the *nullah*. I was hardly aware of the cold or the fact that I was bareheaded and without a coat as the rain soaked me to the skin.

I had run as best I could for quite a distance before I became aware of another lantern bobbing behind me. It was Thangavelu, carrying the other light. He loved Donald, and

I was grateful for his presence. No other servant would have dared to venture forth on that foul night, in pitch darkness and unarmed, to a place where a wild elephant was rampaging in fury.

Then we heard a tearing, rending sound, and a crash, and I knew the elephant had pushed over the tree on which Don had his *machan*. I tried to run faster and Thangavelu ran beside me. But I could not make the pace, so we resorted to shouting as we jog-trotted along, hoping to attract the elephant's attention and draw him away from Donald.

This is how Donald himself tells his part of this story: 'I don't know why my father, when he writes his books, brings me into them. For one thing, I hate writing and talking about myself. Actually, the entire incident appears to me now as "much ado about nothing".

'Dad had told how it all started and how I came to be seated on the soap-nut tree with Dudhwalla's flashlight camera to try to photograph the tiger that had killed and devoured our bait the previous night. There was so little left that I had decided to tie a live one near by to tempt the tiger when he prowled around, as tigers generally do, before approaching their kills.

'The *machan* was a comfortable one; the head and feet of the first calf lay in a ditch some thirty yards to my left, while below me was the *nullah* that Kunmarie, our *shikari*, said was a regular route for tigers and panthers on their way to the river. Entering it was a smaller watercourse which the tiger used the night before. A shade to my right, and in clear view, was our third bait—a live one—another buffalo-calf. The second bait was killed by a panther across the river the night before.

'Darkness had just fallen when the deer and langur monkeys sounded their alarm cries and I knew that a tiger or a panther was afoot—probably a tiger, to judge by the amount of noise the animals were making. Then the tiger roared fairly near, and soon afterwards I could hear a panther answering in the distance. Most likely it was the one that killed our second bait.

'I got ready to take my picture. All the same, I wished I had a rifle in my hands instead of a camera. The old man is always talking about taking photographs instead of shooting, and I guess he is right, but the temptation was there nevertheless. I felt strongly now and wished I had my .423 with me.

'The next sound I heard was a thud and the cry of the live bait. I knew it was a tiger and not a panther that was killing the calf, for a panther has to choke his victim, who naturally struggles. There was no sound of a struggle whatever, for the calf was already dead with a broken neck.

'I pointed the camera downwards and to my right, in the general direction of the live bait, and pressed the switch-button. There was a blinding flash and the tiger uttered a startled 'Gr-a-ahm!' This was followed by the faint crash of undergrowth. I knew that it had gone.

'There was nothing more for me to do and I stretched out to sleep, contented with the hope of a good photograph. The *machan* was a bit hard and I wished I was back in our bamboo cabin.

'I must have fallen asleep after that, for I woke with a start to find my *machan* swaying crazily as the tree bent and threshed in a mighty wind. The night was extraordinarily dark till a flash of lightning, followed almost at once by a crash of thunder, told me we were in for a storm, and a big one too. Branches and leaves were torn from the trees and they whipped past my face, while my tarpaulin roof was partly blown away. One end held, the corner that we had lashed to the tree-trunk, while the other threshed loudly in the wind, whipping against the branches and making a great noise.

'Then all at once the wind fell and the rain came. It was more like a waterfall than rain. I closed Dudhwalla's camera and flashlight apparatus and put them away in their case and hoped the water would not get through. I was like a sponge myself; so full of water that it seemed to be running through me. And the rain went on falling.

'Now something unusual occurred. The tiger came back. Probably the lightning had made it think himself a fool for running away in the first instance. What it had seen must have been only a flash of lightning, no more. So it came back and started tearing at the calf it had killed a short time before.

'I dared not attempt to take another picture. God knows what would happen to Dudhwalla's camera, I thought, if I opened it in the torrential rain. There was no point in trying to do anything; even the beam of my torch could not reach the tiger through the falling rain.

'Eventually the rain eased off a little and I could hear the tiger's gnawing more clearly. Then I heard a fresh sound: the squelch of giant footfalls approaching along the *nullah,* wading through the rushing water that I could hear gurgling down the watercourse below. An elephant!

'Probably is was too wet for it to eat and it just wanted to shelter, for he was breaking no branches. It squelched nearer and nearer.

'The tiger heard it too and did not like it. It let out a terrific "Wr-aah!" Ordinarily it would slink away, for tigers and elephants avoid one another as much a possible. But this tiger was an exception. It was eating.

'Moreover, it was angry. So he snarled again and again: "Wr-aah! Wr-aah! Wr-aah!"

'The squelching stopped abruptly. The elephant attempted to strike its trunk against the ground in the usual note of alarm and warning. But its trunk met mud and water instead of firm

219

earth, and the resulting noise sounded more like somebody with a severe cold blowing his nose.

'This annoyed the tiger more and he growled louder than ever, and the elephant would have as likely as not gone away then and left the tiger to its feast, and me in peace, but for an unfortunate turn of events.

'There was a sudden gust of wind and the end of the tarpaulin waved like a flag, banging against the branches of the tree almost above the elephant's head. The tiger took off with a leap at hearing this new sound and crashed into the undergrowth at the elephant's side. This startled and angered the great beast; confused and alarmed, it did not know whether the tiger meant to attack it or if the strange object that was lashing about above its head spelled danger. It looked up and saw everything: the tarpaulin, the *machan*, and me!

'Jumbo let out a terrible scream and rushed straight at the soap-nut tree, its forehead banging against the trunk with a sickening thud. The heavy rain had saturated and loosened the earth, the tree-trunk went off the perpendicular and assumed a slant, and I knew well enough that with another push or two it would come crashing to the ground.

'Jumbo screamed again, backed a little and was obviously gathering itself for a further assault. Although it was very dark, I could faintly make out his shape, so close as to be almost within arm's reach, directly to my left. A faint streak of whiteness against that inky-black background indicated its tusks and confirmed that it was a bull. Moreover, I could smell him now. In spite of the rain that must have washed him well, his body gave out the rank, unmistakable odour of a wild tusker, especially strong when the animal is angry.

'In the next rush the soap-nut tree would fall to earth and take me with it. so I started shouting madly, at the top of my lungs, the first words, just any words, that came into my mind.

My voice had the desired effect—at least for the moment. The elephant delayed his charge and screamed again. The next second would decide my fate.

'My electric torch! Why had I not thought of it before? The light was sure to frighten him off. Hastly I grabbed it and shone it directly into the elephant's face.

'By all the rules of the game he should have beaten a hasty retreat. Instead, he screamed louder than ever, and a second later I felt as if a steamroller had hit me, when he dashed his forehead a second time into the trunk of the soap-nut tree. In slow motion, as if deliberately staged, the tree heeled over to the accompanying noise of rending roots. Then, gathering momentum, it crashed to earth, carrying me, *machan* and everything with it.

'When I felt myself falling I grabbed at the branch above my head so that, apart from the shock, I should receive no physical injury. I thought fast. The first idea that came to mind was to dash for it; but I was enmeshed in the branches of the blasted tree and could not find my torch. In falling I had let go of it in order to grab the branch. God knows where it had gone. It was pitch-dark and to escape from the entanglement of bamboos that formed the *machan* and which were now jumbled all around me, and from the branches of the tree itself, would take a considerable effort, and would lead the elephant to where I was.

'The elephant solved the problem by finding the end of the tarpaulin that had been threshing about in the breeze and seizing it with his trunk. One end was still tied to a branch, so he tore it in two and I could hear him tramping and stamping upon the other piece a few paces away.

'I cowered among the branches, but peeped out to see if I could discover how close he was. It was utterly black everywhere, but his movements betrayed that he was within fifteen feet. I could smell him strongly and hear him breathing as he slogged the end of the tarpaulin against the ground with his trunk, stamped upon it and tore it to shreds. The noise continued for a full minute or two when another noise reached me. I could hear men shouting.

'They appeared to be approaching, and soon I could make out dad's voice and another, which I recognized as Thangavelu's. The twinkle of lights in the distance showed that they were carrying lanterns or torches. Abruptly the bull stopped beating the tarpaulin. He was silent for a moment and then banged the end of his trunk against the ground in alarm and anger. I heard him turning around to face the approaching men.

'Dad and Thangavelu were coming in at the run now, shouting as they did so. I knew my father was unarmed and that it was going to be touch-and-go whether the enraged bull decided to charge them or beat a retreat himself. Perhaps if I started shouting it would help to confuse the dammed beast.

'Just then, stumbling and squelching down the water-filled *nullah* the two men came, holding their lanterns in front of them and shrieking like banshees. The old man was yelling "Don, are you all right?" but I dared not answer. The elephant was far too close and the sound of my voice would bring him down upon me.

'The flickering lights showed me the towering form of the creature as he faced them, his trunk curled inwards, the inevitable sign of an elephant on the verge of a charge. I would have to do something to divert his attention, so I let out a yell and kept on yelling.

'The elephant trumpeted shrilly. Dad and Thangavelu, who had now seen him, stopped running and held their lanterns aloft, to join in the general pandemonium, by yelling too. Dad was doing something so ridiculous that I almost laughed in spite of the danger we were all in at that moment. He was brandishing a stick.

'The screeching sounds we were all making must have sounded hideous. But, thank God, the bull thought so too and lost his nerve. He wheeled abruptly and thundered up the bank I lost no time in getting free of the tree and getting to Dad and Thangavelu.

'"Are you all right?" the old man asked.

'I could not help smiling. He appeared in worse shape than I was and his voice was hoarse from screaming.

'"Thanks. I'm fine." I assured him.

'"Thank God," he said, and then, "Let's get out of here."

'"That's a sentiment with which I fully agree. And fast," I added, rather unnecessarily.

'We stumbled away from the soap-nut tree as quickly as we could. Elephants are individuals after all, and this one could change his mind and return.'

The following morning we went back to recover Dudhwalla's camera and Don's torch. A sight awaited us.

Perhaps the camera had been thrown clear of the falling tree, or perhaps it had got caught up in the tarpaulin. Anyway, either deliberately or by accident, the elephant had stamped it flat. Gone was Dudhwalla's camera and Donald's precious flashlight photograph of the tiger eating its kill! But we found the torch unharmed.

Later that day we sat by the swollen banks of the river, watching the spotted deer and the langur monkeys feeding and playing upon the opposite bank. The wind of the previous night had knocked down the wild figs by the thousand from the great tree on the other side of the river. A herd of about thirty spotted deer were feasting upon them, while the family of langur monkeys that had found the figs earlier and had been tucking into them were now too full to eat any more.

They were frolicking and playing with one another and the spotted fawns like children. Now and again a half-grown langur would leap from the branch of a tree onto the back of a startled spotted doe, tweak her ears or pull her stumpy tail and then jump back again. The spotted stag was indignant at such activities and so were the older langurs, but the fawns frisked about, trying to play catch-as-catch-can with the younger monkeys. It was an unusual and pretty sight.

But as we were looking, death struck where all had been so peaceful. The herd of deer had moved away but the monkeys were still gambolling when a rusty brown streak leaped out of the jungle upon a half-grown langur that had strayed a short distance from the band.

For once the langur watchman had failed in his duty. Perhaps he had been too distracted in watching us to notice the lone, slinking wild dog that had successfully stalked the happy monkeys and now stood upon the opposite bank of the river with one of them dangling from his jaws.

Most of the monkeys scampered to the tree-top, screaming invectives, but the langur watchman and the big males leaped down in concerted attack, voicing the harsh langur war-cry: 'Hok! Hok! Hok! Hok!' They were too late. The young langur was already dead.

Don and I stood up and shouted in unison. My voice, already strained by my efforts of the night before, must have sounded ghastly, for the wild dog dropped the dead monkey in fright and ran a few yards away. There he stopped to gaze at us stonily. These creatures are exceptionally bold, far more so than the great cats of the jungle. They hardly fear man, although they do not attack him as a rule.

The river was swollen and too deep to wade across, but while still shouting to keep the wild dog at bay, we made it by clambering along the trunk and branches of an ancient tree that had fallen years ago and still spanned the stream. The silver-grey body of the black-faced little langur was warm when we picked it up, the great tail, nearly a yard in length, hanging limply from the carcase.

The monkey tribe was still on the tree-top, screaming invectives at the watching murderer, while the watchman and the other males bared their teeth at the wild dog and us alternately. Then they appeared to understand that we were not responsible for the little creature's death and fell silent as we picked up the lifeless body and placed it as high as Don could reach on the crotch of the tree where the monkeys were grouped. After that we returned to our side of the river.

The langurs came down now and surrounded the carcase of their companion. Some smelled it, others handled it. An old female, who might have been its mother, picked it up and kissed it. The large black eyes in those jet black faces seemed strangely shiny and moist. Do langurs weep?

We left 'tiger-land' that afternoon, disappointed but richer in experience for our little adventure with the elephant. The geese had come down from the Himalayas in larger numbers than usual this year, and Don had planned a geese-and-duck shooting expedition with some friends. So we had to return in time to meet them. I did not join the party.